I'M A
CHRISTIAN ON MY
WAY
TO HELL

by Karen R Williams

Book cover by LLPix Photography LLPix.com

Library Of Congress Control Number: 2013911049
ISBN: 978-0-615-81882-5

Scripture quotations:

New Spirit-Filled Life Bible® New King James Version Copyright © 2002 by Thomas Nelson, Inc

The Holy Bible, New King James Version Copyright © 1982 by Thomas Nelson, Inc.

Acknowledgements:

All Praises, Glory and Honor to God the Father and Jesus Christ for which ALL things are made possible for me! Without Him I am nothing. I would like to give a sincere thank you to all, especially, my big sister Monica R. Lett who God has used in my life to be a constant support and Godly encouragement. Thanks for having my back when others didn't! MUAH!! Lastly, I thank those who were used as obstacles in my life. Seriously, without you I would not have been able to see that I can STILL FORGIVE and operate in GOD'S love AND be who HE wants me to be. GOD BLESS each and EVERY ONE of you! Amen and Amen! SHALOM!

Table of Contents

APPEARANCE IS EVERYTHING

There is a way that seems right to a man,
But its end is the way of death. Proverbs 14:12

DANIELLE

walked into her lavishly decorated townhouse fuming. She was so angry that she shut the door with so much force, you thought it would break off its hinges. The walls shook and rumbled like it was an earthquake of a 3.5 magnitude. Danielle tried to calm herself down while her mother's words flooded through her mind taking over her thoughts,

"*...a lady must never draw negative attention to herself no matter what.*"

The statement vibrated through every crevice of Danielle's conscious whenever she wanted to kick, scream or shout her displeasures about life's mishaps. Like when she walked into her dorm room only to find her friend straddling her boyfriend and he looked like he was enjoying it, or walking pass her father's office and catching him pressed up against her aunt, his wife's sister, kissing and fondling one another. Instead of venting and drawing unnecessary attention to herself, Danielle learned to swallow the hurtful truth and never think about it again. A lady who is well-mannered lady would try her best not to cause anyone discomfort by rehashing unsettling memories of the past.

Danielle lives in a lovely quieted gated community. She cannot stand nosey neighbors. Danielle kept to herself, not meddling in anyone's business and she'd like the same respect.

Mind yo' business! Ain't nobody paying bills over here but me! she'd say to herself during her inner rants.

Danielle is a 30-year-old single very attractive, highly intelligent and very fashionably conscious successful junior advertising executive in one of L.A.'s top advertising firms. You could say she has worked as hard as anyone else has in order to secure her lucrative position. She quickly learned how to duck and dodge the hate that was thrown at her by backstabbing colleagues and people she considered friends, it came along with success. This explains the reason she didn't mind being propositioned by several superiors who were responsible for promoting her to the position of junior executive because it came along with the territory.

On several occasions, Danielle had been an arm ornament for a number of executives by accompanying them to annual functions and special events. She didn't mind being used in that manner in the least. As a matter of fact, she thought it was flattering that an exec would call upon her to adorn them with her presence.

I know I look good; she'd say to herself as posed in front of a full-length mirror. Danielle was making sure she looked tight in all the right places as she prepared herself to get ready to shake hands and entertain whomever her superior had to play nice with.

"It ain't my fault that his wife isn't good enough for this occasion." She laughed as she pressed out slightly visible wrinkles in her fire red strapless backless Vera Wang cocktail dress. "Hell! Or any occasion for that matter, *humph!"* she boasted as she teased her hair. "That's why he calls, *moi!"* After blowing a kiss to herself she shamelessly struts off. Their lost is her temporary gain. Besides, she only rents them long enough to get what she wants. *What's the harm in that? I always give them back.*

Don't get me wrong, Danielle was quite the empathetic one. It wasn't hard for her to understand just how lonely her married suitors become when their wives are out of town and they loath sleeping alone. Her justifications were as follows, "He is lonely! *Why should* he have to sleep alone in that king size bed while *his*

6

wife is probably out there somewhere making horizontal moves herself!" That was her M.O. In order to feel guiltless, she convinced herself that the other party, *must* be doing something wrong, and their wrong, made her wrong, right.

Danielle believed she's worked hard for what she has. And getting a little help every now and then by committing such small acts of harmless indiscretions never hurt anyone. Her mother seemed to be fine with her father's many indiscretions, after all these years. To further justify her corrupt way of thinking, Danielle saturated her mind with unconscionable statements like, "…if you want to accomplish great things in life you just *might* have to get a little dirty." Danielle was no dummy, she's far from it. Her parents made sure they provided their daughter with the best education that money could buy. Her life was centered on education. She might have recalled learning how to fill out a college application at the tender age of five. Failure was not an option. She came from a long line of established professionals. Her family, the Stevens, are well regarded individuals who pay their taxes, well at least some of the times. They never hesitate to help the poor, most of the time. They are members of various highly *recognized* charities. They would *never* make the mistake of getting involved with *any* charity that wasn't widely known! To further show just how impressive the Stevens' are in their *own* eyes, they attend church every *single* Sunday. To Danielle's family, church was seen as a place where they are taught "good" morals. Church was where they are reminded that *even* Jesus Christ helped the poor, so they're in good company. They've obtained principals like forgiving those who have hurt them. The Stevens have kept some of these teachings of the Lord near and dear to their hearts *but* not without applying their own twisted versions to it.

"You *can* forgive honey…," Danielle's father said to her one afternoon when she walked into his study thinking he hadn't yet arrived home. Danielle looked like a deer caught in headlights when she walked into his office and saw him sitting on his wine colored soft leather executive couch holding a glass of brandy staring off into space, "...but *don't* forget what the bastards have done. They'll come running back. They always come crawling back and don't hesitate to help them baby!" he says with eyes of fire. She doesn't know if the menacing look in his eye is from the alcohol or intense hate he has for those who dared to betray him. "I want you to help them baby girl. Never, *ever* let them forget what they did to you in the first place!" Sad to say Danielle retained the ungodly advice without questioning its origin. It came from one of many dark places in her father's heart. He handed over the ill-advised directions to his daughter because his former accountant revealed to him that he had stolen money from Mr. Stevens throughout the years. His ex-accountant decided to ease his conscious hoping his revelations would soften Mr. Steven's heart and cause him to reach out to him in his time of need. Being the good "Christian" that Mr. Stevens is, he accepted the rogue accountant's admission. He even offered to help him. Of course, his help came with penalties. Mr. Stevens made sure not one day went by without reminding his old account how lowly and treacherous his actions were and how glad he should be to have such a kind friend like himself.

Church and God's word helped the Stevens to truly embrace how blessed they are and how they should always appreciate everything they've accomplished in life. They learned that there's nothing wrong with having an abundance of wealth. Owning homes throughout the four corners of the earth, luxury cars that aren't available to the working class. Custom made clothes designed by top designers and purchasing yachts to sail the great seas. As I stated, the Stevens are Christians in name *only*. As long as they appeared to be upstanding citizens of society and attend church regularly they were sure to have their names written in the Lamb's Book of Life.

Danielle kicked off her Jimmy Choo stilettos and threw her soft leather Italian brief case haphazardly onto her expensive olive green suede sofa.

"Ooh!" she exclaimed with her fist balled tightly. "God! Please help me forgive that dirty bastard!" She took a deep exasperated breath. "I know that's one of your principles but slashing his damn tires would bring me so much joy! It'll make me really happy right now!" Danielle demonstrated her frustrations by slamming her house keys down on the table. "*UGH!* Damn a conscious! That fool doesn't have one! I need a drink.*"

Danielle marched to the bar that sat to the left of her large living room. Her mini bar housed only the best brandies, cognac, vodka and gin that money could buy. Danielle reached for a bottle of the clear intoxicating liquid joy.

"Hello friend, I've been thinking about you all day!" She reached for a glass from the top shelf twisted off the cap watching in sheer delight as the liquor filled it. "Such a lovely sound." She sat the bottle down screwed the cap on, not too tight, and made a beeline for the sofa.

Danielle dropped down on the couch, raised the glass to her lips, took a long sip, instantly feeling the effects of the alcohol streaming through her body. She leaned her head against the sofa allowing the liquor to continue working its magic throughout her system. All her troubles slid far away for the time being, that is, until the phone rang temporarily interrupting her relaxing mode.

"Ah!" Danielle groaned as she sat her glass on the table. "Let me get that, it might be Justin." She answered the phone on the last ring, "Hello?"

"Hello?" Justin repeated in his satin sexy voice. "How are you, baby?"

"*Ummmm,* better now that you've called."

"Am I going to see you later tonight?" A seductive smile spread across Danielle's face at the thought of seeing Justin.

"Of course," she purred. "What time will you be here?"

"What time do you *want* me there?" he asked, she laughed softly.

"You know where I live." Danielle hung the phone up avoiding his question. This was *her* form of psychological foreplay. Anticipation was the force behind pursuit and desire.

As Danielle spun on her heels, heeding in the direction of the sofa, the phone rang again. Now she's annoyed because

9

she's been kept from her drink far too long. "Come on baby, do you need me to draw a map for you?" Danielle angrily lifts the phone to her ear, "Hello!" She did not bother to hide her agitation. "I hope you're calling back to ask what kind of wine I want to drink?" She giggled trying to release tension.

"What kind of wine you want to drink?" a voice said back, sounding confused.

Danielle's mind drew a blank. She's buzzed from the liquid joy. *Who is this!* She removed the phone from her ear and stared at it incredulously. "Who is this?"

"Who do you think it is?"

"Cynthia!" Her eyes squint giving that infamous look that people are known for when they're not sure about something.

"Duh! What wine? And when did you ask me to bring you some?"

"Gurrrl! *Noooo,* I thought you were-" Danielle's cut off.

"Justin! Humph!" Cynthia sneered. It's no secret that she's not fond of Justin at all. She thinks he's a cheater.

"Cindy," Danielle said exasperatedly, "...not today, okay?"

"What's wrong?" Cynthia asked, her voice filled with concern.

"Mr. James, gets-on-my-damn-nerves, ole beast!"

"That's nothing new, he's always getting on your nerves. What did he do, now?"

"I made plans to spend the weekend with Justin but now, I can't because the idiot threw a last-minute assignment at me. I'm stuck in this house all doggon' weekend!" Danielle let out a hard sigh through the phone.

"Okaaay! It doesn't sound *that* bad."

"Yeah! To *you,* it doesn't sound that bad because you don't like Justin anyway."

"True, but what I'm saying isn't about him. All you gotta do is get the assignments done and out of the way. Then, you'll still have time to do *whatever* it is that you do with him."

Danielle rolled her eyes at Cynthia's condescending tone towards Justin and her 'know it all' attitude about Danielle's work. "It might sound simple to you but I have to come up with *three, new* campaign ideas by *next* Wednesday. Now, do you have a magic wand for that?"

"Don't trip, what are the new campaigns?"

"One is for a new liquor campaign, the second is a new SUV and the third is an ad for diamonds."

"Like I said, it's no biggie! You got enough liquor to come up with new liquor campaign ads for the next two years."

"Whatever silly," Danielle said as she laughed at the obvious. She did a quick scan of her well stocked liquor cabinet. *That is a lot of liquor.*

"And speaking of liquor! *Gurl,* I need to come over and take some off your hands for this weekend, since you won't be needing much of it." She chuckled.

"Whatever Cindy, ha! Ha! Thanks for reminding me."

"Anytime, anytime. You know I'm only playing with you. *But* I'm serious about retrieving some of that expensive liquor though."

"Help yourself, what do you need it for anyway?" Danielle braced herself for Cynthia's response. Nothing was inappropriate to her friend.

"Well, since you've asked." Danielle could picture her friend grinning from ear to ear. Although she couldn't bring herself to admit it, Danielle enjoyed listening to Cynthia's animated descriptions of her sexual conquests. "While you are working Saturday, I will be playing with one of my boy toys. *And,* I will end my night with a very ripe and eager to please young lady who's new to the life. Might I add, she's very excited to be having her first experience with *moi!* Thank you! Thank you *very* much."

"Sorry I asked," Danielle said with mocked distaste.

"I keep telling you that you should try it," Cynthia added mischievously. "You know the statement *'don't knock it till you try it'* is *soooo* true! My invitation will always be open to you. *But,* you should take advantage of this generous offer before you get too old and then I won't want cha!" Cynthia burst out laughing at her own joke.

Danielle couldn't help but to laugh too. *"Anyway!* Now that's a bold face lie! You will *still* want me toothless and all."

"Seriously Danielle, I can introduce you to a world filled with insurmountable pleasure that you won't be able to describe, let alone handle."

Danielle *was* secretly interested in this world that Cynthia spoke of but she didn't want her friend to know about her subtle curiosity. "You've only offered the invitation about one billion and one times and I always say *noooooo!"*

"And I'm going to keep throwing it out there until you come to your senses and say *yessssss!"*

Danielle heard keys jiggling at her front door. "That's Justin," said more to herself. Danielle knew Cynthia couldn't care less. "I'm going to have to call you back."

"Humph! Saved by the bell…literally."

"Byyyeeee!" Danielle hung the phone up and ran to the door like an excited child swinging it open and was greeted with the most gorgeous smile.

"Hello angel," Justin purred holding out a bouquet of red roses and an expensive bottle of champagne.

"Just what the doctor ordered," Danielle said as she smiled at the man she's in lust with planting sweet kisses on his lips, "…a man and a bottle of chilled champagne." Every reservation she held about Justin possibly being a cheater, flew out the window. She hiked up her tailor-made skirt and jumped up on Justin's waist covering his face and neck with more wet kisses.

Danielle rolled over on her side to glance at the alarm clock that read 11:48 PM. Justin was about to leave soon. She gently turned to face her lover taking in his magnificent physique and deeply inhaling the intoxicating scent of his cologne. Justin was sound asleep and she almost didn't want to wake him. Whenever Justin stayed late he'd ask Danielle to not let him sleep pass twelve midnight.

I wonder what he'd do if I just let him sleep and not wake him? She contemplated as she twisted his curly ringlets around her finger. Danielle was tempted to find out but she feared the repercussion she might face by not honoring what he's asked. In addition, her body fiends for his extraordinary love making. Danielle couldn't bear the thought of jeopardizing what they have just for the sake of curiosity.

Why does he always have to leave at twelve! The question resonated through her mind. Danielle quickly brushed it off not wanting to spoil the tranquility and protection she felt at that moment even if it's temporary. A smile spreads across her face as she reminisced about the first day they laid eyes on one another. Drenched in sweat, Justin *still* looked good.

It was a lovely mellow day in Los Angeles, days like that are not unusual in sunny Southern California. You will never cease enjoying them. Danielle was seated in her favorite spot near the tennis court at Ladera Park so engrossed in her work that she didn't realize someone was standing beside her waiting to get her attention. *Ring! Ring! Ring!* The ringing of her sophisticated smart phone does nothing to draw attention away from her work. With her eyes still glued on the laptop monitor, Danielle reached for the device but it's no longer there. Her heart pounded against her chest. *What did I do with my phone! I know I brought it with me.*

Danielle studied the spot where she thought she placed her phone, then she heard a deep baritone voice say, "Are you looking for this?" She quickly snapped her head in the direction of the hypnotizing voice and her eyes fell onto the phone sitting in the middle of a large moist palm. Danielle was suddenly startled and excited. The welcoming, eye-candy, distraction studied her closely, wondering if she was going to snatch the phone out his hand and run like a track star for help. "Here," he said encouraging Danielle to make a move, any move.

By now, Danielle's brain had processed what had taken place. She didn't know if she should be upset by his antics and invasion of her personal space or, if at all, slightly impressed by his boldness. She reclaimed her phone from his large hand and sat it where it was. With a look of mocked anger covering Danielle's face, she looked her potential candidate up and down taking her sweet time, examining him from head to toe making, him feel very uncomfortable. Danielle couldn't help but to be taken aback by his handsomely chiseled face. His 5 o'clock shadow is just how she liked it-easy hair and well-manicured. His muscular frame stood at 6'2.'' Danielle could tell by the way his Nike sweat suit fit him

13

that he was tantalizing eye candy. He would be nice to look at with or without clothes.

If only I had x-ray vision! Danielle said to herself filled with such lust that even *she was* surprised by her own thoughts. His caramel complexion glistened from the thin layer of sweat covering his visible skin. He looked radiant, healthy like he really took pride in what he put into his body. And his teeth are white as snow!

He interrupted her day dreaming when he cleared his throat, smiled embarrassingly and says, "I guess it wasn't that important?"

Danielle tried to fight the seductive smile that threatened to make its way to her face. "I guess not," she said challenging him with a stare that was meant to bring any man to his knees. "If it's important they will call back," she threw in a little too flirtatiously. Danielle silently admonished herself for revealing just how much she was into him as well. A sultry smile covered his face and her heart skipped a beat. He glanced down at the empty seat next to her.

"May I?"

Uh, uh, I like the view just the way it is. Danielle was a little embarrassed by her instant attraction to this man. She rested her forehead on top of her hand and giggled. "Go ahead." He laughed because he knew why she was blushing.

Ahhhh! She's interested in me too. He straddled the bench like a rodeo star with renewed confidence looking directly in her eyes. Danielle gave him her undivided attention. The smell of his cologne mixed with a hint of sweat was intoxicating.

Lawd! He even smells good during a workout! She shook her head and silently laughed at her high school excitement.

"Are you gonna let me in on what's tickling you?" he asked confidently, a little too confident.

"Maybe, it depends on how I feel about you after you leave." His interest grew stronger by the second. He loved a challenge, especially from a sophisticated lady.

"Not only is she beautiful, she's bold as hell. That is a one-of-a -kind combination, I must say." Danielle put on a poker face.

He is smooth. Okay! I'm game. Show me what you got, baby.

As if he read her mind he says, "I prefer not to further embarrass myself by telling you how nervous I am but you strike me as a woman who is easily turned off by bogus games. You want real and straight to the point." He paused waiting for Danielle to indicate whether or not he is on the right track. She gave him nothing, he continues, "I'm totally stricken by your beauty." He paused again taking in her physical attributes. Danielle's shoulder length hair is what turned him on the most. He could tell that her hair is real. With so many women sporting weaves nowadays, when he came across a woman rocking her own hair it was equivalent to the 8th wonder of the world. His heart fluttered as he watched the sunlight radiate through Danielle's hazel brown eyes that went so well with her light tone. He had to fight with all his might to keep from staring at her perfectly shaped ample bosoms. Her impeccable shape let him know he has *a lot* to look forward to when he's given the chance to help her undress.

Danielle was well aware that he's checking her out real tuff. She obliged, by giving him all the time she felt he needed to take it all in. Danielle never grew tired of hearing men tell her time and time again just how beautiful she is. But what Danielle had grown tired of, were the *reasons* behind the wonderful compliments. Most men learned that the way into a woman's *body,* was to saturate her with compliments causing her to be interested in their pursuit. After the man gets what he wants, he'll walk away like their encounter never meant a thing. It's fair to say that even with all of Danielle's beauty and intelligence it hasn't prevented her from having her share of playas. But she thinks there might be something genuine about this man. She decided to give him a chance just to see what he planned to do with it.

Danielle secretly enjoyed the little hint of insecurity he displayed while he shared his feelings. When he admitted that her beauty caused him to lose confidence, she pretends to not be fazed by his admission. It's a game that she enjoyed to play, of not letting on how vulnerable she is for fear of being taken advantage of. Regardless of the games she played, Danielle can't deny that she's drawn to this tall dark fine stranger. He continues,

"I would love to get to know you in every way possible, including your exquisite mind. That is, if you will permit me to?" He flashed his boy like grin and his green eyes sparkled. It's sealed, Danielle was open.

"When?" she asked. He's taken aback. His smile was suddenly replaced with confusion. He didn't expect her to be so direct.

"Huh? When? I'm-I'm sorry. I-" she cut him off.

"When were you planning on taking me out?" She smiled. He's nervous and relieved. "You were asking me out, weren't you?"

He finally loosened up, letting a smile reclaim his charming face. "Whenever it's convenient for you," he said. Then he looked as if he's forgotten something important. "Um, I'm sorry, what is your name?"

"Danielle."

"Danielle," he repeated, reaching for her hand stamping it with a kiss. "I love that name, it's a very intriguing name. That's the cherry on top of my sundae." His last statement was a little corny although it kept Danielle interested, to say the least. She just stared at him for a few minutes before she says another word. As Danielle remained silent, the rapid thoughts running through her mind would make a foul mouth truck driver blush. She dared not reveal those thoughts to him, well at least not yet.

"Hmmmm, let's see." Trying not to appear desperate, she picked her smart phone up pretending to check her calendar. Danielle really doesn't have to pretend like she has a full schedule because she does. Regardless of her full schedule, she would most certainly make time for him even if important meetings with special clients had to be cancelled.

"Take your time," he said jokingly, hoping to mask his anxiety.

Danielle wanted to tell him she's available tonight but she could hear her mother's voice in her head saying,

Never present yourself as a cheap desperate woman to any man because he'll never see you as anything different. She wished she could ignore her mother's echoing words of caution and be shamelessly desperate as other women. But Danielle knew she would not be able stand herself if she acted like she had no self-respect.

"Okay!" she said, feigning exasperation like the fake task of looking through her calendar was the hardest thing to do. "It looks like I'll be free next Friday." Danielle stared in his luscious eyes and asks, "How does your calendar look?" She felt butterflies swarm around her belly like angry bees. *Please say you'll be free! Please!* When he took a millisecond too long to answer, Danielle was seconds away from blurting out a much sooner date.

He beat her to the punch, *"Awwww, I was hoping for something sooner than Friday, like tonight?"* he said with a glimmer of hope in his eyes. He knew she wasn't going to agree to go out with him so soon but it didn't hurt to ask. A woman like Danielle was too classy to be desperate, so he thought. She quickly turned away from his mesmerizing stare before she stumbled and fell into his trap of lust.

Is it too soon to get bucket naked and roll around in the hay together? "I'm-" Danielle stopped speaking as if she instantly remembered something. With all his blatant, but welcomed flirting, he forgot to say his name, "...oh! What's your name?" His face was flushed. To say he was embarrassed was an understatement.

"Excuse me for my absent mindedness, I'm Justin." He offered his hand and Danielle graciously took it.

"It's nice to meet you, Justin." He nodded his head.

"Likewise, see..." he said pointing at Danielle like she did something wrong, "...this is the affect you have on me already and we haven't even been intimate...yet."

Danielle's heart felt like it was about to explode in her chest. She cleared her throat, his forwardness caught her by surprise. Danielle suddenly felt aroused.

"As I was trying to say, Justin..." she said purposely avoiding his last statement, "...unfortunately my work schedule does not permit me much flexibility. I've been literally swamped with work non-stop for the past two months. The only reason I am at the park today, is to take advantage of this gorgeous weather."

"Yes, the weather is breathtaking but not as breathtaking as you are." Justin licked his lips sensually, like LL Cool J. *"Humph!* I should thank your boss and send him tickets to the next Lakers' game."

The mere mention of Danielle's boss made her flinch. Her whole disposition changed in an instant. She didn't know if she should be offended or flattered by what he said. Justin saw the perplexed look on Danielle's lovely face and he immediately wanted to find out what was wrong.

"What I-I," he stumbled, "...okay, what I meant is, if it wasn't for your boss being a *cruel* task master, I would not have had the pleasure of meeting such a lovely creature as yourself." Justin poured it on real thick but it was something about the way this man smelled, looked and the chemistry Danielle felt emanating from him that made her throw caution to the wind. She rested her chin on her hands, smiled and says,

"You're smooth." Justin blushed like a twelve-year-old who had just entered puberty and says,

"Should I be rough?"

There he goes again! Danielle took the bait and dived in head first. "Well, it depends on the task." They held one another's gaze for a moment which felt like an eternity. Both basked in their lustful thoughts for one another. Their self-induced trance was broken by the sound of Justin's voice,

"I don't expect a beautiful lady such as yourself to have an empty calendar." He desperately hoped she was single.

"Don't be too surprised, my calendar isn't always filled, silly."

Yes! She's single! "Okay! It's a date," Justin said trying to compose his excitement as he stood to his feet. Danielle was captivated by his Adonis like body. She never saw a man stand up so seductively before.

This man ooze lust!

"I look forward to seeing you in your *red dress* and *your red high heels,*" he said with a Cheshire grin. "No seriously, I'm looking forward to spending a night out on the town with you."

Danielle saw his lips moving but she heard no sound because she was lost in thoughts of picturing him naked. She couldn't stop the carnal desires raving through her loins for this man! It was like, he pulled out the most sensual urges she had ever known! "Until we meet again, Mr. Justin."

18

He took a hold of Danielle's hand and gently caressed it. With a smile that's meant to break hearts, Justin kissed her hand one last time. Then, he took deliberate steps backwards, making sure Danielle's eyes remained on him. He slowly turned around, breaking into a full jog, keeping his new lady friend captivated.

That was one and a half years ago. Danielle's and Justin's relationship had been good for the most part, except for one thing. When Danielle wanted to visit him, she could *only* do so on the weekends. That was the reason Cynthia didn't like Justin, she thought he was married.

"I mean for one, he always tells you to wake his ass up at midnight, every time he spends the night with you. *Two;* you've been with this man for *one whole year* and you've *never* been to his house, during the week days! Conclusion; *he is* a lying, cheating ass, *married* male-whore*!"* Cynthia loved making Danielle feel dumb as hell. It's her way of making Danielle think, so she said. Of course, Danielle didn't see it that way. She thinks Cynthia berates her to be mean and psychologically abusive. To add insult to injury, she'd say, "Open your eyes Danielle! Stop thinking with your vajayjay! He is playing you like a floozy!"

There was no doubt that Danielle believed her best friend was looking out for her best interest. Although, she couldn't help to feel that Cynthia's feelings for her well-being, were a little biased. Danielle thinks her best friend might be envious of Justin because she wants to be more than *friends*. Hidden desires would eventually make themselves known in the most obvious ways. Danielle hoped she would be ready when Cynthia's undisclosed desires actually manifest.

The clock read, 11:59 PM and 23 seconds. Justin nestled his body closer to Danielle's. The warmth radiating from his flesh was scrumptious. She secretly hated that he had to leave her side during the night.

I would love for him to stay the entire night with me so we could have breakfast in bed. "Justin," she whispered. He grunted and let out a series of snorts. She gently shook his shoulder. "Justin? It's time to wake up."

He stirred awake. "*Ooooooh!*" he said as he stretched his lean body against hers. "What time is it?" Justin squint his eyes looking at the clock. "Twelve on the dot, thank you, baby." He wrapped his strong arms around Danielle and kissed her forehead.

A fohead kiss! What the hell! We just fornicated, now he wants to act like Mr. Rogers'? If his intentions were to make her feel sexy, brotha failed! Danielle felt like a ten-year-old being kissed by her grandfather. Oblivious to her feelings, Justin says,

"I gotta run, baby. I'm going to jump in the shower, you wanna come with?" As much as Danielle wanted to get down with him one more time before he left, she declined.

"Go ahead baby, I have a long day ahead of me."

"Okay, suit yourself." He grabbed his clothes and hustled into the bathroom.

Danielle pulled the covers up to her shoulders and turned on her side. All of a sudden, she felt a cold chill. Where she once had thoughts of fulfillment by her lover, they quickly turned to heavy condemnation. Something was wrong but she couldn't quite put her finger on it. She abruptly sat up in her bed feeling uneasy. Danielle scanned her dark room barely, able to make out the silhouettes. The only dim light that streamed through the room came from underneath the bathroom door. She tried to shake off the unwelcoming creepy sensation by telling herself she was just tired. No matter what she convinced herself to believe, she couldn't escape the subtle condemnation that rose in her soul. Danielle didn't know why she was having these feelings or where they have come from. As she laid in the bed pondering these new confusing emotions she slipped off to sleep until the alarm sounded at 5:30 in the morning.

IT'S A NATURAL THANG

Do not love the world or the things in the world. If anyone loves the world, the love of the Father is not in him. For all that is in the world-the lust of the flesh, the lust of the eyes and the pride of life-is not of the Father but is of the world. And the world is passing away, and the lust of it; but he who does the will of God abides forever. 1John 2:15-17 NKJV

CYNTHIA

had been sitting on the sofa staring at the phone, forever, after she got off the phone with Danielle. She shook her head trying to snap out of the daze.

"Humph!"

Finally, Cynthia stood up and walked to the counter to put the cordless on the base. "One day Danielle, you will come over to the dark side," she said jokingly but her intentions were not to be taken lightly.

Cynthia lived in a small comfortable two-bedroom house north of Downtown Los Angeles. Her reason for having such a small abode, was to keep unwanted houseguest at bay. Whenever someone needed an extra hand by asking if they could crash at her place for a couple of days, that usually turned into months, Cynthia could easily say, without guilt, that she didn't have the room. She conveniently converted her second bedroom into a dark room studio. So, Cynthia wasn't lying, not really.

Of course, there were *no* plans for child rearing in her future. Children would definitely cramp her uninhibited lifestyle. Cynthia wouldn't be able her to express herself sexually the way she was

21

comfortable doing. When a person chose to live a carefree sexual lifestyle without boundaries, children must be kept out of it. Even though Cynthia chose to live life without a conscious of right or wrong, she knew that a child needed to be brought up in an environment filled with love and discipline. Those were the two most essential things that Cynthia lacked in her life.

When Cynthia wasn't trekking through the streets of Los Angeles looking through camera lenses, trying to capture tomorrow's headline, she prowled every hip and sheik club, bar or social scene known in L.A. looking for someone or multiple partners to satisfy an unquenchable desire that lie deep within. She made a vow to never be lonely and never to settle down.

Cynthia grew up feeling she was dealt a bad hand. One day while walking home from school, she began experiencing an overwhelming foreboding feeling that took a hold of her causing her to become temporarily frozen. Her feet felt like chunks of concrete, every step was laborious. Cynthia felt terror swelling up in the pit of her stomach. As she got closer to her house, the dreadful feeling intensified. Fear engulfed her! As Cynthia took a step up the stairs, panic gripped her causing her not to want to enter the house. She didn't understand where the fear came from.

Why do I feel this way!

The fear of being ridiculed by her parents overshadowed the dread of entering her home. Cynthia slowly turned the door knob. The sounds of the squeaky door hinges were unusually loud for some strange unsettling reason. Now that the door was completely open, she began hyperventilating as she stared at her parent's lifeless bodies sprawled out on the living room floor. Cynthia's parents have both OD'd from heroin. After that horrific experience, she knew her life was headed down a troubled road of misery. No matter how rough life became she, said she would never turn out to be like *them.*

Cynthia prided herself on her smooth complexion and strong dancer legs. Taking modern dance as a minor during her sophomore year at Howard University was the best decision she ever made. Her legs were her greatest assets when she needed to run up and down the streets, capturing pictures to solicit to periodicals and newspapers. And the bedroom was where Cynthia really appreciated the flexibility and strength of her "assets" when showing off cleaver skills, leaving her partners breathless and awestruck.

Cynthia's philosophy was, "Always look out for number one and always have fun even if it kills you. As long as I don't intentionally hurt anyone, what's the problem?" What was so wrong with living without restraints? Nothing at all, was her rationale.

Cynthia's happiness was solely contingent upon sex and people. Those two components, were the key to her pseudo contentment, this was what she told herself. The real truth was, loneliness and lonely days were what Cynthia hated the most, with a passion. They always let her know there was no real happiness that existed in her life.

It's Thursday night, the air was filled with enough electricity to bring the dead back to life. Cynthia never looked better, sporting a new black strapless dress that stopped four inches above her knees, giving off all the right signs. She wanted everyone who looked at her to know she was *hot, single, ready* to *mingle* and *willing* to try *anything,* once and repeat it if she loved it.

Cynthia had only been sitting in the VIP section of the popular nightclub, The Dragonfly, for a few moments before a very tall dark and handsome distinguished gentleman approached her.

"Are you waiting for someone or is this your way of making sure everyone in here sees you?"

Cynthia couldn't help but to be impressed by his cleaver icebreaker. She smiled and looked over at the seat next to her, indicating that it was okay for him to sit down.

The instant chemistry between the two was hypnotic. Cynthia knew they won't be sitting in the club for long. One thing she did not do was play coy games. When it came to Cynthia getting exactly what she wanted, there was nothing off limits. Needless to say, her insatiable sexual appetite held no bounds.

Casanova boldly undressed Cynthia with his eyes. She *craved* that kind of attention, Cynthia loved being desired. Sensuous desires intensified between the both of them every second.

He's about to have the time of his life, Cynthia thought to herself as she stared into his sexy eyes. When it came to sex games she had no shame. As time went by, Cynthia could not contain the heat that raged inside. She indicated this, by seductively reaching for her drink, slowly bringing it to her lips, licking the rim sending off all sorts of sexual signals to her soon to be bed-buddy.

He took a hard swallow. "Let me refresh your drink," he offered. There was a long pause.

Cynthia took a slow sip from her nearly empty glass of brandy and placed it on the table. She enticed him by biting her bottom lip and says,

"What is your name?" He smiled embarrassingly, he couldn't believe he didn't introduce himself when he initially approached the table. In a satin laced voice dripping with seduction he says,

"Everybody calls me GQ."

"Well GQ, I have a better idea." He arched his eyebrow as he took a sip from his glass, letting her know she had his full attention. "How about you...and I...go back to my place? And you know what, GQ?"

"What, baby?" his voice was barely above a whisper.

"I believe you and I will have *a lot* of fun in my bed. That is," she reached over and squeezed his inner thigh, "...*if*...you can handle the task." GQ emptied his glass in one gulp, returned it to the table and hastily stood to his feet. Extending his hand to Cynthia, he says,

"I was waiting for you to ask." He cradled Cynthia's arm in the crock of his arm, smiling charmingly as he thought about what's about to go down tonight!

While GQ escorted Cynthia out of the VIP room, she locked eyes with an attractive model type looking young lady. Instant lust passed between the two. Cynthia winked at the young lady, who was probably no older than twenty-two, and she winked back, blowing a kiss. Cynthia had a mind to dismiss the old man for the strikingly beautiful young lady.

But that would be rude, she told herself.

Instead, Cynthia beckon for the young lady to come to her. She stood mesmerized as the young lady walked provocatively towards them. Cynthia's mind was blown!

Damn!!! That's a sexy mutha...! The young lady stood face to face with Cynthia. *You gotta come home with me, you just have to!* "If you have any plans tonight, would you mind cancelling them and joining us in a private party, please!" Cynthia asked in desperation, as she yelled over the music, booming through the club's high tech digital speakers. The young lady smiled enticingly. She was very much excited about the personal invitation.

"Give me a second, I have to tell my friends that something has suddenly come up." She looked the two over desirously before walking away. Cynthia and GQ turned away heading for the exit.

A DIVINE RELATIONSHIP

Oh how I love Your law! It is my meditation all the day. You, through Your commandments make me wiser than my enemies; for they are ever with me. PSALM 119:97-98 NKJV

LISA

lounged on the sofa looking at her favorite reality show when the Holy Spirit urged her to pray in her heavenly language. She turned the television off and all was silent in the two-bedroom house that Lisa shared with her mother. She had no clue as to why there was an urgency to pray but whatever it was, she knew it was serious.

Lisa stood up from the sofa and began praying with her hands lifted towards heaven. Immediately she felt the anointing from the Holy Spirit surrounding her like a warm comforter. Lisa prayed earnestly, intertwining verbal prayer with her heavenly language. A miraculous wonderful language that only her heavenly Father understood.

"Father God, Jesus Christ please have mercy on the saints! In the name of Jesus Christ, I rebuke you devil and bind every wicked foul assignment that you try and send against God's children tonight. No weapon formed against us shall prosper in the mighty name of Jesus Christ! You hear that devil! You are and will always be defeated in the name of Jesus Christ of Nazareth! Jesus defeated you at the cross when He went to hell for three days and nights and took back the keys of death and life!"

Lisa continued to pray with boldness and power in the name of Jesus, until there was a release in her spirit. "Father God, thank You for Your mercy and grace! Praise You Jesus! Thank You Jesus! Hallelujah! God, You are more than worthy to be praised! Thank You Father God for Your wonderful love! Thank You Jesus for dying on the cross for our sins. Father God I thank You that whomever I am praying for they are covered in the precious blood of the Lamb! Thank You for putting a fiery hedge of protection around them and their families! I thank You that whatever the devil has planned against them is defeated and is crushed under their feet because it's crushed under Your feet Father God! Praise You Lord! Hallelujah! Praise You Father! Thank You Holy Spirit! Jesus! Hallelujah! Praise Your Holy name Father God! Thank You for your tender mercies!"

Lisa felt the presence of God in the room, she knew He was pleased. The urgency she felt earlier had dissipated and now her soul is filled with utter peace. "Father God You are so merciful!" she said as tears streamed down her face. She immediately wanted to pick the phone up to check on her friends but she decided against it. She has to know and believe that whomever she just prayed for was all right. Calling them would indicate fear and a lack of faith in God to take care of the matter at hand.

Lisa went into the kitchen to get a cup of water. Then she went back into the living room, sat down on the sofa and opened her Bible to her favorite book, Proverbs. "Reading the Bible is better than watching a movie on any given day."

Lisa lives with her mother who became disabled due to an injury she suffered on the job, over ten years ago when she was employed by the City of Los Angeles. The injury Lisa's mother suffered, limited her day-to-day activities.

Lisa and her mother had not always had a loving and caring relationship but she knew that sharing dwellings would not be an issue. The only ones who seemed to have a problem with how she lived *her* life, were the ones who really weren't doing anything productive in their lives.

Lisa found that choosing to walk on the path of the straight and narrow has brought much harsh ridicule and relentless persecutions in her life. She suffered much persecution, not *only,* from the world but also from the Body of Christ, her family and her so-called friends. When she chose to rededicate her life to Jesus Christ, over twenty years ago, she made a firm decision never to turn away from God again. Lisa is sold out to Jesus Christ 100%! Her walk with God hasn't always been joyous but it sure does feel good knowing that Jesus will never leave her nor forsake her. She knew that God would always be by her side even during the storms. People have since come and gone from her life but God continued to remain a constant friend.

During trials and tribulations, controversy was always present. People will want you to do it *their* way when God is telling you to do *it His* way. Trusting God completely and not leaning upon your own understanding was a sure way of being ostracized. Whenever you choose to go against what's *popular,* deemed *acceptable* by the world, you will always be alienated. When God loves you, and shows you great favor, the world will always hate you. Lisa would rather be accepted by God than have the acceptance of man.

Walking the straight and narrow path wasn't always Lisa's first priority nor was it her heart's desire. There was a time in her life that she *willing* participated in a lifestyle that went against God's word *but* was condoned in the world. She had always felt God's hand on her even when she refused to acknowledge Him. There were times Lisa rejected certain things that she felt was *too* far off the path and would only lead her further into darkness. She had always known that God was with her even in her life of sin. There are many who have chosen to live a lifestyle propelling them deeper into darkness and some are lost forever. Every day, Lisa thanked God for not leaving her to perish in her sins.

Lisa looked at the clock, it was 6:50 PM. Her favorite reality show, about four successful singers and their superstar oldest sister will end in ten minutes. Lisa always found herself laughing hysterically at the antics of the youngest sibling who was always getting on her sisters nerves.

The cell phone rang as she watched the show's ending credits roll down the screen. She was too busy contemplating about what she's going to watch next to answer the phone. Lisa's phone rang once again and she examined the caller ID. It's Regina. She pressed accept and put the phone to her ear,

"Hello?"

"Hey Lisa," Regina said sounding a little down which was not unusual. What *is* unusual is if she called sounding happy. Then, Lisa would be pressed to find out what was really going on.

"Hey gurl, what's up?"

"Nothing, I'm feeling depressed about my statistics class. I have to take a test tomorrow and I don't think I'm going to do that well." Lisa rolled her eyes and was immediately convicted. She covered the mouth piece with her hand and asked God for His forgiveness,

I'm sorry for being impatient with Your child, Father God. "Regina...you read God's Word, right?"

"You know I do, Lisa."

"Okay, you go to church too, right?"

"Yes, almost every Sunday. What does this-" Lisa cut her off.

"What I'm saying is, you don't have to accept low-self-esteem, Regina, you know God's word. You'll be set free, *once* you take authority over those demonic spirits that are making your life miserable." Both parties go silent as they ponder what the other was going to say. "The devil is stealing your peace. There is no reason why you should be walking around feeling defeated. You're not defeated Regina; the devil is defeated! You're suppose to prosper at whatever you put your hands to in Jesus name." Silence. Lisa exhaled letting out a loud stream of air. She could detect Regina's agitation but she didn't care. She had become irritated by Regina's defeatist attitude. *When is she going to walk in victory Lord!* "You can choose to walk in victory or defeat."

"Everything you are saying is true," Regina said as she exhaled. "I don't know what's wrong with me! One minute I'm fine, I feel real confident like, *I know* that I can do all things through Christ Jesus who strengthens me, Then, this intense fear and anxiety comes over me and, and-" she broke off. Lisa could hear Regina sniffling through the phone, "...I second guess *everything,* I don't know." She sniffled again. "I don't know," Regina repeated. Lisa had compassion for her friend.

"It's an unclean spirit, Regina," Lisa said with a softer tone. She knew exactly how Regina felt. Lisa was tormented by the same spirit of fear years, until God told her what to do to be delivered and set free from the oppressive spirit. She hasn't had a problem with fear ever again. "I've shared with you what God had me to do to be delivered from fear. You have to get alone with God, Regina and seek His face. Let Him know how much you want to be set free and He will deliver you. You have to *want* to be delivered, honey. God doesn't want us bound by anything. When we are bound, we are limited in our walk with God and when we're limited, how will we be effective witnesses for Jesus? We can't."

"I know," Regina said.

"Ask God, to reveal to you what door has been opened that has allowed that spirit of low-self-esteem to have a stronghold in your life." Regina hated to think about the past but she knew God had already given her the answer. Tears welled up in her eyes just thinking about how cruelly she was treated.

If I can just say it! Just let it out! Forget it! She won't understand anyway. She'll think I'm just whining.

Lisa broke through Regina's mental rant. "God is waiting on you to cry out to Him, dear."

And that's what I'm doing now!

"Aren't you tired of being oppressed?" That was a question Lisa really didn't need to ask. She wanted Regina to ask *herself* that question, to know if she really *is tired* of being oppressed. Misery is a part of life, for some people. They wouldn't know what to do if they were rid of it. It's like an uninvited guest who's come to visit and never left.

"Yes, I am tired!" Regina yelled with conviction. She sounded genuinely sincere, that she *actually* believed herself. "And frankly, I'm tired of praying to God asking Him to help me!"

That's right girl, let it out! At least, you're being honest, Lisa said to herself.

"I ask God to help me *all* the time but nothing ever changes! I mean, what do I have to do to get help from Him, kill someone!" Regina knew she went too far but it's better to let it out than keeping it in.

Lisa let out a hefty sigh. Regina prepared herself to get chewed out by Lisa for what she just let spill out. In actuality, Lisa didn't have anything to say. How Regina felt, is how she felt, even if it's wrong. Instead of preaching, Lisa decided to pray silently expecting Holy Spirit to give her the words of comfort to sooth her friend's tormented soul. Her silence made Regina uncomfortable.

"Hello!" she blurted out uneasily. "Are you still there?"

"I'm still here, Regina."

"Oh…"

"All I can say is, just be patient, God sees your heart. There are things He's getting ready to reveal to you. Pray and ask Him to prepare your heart for it." A tinge of fear passed through Regina. She had an idea, of what God was getting ready to show her. Lisa continued, "All that matters is that you let Him do whatever is needed to be done so that you'll be healed from all forms of emotional scars and rejection."

Regina was taken aback. *How does she know!* She never shared with anyone about the pain and rejection she went through as a child. The uneasiness Regina felt started to intensify. She was thinking that Lisa would try to convince her to talk about the past and reveal things she's not ready to discuss. She quickly came up with an excuse to get off the phone.

Before she had the chance to fabricate a story, Lisa surprised her by saying, "Don't worry about it. When it's time to release it, you will." Regina inhaled.

"I'll try, it's just that I'm tired of this."

"Instead of saying you'll try, start saying you can do all things through Christ who strengthens you."

"Okay, I will in Jesus name."

"Exactly! When you say it, believe it and know that His Word is working in your life, you hear me?"

"Yes."

"Well look, I am exhausted and I need to get some rest. Call me tomorrow and remember that everything you put your hands to will prosper in Jesus name! Go to school tomorrow, full of boldness and confidence knowing that you *know* you're going to pass that test in Jesus name! With God, you have more wisdom than your professors."

"Okay." Regina didn't sound too confident. Lisa had to believe that she planted into good ground.

"Okay, talk to you tomorrow."

"All right, good bye."

Lisa got up from the sofa and stretched, she was tired. "Lord God, I ask that you help Regina, Father. Deliver her from all her troubles. See her heart Father God. I rebuke you devil and command you to get your filthy hands off Regina right now in Jesus name! You're hold on her is broken and she is set free in the name of Jesus Christ! Thank you Father for delivering her from the spirit of fear. I thank You that the words I speak are Spirit and truth and they do not return unto You void but accomplishes what they were sent out to do! She's set free in Jesus name! Amen!"

As far as Lisa was concerned that prayer sealed the matter. She was ready to go to bed just like, she told Regina she was going to do. One thing about Lisa, she did not say what she didn't mean and she did not take too kindly to people who do. There was no room in her life for hypocrisy. But she often found herself surrounded by people, be it in church and the world, who have *no* problem with being blatant hypocrites. You would think that one would become use to people saying one thing and doing something totally different but when your heart is right you never will. Lisa's pet peeves were women, her age and younger, who were in sexual relationships outside of marriage, dropping babies like it is a fad. These same women would sit on the first pew in the church, every Sunday morning screaming and shouting, "Amen!" at the top of their lungs when the minister read the scripture, "...thou shall not fornicate." Lisa didn't understand the mentality of these women and they don't understand hers either. Why should they, when the pastor condones their lifestyles? These pastors saw nothing wrong with their parishioners giving into the weakness of the flesh over and over again, so why was she so uptight?

Some might think Lisa felt this way because she couldn't get a man, that was quite the contrary. She could pull *any* man that she wanted. She's 5'10, medium frame, dark brown healthy skin that glows bright from a proper diet and exercise. Lisa has extremely long hair. When she lets it down and rocked a natural hairstyle you better watch out! Men couldn't help but to do a double take marveling at her natural beauty from her head to her feet.

The beauty emanating from Lisa, shined from the inside out. This radiance came, *only* from living righteously and it amplified her physical attributes. Again, she had *no* problem *getting* a man. And Lisa was not in a relationship with *anyone*, because she *chose* to live her life as a *real* bona fide servant of the Most High God. Having a sincere relationship with God, meant not giving into the desires of the flesh that could and will separate you from Him. Besides, Lisa really didn't see what people got out of having illicit sex, especially when there was no commitment. When there is no love in a relationship, all that's left is emptiness, rejection and dejection, that will leave you tugging around emotional baggage.

When some people are tired of being empty and battling loneliness, they will finally go searching for God. Once they find God, they will eventually have to deal with the many layers of hurt that they used sex to mask the pain. Peeling off layers from numerous wounds, on top of unhealed wounds, will take time in order for you to have a successful personal relationship with God. He is willing to take time and go through the process of allowing you to heal, so that He *can* have a successful relationship with you, because He *knows* you are worth it.

Sin *is* pleasurable in the beginning but when the end comes, it brings unspeakable misery and turmoil. Hence; "Nothing last forever."

WHERE IS THE LOVE

...God anointed Jesus of Nazareth with the Holy Spirit and with power, who went about doing good and HEALING ALL who were OPPRESSED by the devil, for God was with Him... ACTS 10:38 NLJV, I can do ALL THINGS through Christ who STRENGTHTENS ME. PHILIPPIANS 4:13 NKJV

REGINA

hung the phone up and fell backwards on top of the bed, looking towards heaven. She wanted God to supernaturally open her rooftop and send down a message of hope and encouragement.

After lying motionless, waiting on God for about ten minutes, Regina sat up and slid down the side of her bed onto the floor. She reached underneath the bed and dragged out her stash of *top shelf* cannabis. The kind of weed that was guaranteed to get *ya hiiggghh!!*

It took Regina no time to roll up a nice size joint for her enjoyment. At fifteen, she rolled her first marijuana joint superbly, might I add, like she had been doing it her whole life. She was first introduced to marijuana by her then best friend, Trisha and she loved getting high. She loved the way it made her feel, especially when she was down and plagued by the many problems that came with being a teenager. Trisha definitely felt, that if *anyone* needed to get high the most, it would be her best friend, Regina. Trisha hand firsthand knowledge of her best friend's afflictions and just how horrible life really was for her.

Trisha experienced many sleepless nights after hearing about the constant turmoil in Regina's home. If she had not heard first,

34

hand she would not have ever believed that people could be so damn cruel! The stories that Trisha was told, sounded surreal, she had only seen them in movies. So, when Regina started buying and smoking excessive amounts of marijuana, Trisha was not at all surprised. Regina's parents never physically abused her, it was far worse than that. She was subjected to relentless psychological and verbal abuse. Everything Regina did was a complete failure in her parent's eyes. The psychological abuse afflicted upon Regina was so horrific, that her mother even felt the need to criticize the way that Regina breathe.

The ridiculous scolding happened one day while they were in the midst of eating dinner. Regina's mother commenced to say,

"Must I sit here trying to enjoy this wonderful meal I prepared for us and be fiercely annoyed by your loud breathing?"

Regina was shocked and dismayed that she almost dropped her fork on the table. She dared not do that innocent act of dropping her utensil or else that would have brought down a far worse harsher criticism by her mother. Or course, Regina was perplexed and didn't know what to do. At that point, she never realized that the mere act of breathing was so offensive!

So, what should I do? Stop breathing!

Regina's mother routinely wore white gloves around the house, after she did her chores. She would go behind Regina to perform an inspection like she was some kind of deranged drill sergeant. If Regina's mother found anything not cleaned to her liking, Regina was forced to clean everything all over again, until she received her mother's seal of approval. If that meant staying up until 3:00 AM on a school night until perfection was reached, so be it.

Regina would repeatedly cry out to Trisha, her best friend, all the time about not understanding *why* her parents were so cruel. Another example of her mother's rigorous ways, was when Regina left a smidge of toothpaste inside the bathroom sink one night after brushing her teeth. Her mother stormed into her room and snatched her out of bed, dragging Regina into the bathroom all the while yelling at the top of her lungs like a mad crazed woman. She violently shoved Regina against the shower doors as she pointed wildly into the sink.

"Look at this mess, you a filthy animal!" Regina reluctantly stepped forward looking into the sink expecting to see something unbelievably horrible! Instead, all Regina saw was a pencil tip of toothpaste sitting at the bottom of the sink! Episodes like this made Regina wonder *why,* she wasn't committed and wearing a strait jacket.

"Why can't I have parents that love me unconditionally! They claim they treat me like this to make me stronger but all it does is make me feel like I'm the stupidest person in the world! I hate it Trisha! I hate it!" That was what she screamed over the phone to her friend on many occasions.

Even now that Regina is a grown woman, whenever she was criticized about the smallest things, she conveniently used that as an excuse to get high. This was how Regina chose to cope with emotional pain. She knew this couldn't be right, using marijuana to escape her issues but she's not ready to give it up.

After Regina took the fourth toke from her joint, she was now relaxed, cool and feeling full of *false* confidence. She stood up from the floor and plopped down on the bed to finish studying.

The time was 8:30 PM. Regina had been reading the *same* line in her text book since 8:00 PM. All the while she's been trying to study, she hadn't gotten any further than the first page that she began reading, *and* she has thirty more pages to go. Regina would repeat the cycle all night because she was undoubtedly *stuck!*

The alarm clock sounded with a revengeful blare, causing Regina to jolt out of bed. It was now 8:20 AM.

"What! How!" Regina screamed. "It was *just* 8 o'clock when I started studying last night! Where did the time go!" She threw the covers off. "I have class in forty minutes!" Regina jumped out of bed and scrambled around in her closet looking for something to wear. She ran to the bathroom to splash water on her face. Regina clumsily snatched up the bottle of mouthwash, took a shot, swished it around her mouth then spat into the sink splashing mouthwash all over the place. "That's the least I can do. I don't wanna get an "F" for knocking the professor out with dog breath."

Regina slid on her shoes, grabbed her books and jack rabbits out the house in 1.2 split seconds. As soon as the door shut, she instantaneously remembered her car keys. Regina flung the door open and ran back into the house shouting,

"Where are my doggon keys! Geesh!" She tossed pillows from the sofa to the floor, feeling in between the cushions, there was nothing. She scanned the kitchen then she ran into the bedroom and snatched all the covers off her bed. Regina still couldn't find her keys.

"Are you serious!" She's stressing, she was tempted to go for her stash underneath the bed and take a very much needed smoke break. Regina couldn't do that because she was already late. The clock now read 8:40 AM. She cried out,

"Please God, where are my keys! Help me Father God and I swear I'll cut back on smoking-for real!"

As soon as Regina ended her desperate prayer, she had a thought to look inside her purse. She ran to her purse and immediately searched the bag and *Voilà!* There were Regina's keys, sitting at the bottom of her purse, right before her eyes. She slapped her forehead remembering that she put them inside her purse when she got home from school yesterday. "I really do need to cut down on smoking, anyway." It was a vain confession. In Regina's heart, she had no real plans of ever slowing down or stopping for that matter. She relied on the mind altering high more than a person with emphysema depended on an oxygen tank to breath.

WHAT DOES IT MEAN

DANIELLE

got ready for work in a blur. Her entire weekend was a complete bust. Danielle spent the weekend, alone in bed stuck on her laptop battling feelings of conviction that lingered on into the next day. A funk, so thick, surrounded her like a shroud. Danielle had no idea *where* the tormenting feelings came from. She's been dating Justin for over a year.

Why am I feeling like what I'm doing is wrong now! Is he married? Danielle's discombobulated state caused her to leave out the house in a daze, forgetting her attaché case. *I'm ten minutes late and that's gonna cost me in traffic.*

There were an avalanche of thoughts bombarding Danielle's mind at once. Fighting to concentrate on the road had become a daunting task as she sailed her sky blue 500 SEL Mercedes down LaCienega Blvd, to the 10 FWY East. The commute would take her into Downtown Los Angeles where her office was located.

Once again, Danielle asked herself a very difficult question, *was Justin married?*

She pondered the nerve wrenching question as she swerved in and out of traffic, on the FWY, like an Indianapolis racecar driver. Justin's marital state would not have been a surprise to Danielle. She had always been suspicious of her boyfriend but like most women, she chose to ignore them. Danielle had no regard for the repercussions that might come from Justin possibly being married *with* children because she is selfish. So, it mostly wasn't guilt that had her in a confused state of mind.

Is it the sex? Danielle continued to ask herself. *Why am I feeling this way!*

She was so engrossed in her thoughts that she nearly ran into the back of a Range Rover. There was an accident off the right shoulder on the FWY. It appeared that a driver of a midsized car side swiped a SUV as he tried to cross over into the right lane. Danielle was so wrapped up in her thoughts that she didn't notice the accident.

I mean, what's wrong with having sex with someone you care about! Justin and I are two consenting adults engaging in sex and expressing our love for one another physically! I don't see anything wrong with that! Sex is natural. That's what lovers do! Her reasoning sounded good but she still couldn't shake the feeling that something wasn't right.

Danielle barely remembered getting to her office, let alone, sitting at her desk staring at a black computer screen. She realized that she had been sitting in front of a dark monitor for the last twenty minutes, with her mind on everything but work. Her thoughts were broken by a soft knock on her office door. It's Chris, the mail clerk. He would politely stick his head inside the office, before he dared entered, making sure everything was decent. Chris had more than his fair share of walking into an executive's office, unannounced, catching a few of them in compromising positions. The things he witnessed, would have given Hustler's magazine a run for their money.

A subtle smile crossed Danielle's face. She had been watching him for a while and she definitely liked what she saw. Chris was medium height with a strong build. He had light brown creamy skin and a smile that could make your grandmother blush.

Chris had been working at the firm for three months and he had already made a good impression on his manage, that was what Danielle was told. If Chris kept his nose clean, he would have no problem climbing the corporate ladder. And it couldn't hurt if Chris learned to be at this young executive's beck and call. Danielle could tell he was a little head strong but that's okay. It will only make it *more* interesting breaking him down. Making Chris her side-piece, just might be something Danielle might seriously consider. The only thing that would cause her to abandon the idea of making him her boo, was his insufficient funds. Danielle knows how much mail clerks earn. Regardless of how much she fancied Chris, his income most likely would be the deal-breaker. Let's face it, a sista had needs. Danielle had to have *all* the money, *plus* his.

But I might have to break my own rule when it comes to this one, right here. And look at it on the brighter side, Danielle, if you catch this bait, before he's thrown in the lake, you are guaranteed to have first dibs on that check, if he becomes an executive.

Danielle was so caught up in carnal thoughts of Chris, that she hadn't noticed him standing in front of the desk, waiting for her to take her mail from his hand. Danielle quickly snapped out of her daydream state, looking directly into Chris's eyes. His face was flushed, and Danielle was embarrassed.

Damn! Why and I staring at this man like I want to eat him alive! Chris cleared his throat,

"Here's your mail, Ms. Stevens." Danielle tried to save face. She sat straight in her chair smoothing out invisible wrinkles in her expensive designer business skirt.

I can't believe myself! Now was the time that Danielle wished she could hide underneath her desk and stay there until Chris left. Instead, she elected to remain cool and calm under pressure. She had been in worse positions. Danielle cleared her throat and ran her hand through her hair, barely smiling as she reached for the mail. "How was your weekend?" she asked trying to act like she wasn't just undressing the poor lad with her eyes only a minute ago.

"Oh, I just relaxed and enjoyed...*myself,*" Chris said mischievously.

Is he fishing? Danielle decided to divulge Chris, by participating in this lil cat and mouse game brewing before her.

"So, how was *your* weekend?" Chris asked with a twinkle of hope in his eyes.

He's bold and cute! I like that combination. Let's see how he handles this. "My weekend was so-so. It could have been *a lot,* better if I had some...company?" Danielle leaned back in her chair and seductively crossed her legs. The tigress was on the prowl. "You know what they say, all work and no play," Danielle abruptly stopped in mid-sentence when she saw Chris licking his

40

luscious lips as his eyes devoured her sexy legs. *What are you doing! This is a lawsuit waiting to happen! You should at least wait until you're off the clock, Danielle Stevens.* She had to get back on track, quick! "Let's just say, I would have enjoyed my weekend a lot better if I wasn't stuck in the house doing work."

Chris was immediately taken aback by the very noticeable change in Danielle's demeanor. She went from hot, to bitter cold right in front of his face. Chris was indeed confused but he took the hint and excused himself. "Well okay, I'll let you get back to work."

"Okay, thanks." Danielle kept her head down refusing to look at him.

"Have a nice day, Ms. Stevens."

"You too," Danielle said closely studying her mail. Chris walked out of her office discombobulated and closed the door shaking his head.

Women! He somberly pushed the mail cart down the corridor to the next office. "God, *please* help me to understand them! How does someone change from hot to cold within a matter of seconds?" *I don't know why I'm even tripping anyway. She probably only date men with money, and lots of it!*

Danielle spent her lunchtime in the office eating a scrumptious turkey sandwich on wheat bread, from the famous Jerry's Deli, with a garden-fresh salad on the side. Danielle wanted to stay in to get some work done on the ad campaigns. That way, if she got enough work out the way, she wouldn't be faced with yet, another long, lonely dreadful weekend. Danielle was hoping to spend some quality time with her boo and not by herself, in bed with only her laptop to keep her warm. But so much for wishful thinking, it's a slim chance that things will not go as Danielle planned. Something always seemed to happen to keep her and Justin apart. It's a wonder how they were even able to spend time together last Friday.

As Danielle took a bite from her sandwich her cell phone rang. She grabbed a napkin wiping her hands off and answered the phone,

"This is Danielle Stevens."

"Hey gurl!" Lisa's voice full of God's sunshine streamed through the phone straight to Danielle's heart. "How are you?" She never failed to put a smile on her face. Danielle loved how Lisa was so dedicated to God. It's very rare to see someone with so much dedication nowadays.

How is it possible for one to be so loyal to someone they've never seen in life? Danielle asked herself that question often but she wouldn't dare ask Lisa, for fear of offending her. Regardless to how Danielle felt, she would always have much respect for Lisa's love and devotion to her Lord and Savior. She saw evidence of something real in Lisa's life that couldn't be explained. "I am fine, and how are you, darling?"

"I'm blessed, thanks for asking. I was thinking about you this morning and I thought I'd reach out and touch basis with you. How's everything going?"

"Everything is fine!" Danielle squealed a little too excitedly. That usually happened when Danielle wasn't being truthful. "I'm just having lunch in the office and trying to catch up on some work." For some reason, Danielle suddenly felt compelled to shed all her deep dark secrets with Lisa, but of course she wouldn't dare.

"Oh! I didn't mean to disturb you while you're eating lunch and working. I just wanted to send some love your way."

"Ahhhhh! That's so sweet. Thank you, lady."

"You're so welcome. Speaking of love, are you coming to church this Sunday?" The Greater Refuge Church was a popular church based in South Los Angeles. Although, Lisa and Danielle went to church for different reasons, they still enjoyed coming together one day out of the week, even if it was only for a couple of hours.

"I most definitely will be there." As a child, Danielle was programmed by her parents and their community to attend church, faithfully, for appearance sake. There wasn't too much emphasis on reading and living God's word *outside* of church.

"Well, have a good day, sweetie and I'll talk to you later."

"You too Lisa," Danielle said smiling. She felt warmth surround her. This warmth she felt, always engulfed her whenever she encountered someone who's heart was sincere. Sincerity was a rare commodity, nowadays. People were so bombarded by life's mishaps that no one really took the time to extend true concern for the next person. When someone actually showed that they cared, it was priceless to Danielle. This was the very reason why she valued Lisa's friendship because she knew Lisa was truly concerned for her wellbeing.

When Danielle's eyes scanned over the pile of paperwork still sitting before her, she was instantly snapped back to reality. She was tempted to toss the massive number of documents into the waste basket next to her desk and walk out the door. But being homeless wouldn't look good on Danielle, at all. She wouldn't last a minute on the treacherous streets of Downtown Los Angeles, on 5th and Main, which is considered Skid Row. That is where all the hustlers, pimps, hoes, drug addicts and drug dealers come out to play. Danielle would be an easy target, looking like a pink elephant with wings flying in the sky. She rubbed her eyes, kicked off her heels and settled in for the long haul.

"A glass of brandy would sure be nice right about now."

SUBSTITUTES ARE WELCOME

CYNTHIA

was forcefully awakened by the sun's piercing rays blaring through the partially opened blinds in her bedroom. For a quick moment, she forgot where she was and how she even got there. It's not until Cynthia looked at the enormous portrait of two naked women entangled in one another's arms while a naked man stood in the background, watching. *Ding!* She knew exactly where she was.

Cynthia sat up in *her* bed staring at an older attractive man and a beautiful young woman, that she was sandwiched in between.

"What the hell!" she said out loud in a hoarse voice.

Out of habit, Cynthia never let *anyone* kiss the morning sun in her bed. She didn't care *how* great they were in bed! "Uh-uh, wake up sleeping beauty and Mr. GQ." She began shaking their shoulders. Her actions only caused Sleeping Beauty to stir a little and turn on her side. Mr. GQ grunted and pulled the covers over his head. Cynthia was not in the mood for this. With the grace of a professional gymnast, she lifts her slim frame up with one hand and with the help of her right foot, she leaped over the distinguished gentleman, landing on the floor with not so much as a small thump. She was compelled to take a bow but fear of her guest waking up catching her in a full-fledge curtsy would have been awkward, to say the least.

Cynthia went into the closet and took out a short black silk robe then she quietly exited the room. A night filled with excessive drinking and uninhibited sex made an individual hungrier than a bear coming out of hibernation.

Cynthia flew into the kitchen like a crack fiend on steroids and searched the refrigerator for something, *anything* to eat. Everything she laid her eyes on, made her salivate. *I'm so hungry I could eat a cow!* Of course, that was only a figure of speech. Cynthia was well disciplined in that area of her life. Having discipline with what she put into her mouth, with regards to *food*, was how Cynthia maintained such a lovely figure.

Quickly regaining her sense of composure, Cynthia decided to settle for a couple of slices of bacon, eggs a piece of toast and a cup of strong black coffee to try to keep the unforgiving hang-over at bay. Now, all she needed was a frying pan.

Cynthia raced over to the cabinet, snatched up a frying pan sitting it on the burner and tossed the bacon inside, wishing it was already done! "Oh yeah! I need a plate." She quickly dashed to the other side of the kitchen to get a plate and trotted back to the stove.

She's mesmerized as she watched the bacon turn golden crispy brown, Cynthia then, cracked open two eggs into the same frying pan.

"*Mmmm!* It smells so damn good!"

Cynthia displayed how excited she was that the bacon was done, by doing a happy dance right in front of the stove. As she calmed down, she felt two arms encircle her waist. Cynthia jumped startled and was immediately irritated. She was about to have a fit! She whirled around to confront the culprit and came face to face with the beautiful young lady she just spent the night with. *See! This is how people get caught up in emotions. I can't have this!* Cynthia took a deep breath and politely removed the young lady's arms from around her waist, the young lady giggled. Cynthia couldn't help but to be taken in by her beauty. *Snap out of it Cindy! Sex 'em and leave 'em! That's what you do! Nothing more, nothing less.*

"You're not a morning person, I see," the young lady chirped.

Damn! Her voice sounds like butter. I am so tripping right now! It's time for the both of them to get out of my house, like rat now!

"Well, good morning to you too," the young beauty smiled as she daringly took a piece of Cynthia's bacon from out of her plate.

Cynthia stared at the you, ignorant, young beauty like she was crazy as hell! *She...den...lost...her...ever...lov—ing...mind! You do not touch my bacon, that's what you don't do! And, as hungry as I am!* "Look sweetheart..." Cynthia sucked in a deep breath to compose herself, "...I don't mean to be blunt," *yes, I do,* "...but-"

"You want me to kick rocks," sleeping Beauty finished Cynthia's sentence. "I know, I'm familiar with the protocol. It wasn't nothing more than a booty call to you, I get it." Sleeping Beauty turned to walk out of the kitchen, but before she left out, she faced Cynthia and says, "Oh! And by the way, my name is Lori, that is, if you even cared to know my name." Cynthia stared at Lori blankly, with her mouth open as she felt a slice of guilt wrap its coils around Cynthia's throat.

Say something fool, before she leaves! No! Let her go! That's how you keep from getting...hurt. Intense fear gripped Cynthia's soul. *Baby girl will learn, one way or the other. If you want to play this game and win, you cannot afford to get attached...to anyone, period!*

Cynthia will be tormented all day by her own tainted rationalization. And for some strange reason, it was getting harder to continue believing her own cock and bull philosophy. It had grown tired, like a broken record that needed to be discarded ASAP!

After Cynthia scarfed down her, barely warm breakfast, which had only been eaten for nutrients, it for damn sure wasn't eaten for pleasure, she returned to her bedroom to wake Mr. GQ. Fortunately, he knew the game better than little Miss Sunshine.

When she stepped into the room, GQ was already up, dressed and ready to bounce. The only thing he said to Cynthia as he left out the front door was,

"It was fun, hopefully we'll run into one another again." A quick meaningful smile crossed his handsomely chiseled face as he exited. He didn't bother to leave a number and he didn't ask for hers. Cynthia would bet her last bottom dollar that if GQ saw her eating breakfast, he would not have dared to remove *anything* from her plate without her expressed permission. That's how much of an

OG he was. GQ knew the game and he obviously respected the game. Get yours and get on! Cynthia liked that.

She tried to convince herself that it was best for all involved to go their separate ways. If they should meet again, it would be purely by fate. But Cynthia still remained powerless when it came to the tinge of guilt that lingered behind, somewhere deep in her heart. In all of her years of being emotionally unattached to those she shared her body with, she was never convicted nor had she ever felt guilt. This new thing that she felt, terrified the hell outta her. There were apparent cracks in the walls of Cynthia's fortress. She was no longer untouchable.

What is wrong with me! she screamed out loud as she removed her robe, letting it fall to the floor. Cynthia stepped into the shower and turned the hot water on at full blast imagining that its cleansing power was washing away her horrible childhood memories down the drain.

Cynthia never engaged in conversations about her past. It was just too painful rehashing the past but she longed to share *some* of her more *fonder* memories of her adolescent years with her friends. The memories that Cynthia would love to suppress, were the ones of being tossed to and fro, by foster parents, to foster parents. But the memories that she absolutely dreaded the most, were the memories of being molested, raped, beaten, unloved and unwanted by almost every family she lived with. How can one share the tragedies that she dealt with, to anyone? Unfortunately, Cynthia's parents left her to fend for herself at an early age. Drugs were their main priority and parenting was on the bottom of the totem pole.

She was in sixth grade when she came home one day from school, to find both her parents sprawled out on the living room floor with syringes protruding out their arms and their eyes were open wide as if they were still in a state of shock. Their mouths were stretched open, forming loud silent screams that were only heard in hell. Any other child, would have run for dear life after seeing their parent's lifeless bodies lying on the living room floor but that wasn't the case for Cynthia. She was cold and emotionless as she stepped over their cold spiritless bodies to go into her room without even a second glance. From that day forth, Cynthia learned to preserve some peace of mind by acting as if nothing was wrong and everything was normal.

That type of behavior is developed when someone is reared in a dysfunctional setting, without love, care and other life learning necessities.

Cynthia had become desensitized at a dangerous age, the early developmental ages. Seeing first hand, how her parents lived taught Cynthia how to prepare for the worse. Prior to her parent's death, Cynthia had heard countless stories about her classmate's parents overdosing from some type of drug abuse. Hearing about someone dying from an overdose in Cynthia's neighborhood was as common as breathing. She knew it was only a matter of time before what her parents were slaves to, would take their lives. When she heard that her classmate, Louis, mother died from a heroin overdose, she began having strong premonitions of her own parent's death.

On various occasions, Cynthia would walk into her house and be greeted by Louis's mom, who'd be sitting in the living room trying hard not to nod off into a drug stupor, until Cynthia was clearly out of view. With a crooked smile on her face, she would slur and barely let out an audible,

"Hello," to Cynthia while trying to hide her sins underneath her thigh.

Louis's mother and Cynthia's parents would be so high that they could never move fast enough to hide their drug paraphernalia before Cynthia saw them. She'd always catch a look at the tools they used for getting high, just as someone tried to reach for newspapers or whatever to cover up spoons, lighters, syringes, belts, cotton balls and small squares of tin foil. Cynthia always felt embarrassed for them when they did this. She'd quickly advert her eyes and mumble, hello as she retreated to her bedroom for the rest of the night.

After the death of her parents, Cynthia had no one to care for her, not even relatives. She became a ward of the state and that was far worse than living with her drug addicted parents. Dealing with dirty old men who tried to creep into her bedroom when they thought her parents had fallen into deep drug nods was a walk in

48

the park compared to living in foster homes. At least her parents perverted male friends were never able to go too far when she lived with her parents. Before the predator could crawl underneath the covers to violate Cynthia, her father would come busting through the door like superman and violently grab him by his throat, tossing him out the room like a sack of potatoes. One time, her father actually caught a man before he opened the door to her bedroom and he beat him to a pulp. Cynthia thought for certain that he was dead. But she never knew how her father always seem to catch the perpetrators before the act was committed. She was always grateful that her parents were there to protect her.

At the tender age of eleven Cynthia barley understood life. Her parents never shared with her the terrible and cruel things people tried to do to little girls. Even though she was young and naïve, she knew that what those men tried to do to her was wrong. Their faces were hidden in the darkness of her tiny bedroom but she always felt something menacing, something evil exuding from them. When she heard, them trying to creep into her room, terror took hold of her small frame, leaving her temporarily paralyzed for a few seconds that seemed like hours. A river of tears streamed down the sides of Cynthia's face, pooling inside her ears. In this coldhearted world, her parents were all she had and they were no longer there to prevent her from being physically and sexually abused.

Cynthia had the displeasure of living in several foster homes before the age of eighteen. And in every home, she was molested, raped or beaten mercilessly. These horrid images plagued her mind whenever her friends shared their childhood memories. Cynthia swore she would never tell anyone about the abuse she was subjected to. She planned to drag her secrets to the grave.

Cynthia got out the shower and busied herself by cleaning her house like she was expecting a visit from the Queen of England. Cynthia secretly suspected that she had a compulsive disorder about dirty floors. When the cleaning was done, she wanted her kitchen floor so sparkly clean that even *she* could eat off the bare floor if she chose to. But that's a far stretch, even for her, seeing that she's a germaphobe.

Now that Cynthia was finished doing her winter-spring cleaning, she made herself a stiff drink, hit play on the CD player and reclined back on the sofa, letting the smooth, melodic sounds of Luther Vandross sooth her. The combination of liquor and music created a peaceful environment for mediation and relaxation to release the tension that was built up from life's twists, turns, crashes and burns.

Most of the tension in Cynthia's life came from choices she made throughout her adulthood. Sometimes, she felt like she was running on a hamster wheel and she didn't know how to jump off.

Some people, unlike Cynthia, do wake up from the vicious cycles they have continually repeated in their lives and cry out for help. Some will seek people for help and others will go directly to Jesus Christ. Many never escape the cycle and sadly, those people end up perishing.

Cynthia was in her zone, singing like a bona fide Luther Vandross background saanngaa! *"...a house is not a home when you're not heerree with meeee...."* Then the phone rang and she stumbled to her feet. "I'ma have to disagree with you Luther, *my* house is *still* a home, even when I'm all alone honey!" Cynthia had no problem lying to herself. "I don't have time for nobody's drama ova here! *Uh-uh!"* She slurred into the phone, "Hello."

"You bent, *already!"* Danielle exclaimed, teasingly.

"Danni?" That was Cynthia's nick name for Danielle since their college days.

"Yeah girl, what's going on with you! I see you hitting the bottle pretty early gurl! Need I stage an intervention?" Danielle laughed, trying to indicate that she was only joking.

"Ha! Ha! Mutha-"

"Uh-uh! Shut yo mouth!" Danielle said with a burst of uncontrollable laughter. "That's how you feel!" she taunted, in between gut wrenching cackling.

"Awwww! So, you're a comedian now?" Cynthia said sourly as she stumbled and fell back onto the sofa. "I thought we were here?" Cynthia emphasized what she meant by beating on her chest with a balled-up fist.

50

By now, Danielle sensed Cynthia's true frustration and tried to contain her laughter.

"Knock it off! You know I'm only playing with you," Danielle teased. Cynthia blew out a heavy stream of air into the phone. *Is she for real?* Danielle was shocked. "Are you serious, Cynthia! You're really angry?" *I can't believe it! She's really angry? Wow, we always play like this. She must have had a bad night.*

"Whatever," Cynthia said pouting.

"If you don't knock it off, Cindy! What is wrong with you? I'm just playing! Really, Cynthia?" Danielle hated when Cynthia acted extra.

"You stop!" Cynthia bellowed out. She almost surprised herself by the force of her protest. "Why do you keep playing with my emotions like this, Danielle?" Cynthia tried to sound assertive but the liquor slowed her speech causing her to sound whiny.

"Emotions!" Danielle sang out. "When did you sprout emotions?" Cynthia yanked the phone from her ear and stared at it in disbelief.

You picked the wrong damn day to play, Danni.

Danielle continued to make light of the situation while Cynthia became enraged. She's had enough, and Cynthia demonstrated this by slamming the phone down in Danielle's face. Yeah, she felt guilty as hell, but she wasn't guilty enough to call her friend back. Cynthia had a point to prove.

Don't play with my emotions when I've trusted you enough to share them with you. "The world doesn't revolve around you, woman! I have problems too but you wouldn't know that, because I haven't shared them with you!" Cynthia screamed from agony and she fell to her knees and then to the floor in a fetal position, crying like a baby. "I haven't told you *anything!"* she said between hard sobs that came from a battered soul. "Momma!" she sobbed. "Daddy! Why did you leave me! *Why!"* Cynthia bellowed as her tears gush out like torrents of rain. Every time she tried to lower the flood gates and pull herself together, she found herself crying even harder. Terrified that she was falling apart at the seams, Cynthia bolted up from her fetal position, ran to her bedroom, threw herself on top of her bed and buried her face deep into the pillow.

"Cynthia." She heard a sweet, loving caring voice call her name but she refused to answer. *"Cynthia!"* The voice grew louder.

"Yes, Lord! I know! I know…but I'm not ready. I'm just not ready! I'm too ashamed! How can you love someone like me? How?" Within minutes, Cynthia fell into a sound sleep. It was the best sleep she had in years.

WHY LORD

LISA

just finished cleaning the kitchen and preparing her mother's lunch. Now she's sitting at the table ready to digest God's word.

Lisa opened her Bible and began to read but then she stopped and stared out the window deep in thought.

Why Lord? Why don't I have friends of like faith walking this walk with me? All the people that I try to call friends live a life opposite of Your word. If I need encouragement they aren't able to encourage me because they are all drowning in their own despair. I don't understand Lord. I mean, I know Your understanding is not my understanding and Your ways not ways but Jesus! Even You, had eleven disciples, excluding Judas, who followed You and had Your back. Can I at least, have one, true friend who is not ashamed of the gospel of Jesus Christ! Who loves You and Your commandments? How does this help me being surrounded by unbelievers? It feels like I'm alone in my walk with You.

Lisa expressed her frustrations to her Father God in silence. Her heart weighed heavy. She desired to be surrounded by righteous people or people who *at least* desired, with all their heart, to walk on the path of the straight and narrow.

As Lisa continued pondering her predicament, perhaps feeling a little self-pity, God burst through her feelings of sorrow and brought comfort to her soul.

"If not you then who? If you aren't willing to allow your life to shine like a beacon in the night for those who cannot see and are stumbling however will they come to know Me or recognize My

53

voice? If you surround yourself with righteous people you will have no desire to extend compassion to those who need it the most. Lisa, continue to walk on the path of the straight and narrow to remain an example for those I have sent into your life. Don't worry. You are where I need you to be."

Lisa was comforted by God's encouraging words. Although her soul may be at ease, she still couldn't help but wonder how it would be to have *one* friend who had reverential fear for God. She wanted to know how it felt to have a friend, who loved God with all their heart, just like she does.

PISSED

REGINA

shoved through the door of her apartment and marched in with fire in her eyes! She could have sworn that she felt the ground scorched underneath her feet, that's how hot she was!

All the contents in her hands, keys, jacket and purse were thrown to the middle of the perfectly manicured living room floor.

"This is some bull! I studied hard for this dumb ass test!" Actually, the only thing Regina studied hard for, was sleep after getting high and dozing off but she must have forgotten that, too. Yup, Marijuana will do that to ya. It will deteriorate your short-term memory cells. "I might as well give it up and be a coldhearted manipulator like Cynthia. At least, she's happy! *Ugh!*" Regina shouted to the empty room.

NUISANCE

DANIELLE

sat in her office chair staring at her cell phone in sheer disbelief.

"No, this heffa didn't just hang up in my face!" She pressed send to call her ungrateful friend back. "Wait 'til she gets her ungrateful ass on this phone!" Just as Danielle was mentally preparing to blow her friend's eardrum out, there's a knock at the door. It's her secretary of two years.

"Ms. Stevens?" Ms. Kingston said as she gently opened the office door.

"Yes?" Danielle hung up her cell phone.

"Mr. James would like to see you in his office." Danielle fought not to roll her eyes in disgust.

Ughhh! What does he want! All kinds of thoughts were running through her head about what she wanted to say to Cynthia and what she *wished* she could say to her whack boss! *He probably wants to load me down with more work so I can't spend time with my man. Ever since he met Justin at the annual Christmas party, he's been intentionally making my workload unbearable. Or, he probably didn't get any from his wife so he wants to get off by throwing disgusting innuendos at me. Lawd, that man!*

Danielle had often times thought about filing sexual harassment charges against her raunchy lewd employer. Unfortunately, she didn't have the time it took to deal with the tedious process of proving one guilty.

WHAT'S BURIED COMES OUT

CYNTHIA

woke up with her hand stuck to her tear and saliva stained face. She was disoriented and didn't remember *how* or *why* she's even lying in bed.

Cynthia quickly turned over and sat up, examining her pillow like it was a weird science project gone wrong.

"What is this? Liquor!" She couldn't believe what she saw. "Why is my pillow soaked!" She turned to the nightstand and saw a half-emptied glass of liquor sitting on the edge. "*Okaaaay*, it doesn't look like anything was wasted." She rubbed her hand across her face, then she looked, once again, shockingly at her pillow. "Are these tears and spit!"

Cynthia was too ashamed to acknowledge that her armor could possibly be cracked. She threw the pillow across the floor in a fury.

"What is wrong with me!"

The constant beeping of the answering machine only added to Cynthia's irritation. She bounced to the other side of the bed, yanked up the answering machine and was about to hurl it across the room, smashing it against the wall but she stopped in midair.

"I need to stop tripping! This might be a work assignment or something important." She pressed play on the machine and walked into the bathroom, listening intently as Danielle's agitated voice filled the room.

57

"What's up with you, Cindy!" Danielle hissed, sounding like a disciplinarian. *"You know I can't stand the phone being hung up in my face! That's immature and childish. I just got out of a meeting with my boss, Mr. Suck Face. Don't make me have to deal with your nonsense too. I'm not happy with you woman!"* Beep.

Cynthia flushed the toilet in response to Danielle's complaint.

"Well, join the club. I gotta few bones to pick with you, myself," Cynthia tossed back to the machine, like she could really give two licks about Danielle's feelings. When Cynthia was about to turn on the shower the door bell rung. "And the grand prize goes to the jerk at my door, for having really bad timing," she said out loud to whoever was at her door, about to interrupt her personal time.

Cynthia loved taking showers. There was something about the sound of running water and its cleansing principals, that created an environment that brought about clear and precise thoughts.

Cynthia marched to the front door not even bothering to peer through the peep hole before snatching it open wide. She was greeted by her best friend. The look on Danielle's face was everything that horror movies were made of. If looks could kill...

"What's the deal with you?" Danielle said through gritted teeth as she barged pass Cynthia, like she owned the place.

"Well, hello to you too," Cynthia said to her angry best friend's back. By the time she closed the door, Danielle was standing at the bar with a bottle of brandy in her hand, ready to pour herself a glass. Of course, the brandy was from *her* private stock *anyway*, so Cynthia didn't say a word.

Danielle walked to the sofa, sat down and kicked off her heels. She was ready to let her best friend have it like, there was no tomorrow.

"What do you have to say for yourself, woman?" Danielle asked as her eyes bore holes through her friend.

Cynthia took a seat on the opposite end of the sofa, studying her friend of ten plus years, looking for a sign. Some sort of secret oath shared between close friends, reassuring them, that they could share *anything* with that friend and there would be no regrets.

"*Hellooo!*" Danielle said, breaking into Cynthia's concentration.

"Danielle...," Cynthia said sternly, "...do you *ever* think about *anyone* other than yourself!" Danielle's eyes opened wide. She could not believe the audacity.

"Are you serious! Ms. Love 'em-and-leave 'em-wont-neva-let-anyone-get-close-to-you-not-even-Jesus!" Cynthia winced, like she had been pierced in the heart with a dagger. Danielle's face softened when she saw the pained expression on best friend's face. Cynthia leaned back against the sofa looking wounded. "I'm sorry," Danielle offered a heartfelt apology. Then she shifted her body to face her best friend. "I do think about others. That's why I'm here, trying to find out what's going on with my bestie! Come on Cindy, you can tell me." She reached out and squeezed her hand. "I'm listening." Danielle smiled and turned her gaze to the more than half emptied glass of brandy that sat on the table in front of her. "Wait a minute, let me refresh my drink right quick, right fast and I'll give you my undivided attention."

She winked at Cynthia as she jumped to her feet to get another drink. Within seconds, Danielle was back seated on the sofa, ready to listen to whatever her dear friend had to say. And knowing Cynthia, it could be *anything*. That was why Danielle needed an extra stiff drink to help brace her for whatever her friend might reveal.

Cynthia wanted so badly to expose the darkness that lurked within. Her soul screamed to *finally* be set free!

Let it out! she yelled to herself. The love and show of concern on Danielle's face only caused Cynthia to be more vulnerable. She feared her friend's reproach more than anything else. She wouldn't be able to stand herself if the love she saw in Danielle's eyes changed to disgust, after she revealed the God-awful things that happened to her. *No! I can't take that chance!*

"What is it honey?" Danielle attempted to reassure Cynthia that everything would be okay, by moving closer to her and holding Cynthia's hand in a show of support.

Cynthia allowed her hand to be held for a second, then she gently pulled it from Danielle's soft grip. The problem wasn't Danielle's genuine act of kindness, the problem was definitely with

Cynthia. Instead of feeling comforted by her friend, she felt lust and that made her more ashamed.

Here I am having carnal desires for my friend, when all she's trying to do is console me. Damn! Damn! Damn! "Thank you for offering your support but I, I can't right now."

Disappointment flashed across Danielle's face but from her personal experience, she knew not to force the issue. Danielle knew all too well, *how* it felt to harbor a secret that you were afraid to reveal. It took her nearly twenty years to tell her parents about her uncle molesting her from the age of three until she was nine years old. Thank God, that her parents believed her but they were in total shock and disbelief. When they finished exacting revenge upon her uncle, her mother's brother, Danielle even felt sorry for the sick man. Other than her parents, she never told another soul. But unfortunately, Danielle's parents pride and concern about what *others* may think, shamefully kept them from allowing their daughter to seek the professional help that she needed. Danielle often times, wondered how different her life would be if she went behind her parents back and sought help for herself. If Danielle had gotten the help she needed she probably wouldn't feel the need to crave so much attention from the opposite sex. But no matter how much attention she received from men and women, it still didn't fill the empty void that sat in the pit of her soul.

"It's all good, just know I'm always here for you whenever you need me," Danielle said as she endearingly squeezed Cynthia's hand.

"I know," Cynthia said with a smile. Danielle pointed her index finger at her friend and says,

"I just have one more concern." Cynthia rolled her eyes, threw her head back laughing out loud. "Please, don't hang the phone up in my face ever again! It's rude."

"Gotcha," Cynthia said trying to fight back laughter.

"Don't laugh." Danielle playfully hit Cynthia's hand and pouted. "It's not funny." They stared into one another's eyes. At first, their intentions were playful, then their gaze became more intense. Danielle felt something pass between them that couldn't be denied and she knew Cynthia felt it too. The sheer desire was apparent in her eyes. They say that the eyes were the windows to your soul. Well, Danielle could see straight, no pun intended, into the future through her friend's eyes. That was how unmasked Cynthia's passion for Danielle was. As much as she tried to fight the feelings stirring inside her loins, it only grew stronger. Cynthia moved her hand causing the tips of her finger to graze the top of Danielle's hand, ever so gently. That simple act made Danielle's heart beat fiercely, she wanted to faint. *What is this?!* Danielle was so nervous that was felt sick in the stomach. *Justin is the only one who makes me feel this way, men period! This is my best friend! And she's a woman!*

Danielle stumbled to her feet. She didn't know if it was the sudden attraction to Cynthia or the liquor in her system that caused her legs to buckle underneath the weight of her body. It was more than likely both. Danielle moved about as clumsily as an ox while she tried to quickly put on her thousand dollar stilettos. Cynthia stared at her intensely.

I know she felt that too! Whoa! Where is she going? She's trying to leave before the show gets started? "What are you doing, Danielle?" Cynthia's voice reflected a world of confusion that Danielle's sudden actions shoved her in.

"Um, um...," Danielle stuttered as she grabbed her designer bag and tossed back the rest of the fiery drink in one fluid move, "...I, I gotta go."

Cynthia jumped to her feet, Danielle was almost at the door. Cynthia moved with lightning speed as she grabbed Danielle's keys from the bar and ran like a track star, trying to beat her to the door. She squeezed her body in between the door and her friend. Danielle was nervous, frighten and excited. Cynthia could see her friend's heart pounding through her expensive silk blouse. She laughed silently. Cynthia was tickled and excited about the obvious affect she had on her best friend.

Wow! This is gonna be good! she gloated. Through a shaky voice, Danielle says,

"Cindy-wha, what are you doing!" Her eyes pled for Cynthia to move out the way so she could burn rubber out the door. Cynthia grinned mischievously. She loved seeing Danielle so darn

61

uncomfortable. "Cindy please!" Danielle pleaded. She caught the tone of her voice, Danielle had never begged for anything in her life and she couldn't believe she was begging now! *What kind of hold does she have on me!* When Danielle touched the side of Cynthia's neck, an involuntary shudder ran down her spine. They were both playing games with one another. But the game that they played, was a treacherous one.

Cynthia finally decided to give Danielle a break. She leaned forward, stopping within inches of Danielle and her breathing became erratic. Cynthia's hand slowly appeared before both of their eyes. There was something dangling from her finger tips. Danielle didn't know what Cynthia held in her hand until she pried her eyes from Cynthia's face and saw that the dangling object were her car keys.

"You think you might need these?" Cynthia said with a child-like grin on her face. Embarrassment showed all over Danielle. She took her keys, dropped her head to the floor and says,

"Oh." Cynthia opened the door, stretched out her hand like an usher indicating that Danielle was free to go. Danielle let a meek, "Thank you," escape through her lips. She proceeded out the door to retreat to the privacy of her car, so she could sit back and try to figure out just what happened!

WHAT JUST HAPPENED

DANIELLE

had been hunched over the steering wheel of her Mercedes for about thirty minutes…stuck.

What did I get myself into and what am I going to do about it! S

Danielle was dazed and confused but still found herself compelled to go back inside of Cynthia's house. She fought the impulse to feed her curiosity and tapped the electronic key on the steering wheel column and she peeled off.

After getting out the shower, Danielle laid down on the bed still trying to process what took place at Cynthia's house.

What did I do to cause all this? These feelings just came out from nowhere! Danielle went to Cynthia's house because she was angry and later, became concern for her friend. But she didn't, in a billion years, ever imagine or even entertained the idea of being intimate with Cynthia! *She's my best friend, and she's a woman!*

Danielle sat up in the middle of the bed feeling discombobulated. "Justin!" His name popped into her head. Saying his name was so soothing to Danielle's spirit. She reached for the phone, Justin would be her antidote. After the third ring, Justin answered the phone sounding out of breath. Danielle's suspicions were aroused. "Why are you breathing so hard?" she asked, not trying to hide her skepticism.

"I'm sorry, baby. I was in the shower at the gym when I heard my phone ringing. It's in my locker and I tried to catch it before it hung up. What's up? What can I do for you?" Justin asked, sounding sexy as ever.

Good answer, Danielle said to herself. She believed her man was being truthful so, she decided to let the inquisition go and continue with her plans. *Besides, he knows what I need.* A mischievous grin spread across Danielle's face and an, innocent naughty girl's voice she says, "Where are you going when you leave the gym?" Her voice oozed with the lust she felt.

"I'll go, *wherever* you want me to, baby."

"Humph, don't make me wait too long." She hung the phone up and rushed to get everything ready for their rendezvous. She sat a bottle of Dom Perignon Rose on ice as she prepared the dessert, strawberries and whip cream.

Danielle woke up the next morning hoping her mind would be free of Cynthia. She wanted her memory scrubbed clean of every lustful thought Danielle had for Cynthia. Unfortunately, the romantic night with Justin did nothing to relieve Danielle from her mental anguish. If anything, Danielle's mind was on Cynthia even *more!* Danielle had to make a decision. Either she would find a way to completely rid herself of these tormenting, implausible desires for her best friend or…eventually, she would give into what *appeared* to be inevitable.

A COMMON BOND

Lisa, Regina and Danielle were seated together in the middle section of the large popular church, Greater Refuge. Of course, Cynthia hadn't arrived yet but that was always to be expected. She didn't care too much for religion or beliefs that made people feel guilty about acting upon their carnal desires. But she wanted to show support for her friends and not come off like a total whoremonger.

Cynthia finally arrived and slid into the seat next to Danielle, just as the minister graced the pulpit with his anointed presence. Both exchanged quick nervous glances but not a word was uttered.

Lisa reached over Danielle and squeezed Cynthia's hand endearingly. Regina leaned forward to give her a smile.

"Let us turn to the book of James chapter 1, verse 22," the man of God says. "I will be reading from the New King James Version." He cleared his throat, took a sip of water and continued, "Church, read along with me, *'But be doers of the word, and not hearers only, deceiving yourselves."* Now turn to Matthew 7 verse 24 and let's read together, *therefore whoever hears these sayings of mine, and does them, I will liken him to a wise man who **built his house on the rock.'"*** There you have it church! The Bible says, God says, don't just *sit* and hear His word without putting it into action people. If you are praying for healing in your body put it into action and know that you *know* that you are healed! Walk around like you are healed. If you are believing for your finances to be straighten out don't walk around like you are defeated and scared that your lights are going to be cut off!" The auditorium erupts in laughter. "You walk around in the authority and the power of Jesus Christ and know that you *know* that you own the electric company and they'll have to start paying you!" People all around the auditorium stood to their feet clapping, praising God and encouraging the minister to continue feeding them the word. "And another thing, God wants us to stop doing church, is walking around full of unforgiveness! Your face is puffed up looking all bitter and mad at the world. When you are asking, and expecting God to move miraculously in your life you cannot walk around holding unforgiveness and bitterness in your heart church! If Jesus operated in the spirit of unforgiveness this entire world would be lost!" The church exploded with praise! Praising the God who sits on high! They yell and scream, jump and shout giving their Lord and Savior Jesus Christ all the glory and honor. "Forgiveness is the key to success in your life church. You can't expect God's goodness to be manifested in your life if you're not obedient, forgiving those who hurt you, betrayed you and deceitfully used you. To be ye doers of His word is to do all that we are instructed to do according to His perfect will."

The next forty minutes were filled with many references to the Bible about how to actively apply God's word in one's own life. Some parishioners earnestly listened with eager hearts ready and willing to please God. Others struggled; trying to understand just how they're suppose to forgive people who have done them wrong. The rest; really didn't care one way or the other. They have no problem with the way they live their lives nor do they feel the need to change it for anyone including God. These are the individuals who go to church to appease man. They only *appear* to be good God fearing people but actually could not care less about God or His Son, Jesus Christ, who died on the cross for them and everyone else.

After the benediction and covering by the pastor, Cynthia hightailed it out of church. She practically knocked over anyone who was in her way, which included babies, the elderly and disabled people as she tried to exit the building. Once Cynthia reached the parking lot, she was tempted to pull out a cigarette but her pride kept her from doing it. The cigarette stayed inside her purse for now.

Lisa, Regina and Danielle were lost in the crowd. They slowly made their way through the sea of people heading in the direction of their vehicles.

Lisa walked to her car with her heart filled with gladness and love for the God she serves.

Regina walked to her car still struggling with thoughts about how to let go of the pain, the mental and psychological abuse her parents afflicted upon her. *How do I forgive my mother and father for what they did to me! I was only a child for crying out loud!*

Danielle didn't have too much of anything on her mind in particular. She just wanted to get back home to complete her campaign ads. The ads were two weeks past the deadline and she felt as though she had not gotten much done. When she casted her eyes upon Cynthia, her indecisiveness quickly vanished. Danielle suddenly had an urge to spend more time with her friends, mainly Cynthia. Their eyes remained locked on one another until Regina spoke.

"*Soooo* ladies, what's next?" she eagerly asked. It's not often that they were able to get together. The other three ladies looked at each other, not knowing what to say.

"I'm not doing anything in particular." Cynthia shrugged her shoulders and says, "It's whatever." She secretly hoped Danielle felt the same and decided to chill with them.

"It would be nice to have a little girl talk over a light lunch," Lisa said. "Let's go."

I really do need to go home and get this work done, although spending time with my fam does sound nice. Well... "...all right, so where are we going to eat?" Danielle asked.

Lisa answered, "I have been thinking about Ethiopian food for a strong minute. You guys want to go to the Ethiopian restaurant on Fairfax and San Vicente?"

"Yeah! I remember that restaurant. That sounds cool, are you guys down?" Regina asked directing her question to Danielle and Cynthia. Regina was stumped when she caught strange looks pass between Danielle and Cynthia. *Humph! Honay, honay! What's going on here!* Regina said to herself. Danielle felt busted, so she blurted out an answer to Regina's question.

"Cool! I can do Ethiopian food."

"Yeah, let's roll," Cynthia said. The four ladies got into their separate vehicles and drove to the west side.

The restaurant they chose to dine in, was located in the most highly populated Ethiopian area in Los Angeles. It's ten minutes from downtown L.A., a few minutes away from Beverly Hills and Hollywood. It's a very busy small area that's always thriving in African culture, tourism and a host of other nationalities.

When they walked into the trendy spot, to their surprise they were seated, immediately, even though the restaurant seemed to be filled to capacity.

"Ooh! I'm glad we were seated so fast, cause this sista is hungry!" Lisa stated. She showed just how hungry she was by munching on the vegetable filled pastry appetizers laid out before them.

"That you are," Danielle said while laughing and tossing a piece of the delicious morsels into her mouth. "You might wanna save some room for the main course, dear."

"I know-I know, I just had fruit this morning for breakfast and it feels like I haven't eaten in days!"

"I feel ya, I just had a piece of toast. So, we *can* get on with the main course!" Regina chimed in while picking up the menu to make a selection.

"Everything looks so good, chile! That's why you shouldn't grocery shop or order food when you are starving!"

Lisa and Regina were so busy studying their menus that they hadn't noticed the tell-tale signs that Danielle and Cynthia continued giving one another. Regina pulled down her menu in time to see Cynthia staring at Danielle and slowly licking her lips right after she took a sip of water. Danielle was totally captivated by Cynthia's actions. Regina was in shock! She cleared her throat and stuttered when she addressed the two,

"Y'a-y'a, y'all figured out what you're having?" The manner in which Regina spoke drew Lisa's attention. She tilted her menu forward, squints her eyes studying the three ladies, wondering why Regina sounded so nervous.

"You all right Gina? Are you that hungry?" Lisa asked, giggling to herself.

Danielle and Cynthia became uncomfortable when they sensed all eyes on them. They quickly picked their menus up and pretended to study them. Regina's head shot behind her menu while Lisa's attention remained on her suspiciously acting friends for a minute longer.

Trying to break the uneasiness in the air, Cynthia announced, rather loudly, what she's going to order.

"I think I'll have the Queen of Sheba salad and some Injera. Uh-huh, that sounds really good," Cynthia said while her face was still buried behind the menu.

Seconds later, a very young attractive male waiter approached their table with tablet in hand, ready to take their orders. Through his bright smile and white teeth, he says,

"Well beautiful ladies, may I take your order?" He continued to flash his gorgeous teeth, with his attention particularly set on Regina. She blushed and patted her head self-consciously, making sure she's looking right.

"Thought you would never ask," Cynthia responded. "I'll have your Queen of Sheba Salad and an order of Injera," said in her best Ethiopian accent. The waiter smiled at her in admiration.

"Ahhh! You sound so lovely!" Cynthia blushed, causing her friends much bewilderment. They were shocked by her shyness. She's the one who always remained cool, calm and collected never revealing her true feelings. Their curious stares only added to her embarrassment. Cynthia cleared her throat and says,

"I shared dorms with an Ethiopian girl during my first semester in college."

"Oooohh!" was said collectively, followed by low chuckles.

"I would like to have…ummmm your Sega Wat and Vegetable Alecha," Lisa said.

"Wonderful selection," the waiter said while writing down her order. "And you, beautiful?" he directed the question to Regina. She blushed, trying to conceal her face with the menu.

"Um, *ahhhh...* I'll try the Ethiopian Tomato and Chicken Salad with some Injera."

"Nice, nice," he said while jotting down Regina's order.

"Oh! And let me please have a glass of Tej?" The waiter chuckled. "Why do you laugh?" Regina asked, suddenly feeling self-conscious. *Isn't it honey wine?*

"I'm not laughing at you dear heart. It's just that, you are absolutely adorable."

Regina's heart melted like warm butter. She wanted to slide to the floor and form a puddle underneath the table. It's been a *loooong* time since Regina received such a genuinely lovely compliment from the opposite sex or the same sex for that matter.

I hope he's not just saying that for a tip. If he is, he's good!

"Well ladies, I must say, you've all done a wonderful job at making your selections. Are you ready to order my dear?" he directed his question to Danielle.

"What you've all ordered sounds delicious. I'm so confused, I don't know *what* to order now!"

"Awww! Poor baby," Lisa said and reached over the table to playfully pat Danielle's hand.

"I see, well, take your time-take your time," the waiter said.

"It's okay, I know what I want to order, now. I'll have your African Chicken and Spicy Red Sauce."

"Hmmmm! another wonderful selection," the waiter exclaimed. Danielle continues,

"And I think I'll mimic you today, Regina. Will you please bring me a glass of Tej, as well sir?" Danielle said using her best etiquette.

"Very well," he replied as he tucked his writing tablet into his apron pocket and took their menus. "Thank you, ladies. Your orders will be ready shortly. Is there anything else that I can get for you?"

"Yes!" Regina almost shouted. "Will you please bring some more pastries? Please!" He graciously nodded his head and says,

"Very well." The waiter turned on his heels, heading for the kitchen. Five minutes later, he reappeared with a plate of pastries and more Ethiopian bread, sitting them in the middle of the table. "If there's anything else, please don't hesitate to let me know. My name is Abel." He took a bow, winked at Regina and quickly exits. She was beside herself and tempted to ask Abel for his phone number but Regina was too bashful to ask for it in front of her friends.

The ladies ate, laughed and joked about old times. It's been a while since they've enjoyed themselves over a good meal.

"I have to tell you ladies, I *really* enjoyed this today, I really did," Lisa said with a bright smile. She loved her friends. They were near and dear to her heart. Lisa silently thanked God for the friends He has given her to pray for, to love and to support.

"Here! Here!" Danielle said as she raised her glass in the air offering a toast. "I enjoyed myself too ladies. It's always fun when I'm with you guys." She reached across the table touching their hands endearingly.

"I did too," Regina added.

"Priceless," Cynthia said. The young handsome waiter reappeared with the check laying it on the table face down. Regina picked it up to examine it.

"Nice and pricey," she said while placing the bill where it was like she never should have saw it in the first place.

"Don't worry about the check, I got it," Danielle said. Lisa looked at her watch then she took a sip of water and says,

"Ladies, although I am sad that our joyous occasion together has come to an end, but I must be on my way. I gotta get back home to check on my mother. Before we part, let us pray together, please." They all nod their heads and held hands. "Father God, Jesus Christ I ask that You surround us with the love and the blood of Jesus. Please protect us Father God from all the attacks of the enemy. Surround us with your fiery hedge of protection Father God and I thank You that the weapons formed against us shall not and will not prosper in the mighty name of Jesus Christ! Father I thank You that we desire to live like Jesus every day. And please take away any and all things that interfere with our relationships with You. Keep our feet on Your firm foundation Lord. I thank You for keeping us securely and firmly in Your hands Father God. Please close any and all doors that are opened against us that are designed to do us harm and open wide those doors of Your blessings into every aspect of our lives. Thank You heavenly Father that Your will is done in our lives on this earth as it is in Heaven. I thank You that we don't try to do anything against Your will Father God. Keep us from stumbling into the traps and snares of the enemy that are designed to destroy our lives Father. Thank You that the words I speak are Spirit and truth and they do not return to You void but accomplish what they are sent out to do. I thank You Father God for covering this prayer with the love and the blood of Jesus so that the enemy cannot interfere with it. Thank You Father God, in Jesus mighty name. Amen." Amen was repeated around the table.

Danielle placed a hundred-dollar bill underneath the check. They gathered their belongings and stood up.

"Thank you love for doing that," Lisa said to Danielle for paying the bill.

"Yeah, I really appreciate that Danielle. I got you next time," Regina said.

"It's no problem. I'm blessed with much and I have no problem sharing it."

"Humph! So, I'll keep that in mind," Cynthia said with an undertone that was not meant to be missed. Danielle blushed and lowered her head.

She is not gonna stop, is she?

The handsome waiter approached the ladies thanking them for patronizing their business. Able told the group that he would bring their change back from the hundred-dollar bill. Danielle declined, telling Able that the extra tip was for him because of his superior service. They exchanged more pleasantries as they exit the restaurant walking to their cars in deep thought.

Lisa's thoughts were about her own personal matters that she had to tend to as soon as possible. She wondered how she was going to be able to take care of them when most of her free time was spent attending to her mother's affairs.

Lord! Please help a sista out!

Regina's thoughts were drawn to school, passing her midterm finals and trying to keep afloat financially. She had to figure out how she would earn money while trying to finish school. And

Regina most *definitely* had to figure out a way to keep her marijuana well stocked. At this point, that's the most important thing to her. She felt that she couldn't survive without it.
Uh-uh! I can't let my stash run low!

Danielle was deep in thought about trying to finish her campaign ads before next week. She's bothered about going pass the deadline but the campaigns have proven to be much more work than expected. No one was really concerned about her missing the deadline because she's known for always pulling things together and coming out on top. The feelings Danielle had about her late assignments, were her personal issues. She believed that missing deadlines were a reflection of incompetence. Plus, the longer it took to finish the projects the longer she had to deal with her obnoxious boss! Danielle yearned to spend more quality time with Justin. The separation from him was starting to take its toll on her. On top of the load that's threatening to smother her, she now had to deal with foreign thoughts about Cynthia that have invaded her mind all of a sudden.

It's starting to feel like she's my dude. What's up with that!

Cynthia's thoughts were about her hysterical episodes the other day. She still didn't know why she's been so emotionally unstable lately. Usually, when she's in the mood to drink, all she did was sit back, relax and enjoy the ride that the liquor took her on. She never experienced an emotional breakdown like she had days ago. The outburst had rattled her nerves.

I hope it doesn't happen again. Instantly, like flipping on a light switch, Cynthia's thoughts took a quick turn down the dark seedy alley of carnality. She started thinking about her *now* known desires for Danielle. Cynthia was overly excited about the way her friend obviously felt about her too. She expected great things to transpire between them very soon. Cynthia licked her lips with anticipation.

Little did they know that Lisa's Holy Spirit inspired prayer were fast at work in their lives to deter the plans of the enemy to utterly destroy them. God loves them so much and He has faith that they will repent and turn from their sinful ways before it's too late.

IT'S INEVITABLE

DANIELLE

After she and Justin shared a night of passionate love making he laid on his back, snoring softly as she rested her head on his solid moist chest staring out the window. Normally, Danielle would be lying next to her man basking in the after effects of her climax but that pleasure was greatly disturbed by reoccurring thoughts of Cynthia! Danielle's thoughts had now graduated to thinking about other women as well as her best friend. Women she had eyed while shopping in the grocery stores, the malls, the boutiques, the gas stations, the restaurants, the banks and everywhere else, were filling her loins with an inexplicable thirst.

How did this dam burst open! I don't recall ever really having these feelings in college. I mean, yeah, I had a few encounters with women in college BUT who didn't! It was just for fun but it never stuck. I am and will always be attracted to men! Then another thought slammed into her cranium like a sledge hammer. *Wait a minute! Am I, is it p, p, pos, possible that I am bisexual and I'm just now finding out! Is that what this ish is! OMG!*

Danielle turned over to look at Justin's beautiful face. *Sorry baby, the heart wants, what it wants,* she conceded.

God's word says; *"The heart is deceitful above all thing, And desperately   wicked.   Who   can   know   it? Jeremiah 17:9.*

The carnal desires Danielle ignorantly claimed as her own were a trick of the enemy to keep her blind bound to more sin. The door had been opened for demonic infiltration through fornication and lust. Lust is the foundation for homosexuality, bisexuality and *all* sexual perversions. Lust wants any and everything that the body

74

desires. It's another form of gluttony. Instead of food, lust wants whatever else the body can have for sensual gratification and it's the basis for all sexual sins. When a person is delivered from lust many things he or she believes they are "naturally" attracted to will NO longer be desired. This is why God warns us to be careful of the company we keep. Their ways can and will spill over into your life without you even knowing it. Where you use to reject your friends' wrong doings you will eventually see nothing wrong with what they do. You will ultimately, uninhibitedly incorporate their sins into your own life. By the time, you realize you have been influenced by their sinful nature, it just might be too late.

CURIOSITY CAN BE THE DEVIL'S PLAYGROUND

DANIELLE

An entire week had gone by since Danielle and Cynthia spoke to one another. The last time they laid eyes on one another was when they attended church and had lunch at the Ethiopian restaurant. Danielle was busy at work and didn't have much time to think about Cynthia. Along with putting campaigns together she still had to meet and entertain new clients, make sure that everything ran smoothly with her team *and* try to avoid Mr. James as much as possible. As long as Danielle's team stayed on top of their game it would be easy to avoid her ratchet boss.

Danielle was scheduled to meet with one of their top clients to regarding updates with their campaign ads. As much money as their A-list client shelled out she was surprised they had not planted a representative from their company's firm to observe her team's work around the clock.

She wasn't seated at her desk no longer than five minutes before her assistant burst through the intercom with a message. Danielle just kicked off her shoes and was massaging her feet when she was notified that her 1:30 appointment had arrived.

"I'll escort her to the conference room, Ms. Stevens," Ms. Kingston said.

"Great," Danielle complained out loud to herself. She pressed the intercom button and says, "Thank you, I'll be there."

Danielle reluctantly put on her shoes, stood up and gathered the folders together that her assistant so neatly placed on top of her desk for this afternoon's meeting. Financial reports, graphics, sketches, designs and everything else needed to give the client's assistant a full synopsis of the job they were paid to do.

"So, glad to have competent help. *Whew!*" Danielle said as she closed her office door on her way to the conference room. "After this, I am going home. I don't care what Mr. James says. I've been working 70 hour weeks for three months straight and I'm about to crash and burn if I don't get some serious rest. I might just have to take Justin up on his offer to the Bahamas."

Danielle seductively strolled down the hallway exuding much sophistication, capturing the attention of every eye that graced her presence. She smiled inwardly loving the affect she knew she had on people. There was nothing more gratifying than looking into a person's eyes and knowing that she was what they absolutely desired. Danielle gave off the persona that she was untouchable, in order to keep the illusion of being desired by all. They may look but not touch. Most people are deceived into believing she was out of their reach, due to her privileged background. And she had no problem letting them *think* she was out of their league.

When Danielle opened the door to the conference room, she was immediately blown away by the beautiful face staring back at her. Her composure went flying out the door. If she didn't have such a firm grip on the door knob she would have stumbled into the conference room.

The beautiful woman remained seated, exhibiting a hypnotizing smile. The assistant was seated at the large conference table with her hands neatly folded on top of her burgundy leather iPad case. She was poised, exceptionally sharp, she rocked the latest short hairstyle which complimented her face perfectly. The clothes the assistant wore, showed her taste was as good as her sophisticated hairstyle.

Danielle could tell this woman was use to the finer things in life. A price tag meant nothing to her, she had money and she was not afraid to show it. Her business ensemble alone, cost more than one of Danielle's team members weekly pay check. This woman was definitely on point, in Danielle's eyes. She was someone that Danielle could easily see incorporating into her life.

77

"Hello, Ms. Stevens," she chimed.

"Hel-" Danielle coughed, clearing her throat. *Whoa! Am I choking up?* "Hello," Danielle tried again, giving the young lady a look indicating that she didn't remember her name.

"Felicia," she said calmly, showing her pearly whites. "Felicia Gilbert," she added. "I'm your client, Mr. Bradley's, assistant."

Danielle finally pried her hands from the door knob feeling composed and confident enough to at least walk to the table without falling on her face.

"Thank you, I've been swamped with work for weeks, so please forgive me for not being better prepared," Danielle said as she placed her folder on the table directly in front of the assistant and offering Felicia a firm handshake. Both found themselves holding onto one another's hands a few seconds too long. Danielle gently pulled her hand away and stared down at the table nervously. "As you know, I am Danielle Stevens. I'm one of the junior executives here." *She is beautiful!* Danielle told herself, unable to hide her attraction to this woman. She hoped she wasn't outwardly showing how much she was smitten by Felicia's beauty.

"I know who you are, Ms. Stevens," Felicia said, seducing Danielle with, yet, another tantalizing smile. *I'm hoping we will get better acquainted,* Felicia thought to herself, then cleared her throat and added, "Mr. Bradley told me all about you. He made sure I was well versed for this meeting today. He feels that you are doing a great job with our account. I'm here to make sure that everything is running smoothly like he believes it is." The two locked eyes for a moment. "He would also like to extend his deepest apologies to you for not being able to attend the meeting himself."

"Oh! It's not a problem," Danielle said. She was cheesing on the inside, glad that Mr. Bradley didn't show up. His assistant was much prettier to look at.

Felicia opened her soft leather portfolio, pulled out a white standard business sized envelope and handed it to Danielle. She was confused as she searched Felicia's eyes for a clue as to what's inside the envelope. Felicia raised her eyebrows and smiled. She studied Danielle's face with such intensity that it caused her to become nervous.

This experience was new and different for Danielle, and she liked it. She opened the envelope with much anticipation and withdrew two tickets. Danielle stared at the tickets with wild eye excitement. They were tickets to the highly anticipated African American play that will be premiering in Los Angeles this summer. The play had gotten exceptional reviews and the tickets were sold out everywhere. These tickets were impossible to cop and no one Danielle knew could even score them. To say she was excited was an understatement!

"I can't believe this!" Danielle shrilled, not at all bashful about her display of appreciation. "I searched high and low for these tickets. *Not* even my most serious connections could get them! How...!" she was at a loss for words. Her child like frenzy amused Felicia. Danielle caught a glimpse of delight on Felicia's face. She tried composing herself by assuming a professional tone once again. "Thank you so much. Please tell Mr. Bradley I really appreciate his kind gesture, really, I do. And tell him that the next time he comes into town his dinner and entertainment will be on us." Felicia smiled and says,

"I will most certainly deliver the message to him. I'm pretty sure he will enjoy hearing it." *But not as much as I'm going to enjoy getting to know you.*

For the remainder of the meeting, Felicia's mind was on Danielle and was unable to focus on the task at hand. If you asked Felicia about the details of their meeting she wouldn't be able to tell you *a thing.* She's totally engrossed in Danielle's physical attributes. Felicia even found herself trying to remember why they were having a meeting in the first place.

On the other hand, Danielle was convinced the meeting went well. Felicia suggested they exchanged phone numbers. She said she would be in town for the next couple of months monitoring the campaign's progress as well as taking care of other important matters of her firm.

As Felicia gathered her belongings, she told Danielle she would be having an early dinner at the exclusive restaurant that all the executives and executives' assistants frequented. Felicia didn't want to dine alone and she would love for Danielle to accompany her for dinner.

"I've been told this restaurant's ambiance is lovely. And it's a nice place to relax and unwind after a long day's work. I would love it if you'd joined me for dinner?" Silence. The only thing Danielle wanted to do after work was relax. Relaxing for her, consisted of a half pint of Ben and Jerry's, Chunky Monkey ice cream, her bed and the remote control to her flat screen TV. Danielle was worn out from working 70-hour work weeks but Felicia refused to take no, for an answer. "My firm will pick up the tab, please say you will join me."

Man! I have a feeling that no excuse I give her will make her back off. Okay, okay...I can wait 'til tomorrow to have a date with B & J. And anyway, I can't complain too much. A free meal is always a good thing. What taste better than food? Free food. "Okay, you've twisted my arm," Danielle said half-jokingly.

Felicia bounced up and down on her tippy toes, clapping her hands showing how elated she was. Danielle was quite surprised by her visual excitement, it's cute. She also found the freckles on Felicia's nose intriguing and sexy.

"So..." Felicia said calmly, demonstrating just how quickly she could regain composure.

Danielle didn't miss a beat. *Hmmmm, she's beautiful, intelligent, mature and well composed, I like that.*

"...I'll send a car over at 5:30 this evening to pick you up. Is that okay?" Felicia asked.

"That will be perfect," Danielle said. "I'll be ready."

"Great, I'll be waiting at the restaurant for your arrival. You have my number, right?"

"Yes, I do." She whipped out Felicia's business card reassuring her that she really did have her phone number.

"Perfect, so if anything, and I mean *anything* comes up, please don't hesitate to call." Danielle looked at the business card and says,

"I sure will. Enjoy the rest of your afternoon and we'll see each other later."

"Looking forward to it," Felicia said confidently as she sashayed right out the door.

Danielle stood still watching her as she strutted down the hall with an array of emotions running rampant through her mind.

Am I feeling her! Danielle thought frightfully. She suddenly became light headed and her legs were limp as pasta.

Danielle collapsed in a chair, resting her head on the conference table. She played the entire interaction between her and Felicia over in her mind.

When I walked through the door I felt an instant attraction between us. Her eyes were intense. It was almost like I could feel her thoughts penetrating through me. For me to feel her desires so strong is that saying that I feel the same way! What do I do? What do I do? she repeated over and over in her head like a mantra.

Danielle leaned back in the chair staring at Felicia's business card once again. She inhaled deeply and blew out a forceful stream of air.

"I guess there is nothing left to *do but* go with the flow and see where this current will take me," Danielle said out loud to the empty conference room.

But Danielle did have a choice. She can choose to go 'with the flow' or run like lightening the other way. God has given us all a free will to do as we please. Just because He has given us that right does NOT mean we will not suffer consequences for making the wrong decisions. Most of the things that feel good to the flesh are definitely not good for the spirit. Our spirit wars against our flesh and vice versa (*Romans 8:7*). The enemy tempts the flesh and God communicates with our spirit constantly. It's up to us to heed God's warnings and directions. When we choose to ignore His directions, we will *always* have regrets.

Danielle's train of thoughts were broken by the buzzing of the conference room's intercom.

"Is there anything you need me to assist you with Ms. Stevens?" her assistant's voice echoed throughout the large empty room.

"She noticed that I haven't returned to my office yet," Danielle said out loud. She pressed the button on the intercom system and says, "No thank you, Ms. Kingston, everything is fine. Thank you for having my folders ready for the meeting today." She could feel that Ms. Kingston appreciated the commendation.

"Thank you, Ms. Stevens, anything to make your job easier." *It certainly makes my job easier,* Ms. Kingston thought.

She never ever wanted to relive the day she forgot to accurately supply Danielle with all the necessary documentations and presentations for her meeting with the top execs. Needless to say, the potentially career damaging error made them both appear incompetent. After the meeting was over Danielle walked out the conference room looking angry and flushed. She called Ms. Kingston into her office and read her from right to left, up and down, back and forth and all around. Ms. Kingston never forgot that chastisement till this day. She still shuttered every time she remembered the day she almost lost her job. Since then, Ms. Kingston made it her duty to make sure her boss was thoroughly prepared for whatever she had to do. Even if it's something as small as reading the directions on how to open a box efficiently, Ms. Kingston would make sure Danielle was thoroughly prepared.

"You can take the rest of the day off and I will see you tomorrow." Her assistant was ecstatic! Ms. Kingston fought the compulsion to hike up her skirt and turn cartwheels up and down the hallway. But she composed herself enough to say,

"Thank you, Ms. Stevens, I really appreciate it. I will definitely see you in the morning."

"Have a good day, Ms. Kingston."

"I will, and you do the same."

IS IT STILL A HABIT WHEN YOU DON'T WANT TO BREAK IT

CYNTHIA

was at The Dragonfly in West Hollywood, seated at her favorite table. There were gorgeous men and women approaching her, looking for a fun-filled night of passion and lust but Cynthia, uncharacteristically, turned them all down. She was *actually* fine with the idea of having a few drinks by herself and going home alone. At least, she wouldn't have to be concerned about asking strangers to leave before the sunrays hit her window pane.

An hour passed and Cynthia only had *one* glass of cognac which was certainly unusual for her. On any other given night, Cynthia would have been working on her third round by now, not including what she had to drink at home. She was mellow and in no rush nor was she desperate for company tonight.

Cynthia spent most of her time in the club being entertained by watching people run throughout the club trying to get laid.

Boy o' boy, that's hard work, right there! Do I look like that when I'm running around here looking like a chicken with its head cut off, trying to hook up? With all the energy, it takes searching for the nooky, it's a wonder that we still have the energy to perform! Whew!

Cynthia's mental conversation ended with a shake of her head. She's turned off by picturing how she must look when she's carrying on like a female dog on heat, outta control!

There has to be a better way.

From the corner of her eye, Cynthia noticed someone bobbing and weaving in and out of her peripheral view. She was in deep thought and really wasn't paying much attention. When Cynthia finally turned her head in the direction of the person who's trying to get her to notice them, she wished she hadn't.

GQ...aw dang! I haven't seen him since the threesome we had with Lori. And speaking of Lori, where is she? I wouldn't mind seeing her tonight!

Mr. GQ smiled when he saw Cynthia looking directly at him. She quickly adverted her eyes, pretending not to see him but her efforts were in vain. Cynthia's dismissiveness would not deter the dapper player. GQ picked up his drink and smoothly made his way over to her table.

"Hey sexy," GQ said in a low provocative drawl as he caressed her shoulder. Cynthia gave him a half-hearted smile as she gave her sexy bed buddy a once-over and says,

"Heeeyy, yoouuu,*" guess it wasn't meant for me to go home alone after all.*

"Well hey, yourself," he said as he took a seat. "You're looking *gooood* tonight, baby. How have you been? The last time I saw you, you were having breakfast and didn't offer a brotha, Nathan."

"What!" Cynthia laughed. "You were-," GQ interrupted,

"Naw, I wasn't sleep. I was paying attention to *everything.*" Cynthia laughed bashfully.

Note to self; next time, make sure you whisper when he's around. And what are we having here, a family reunion! It's no need for all this small talk. We're just smashing buddies. We hit it and quit it, toot-it and boot-it, that's it that's all. "Thank you for the compliment and you're looking mighty fine yourself. But to answer your-" once again, Cynthia was distracted.

This time, it was Lori who commended her attention. GQ was curious to find out who or what pulled Cynthia's attention away from him. He looked in the direction of the diversion and saw that it was the beautiful young lady that participated in their threesome. Cynthia was completely captivated by Lori's presence.

"I saw her earlier, when she walked pass me going to the restroom," he said.

"Have you two been in contact with one another since the last time we played together?" she asked with a tinge of jealousy. *For real, Cynthia? Are you really playing the jealous card?*

"Yes," GQ admitted, reluctantly. "We've met up a couple of times and had a ménage à trois." Cynthia gave him the coldest glare. She could have ripped his heart out his chest. Her deadly eyes made chills run down his spine. "Whoa! Wait a minute, we wanted to invite you, *but you* made it quite clear you didn't want to be contacted, *outside* the club arena. So...," GQ shrugged his shoulders. Cynthia felt an impulse to throw her drink in his face, "...we were left to our own devices." He smiled innocently and adds, "I wish you were there, baby." GQ threw Cynthia a wink for good measure.

Sure, you wanted me there, like my ass miss warts. Cynthia was seething. She wanted to slap the taste buds out of his mouth. It's true, that she didn't want to be contacted outside the club but that didn't change the fact that she was *still* jealous as hell! *I should have kept her to myself,* Cynthia thought bitterly.

The object of her attraction cavalierly walked up to their table. Cynthia pretended to be cool and laid back but she's actually more nervous than a sixteen-year-old on a first date. She wanted to grab Lori up and get out of dodge, leaving GQ in the dust.

But that would be rude, or would it? I mean, he had time with her, without me, so why can't I have my time alone with her? Cynthia tried to convince herself. *I made the rules about not wanting to be contacted outside the club, why am I so bothered?* No matter how hard Cynthia tried to rationalize, she still couldn't shake the funky feelings of the them hooking up without her. *Get it together girl!* Lori offer Cynthia a sexy smile.

"Hello, stranger." Being called a stranger, stung Cynthia. It made her even more frustrated. She was forced to think about the time that Lori and GQ shared together, without her. "I didn't expect to see you so soon," Lori said, as Cynthia tried to pull herself together. Cynthia made an attempt at being copasetic, by acting like all was well. She winked and says,

"Hello, Lori."

"Oh! So, you remember my name!" Lori was genuinely surprised that Cynthia hadn't forgotten about her. Judging by the way they departed, Lori thought she had. Cynthia blushed, making it obvious that she had been thinking about Lori since their last encounter.

Better start taking notes, old man. Cynthia's feeling herself a tad bit too much. "Why are you so surprised? Who could ever forget a woman as beautiful as yourself?" Cynthia said, as she looked Lori up and down to emphasize her point, desiring every inch of her amazing body.

Lori's face turned bright red, which wasn't a difficult task to achieve, seeing that she had a light complexion. Cynthia couldn't resist the chance to gloat in GQ's face. She was beyond hyped about the obvious affect she still had on the absolutely gorgeous young lady. GQ turned away, he had seen enough.

Doesn't feel so good to ya, huh old man? Cynthia boasted to herself.

"Stop it, I bet you say that to all your conquest," Lori retorted, secretly hoping she was the only one.

"I'll tell you one thing, I don't say things that I don't mean and I don't like repeating myself like a broken record." Lori's eyes lit up like Christmas tree lights. She couldn't contain her excitement.

GQ interrupts, "*Sooooo!* Are we going to take this back to your house, my house or Lori's house?" When GQ mentioned Lori's house, Cynthia was consumed with fury again. Of course, GQ didn't say it to offend Cynthia. He just wanted to make sure he was *included* in the threesome once again.

Cynthia lifted her glass to her mouth and finished the last of her drink before even attempting to answer GQ's question. She wanted to make her possible competition squirm, just a bit, before she gave him an answer. Her defiance was sheer payback for thinking he could have a night of pleasure without her. Cynthia banged her glass down on the table, clutched her purse with one hand, while pulling Lori close with her free hand. Cynthia turned to GQ and says,

"Follow me, you *do* remember the way, right?"

"I sure do, I'll be right behind you." The three raced off to Cynthia's house for a night of ecstasy.

GIVING UP IS SO MUCH EASIER TO DO

REGINA

Class was over and everyone had abandoned the classroom, leaving Regina sound asleep at her desk. The professor humiliated her in front of the entire class and she couldn't take it anymore. Professor Henry called Regina to the front of the class to pick up her test. With a stone-cold expression on his face, while using no discretion, professor Henry says,

"I don't think this class is for you, Ms. Byrd. You should consider retaking Critical Thinking 101 or better yet, dropping out of school altogether. It appears to me, that you can't seem to grasp the fundamentals." Professor Henry flung her test papers on his desk, before him, like he was too through.

A morbid shocked Regina, picked the paper up, dropped her head, reluctantly turned around and slowly walked back to her desk, trying to drown out the snickering. Regina looked up to see two of her classmates covering their mouths with their hands trying to stifle their laughter. She wanted to crawl under a rock and the pious professor went back to teaching as if nothing happened.

Regina desperately tried to suck down her tears until class ended. When the last student cleared the classroom, Regina began to sob uncontrollably.

"My mom and dad always told me I was a dumb ass and I wouldn't amount to anything," she said while rivers of tears streamed down her face. "I guess they were right, mommy knows best!" Her heart was broken.

Regina had no recollection of falling asleep until she heard the sound of footsteps coming towards her. She snapped her head up and she stared at the faces of strangers walking pass her as they filled empty chairs. Regina was confused.

What! 4:30! This must be the professor's next class. An older woman approached her as she collected her things.

"Excuse me young lady, are you sitting there? I usually sit close to the chalkboard on the account of my bad eyes," the older woman paused waiting for Regina's response but she's too busy rushing, trying to get the hell outta there. She paid the old lady no mind as she tossed her books into her backpack. The older woman noticed Regina's frantic behavior and she asks, "Are you all right, baybae? You seem rather rushed, it's okay. You don't have to move so fast on the account of me. I can find another seat, baybae. *Hehe,* I need to be making my way to the back of the classroom anyway. So, when I do walk up to the front of the class at least, I can say I'm getting my exercise." The older woman gave a little chuckle but quickly went silent once she realized her audience was not giving her the time of day. "I don't recall ever seeing you in this class. Are you new honey?"

Regina continued to ignore the woman as she zipped up her backpack and damn near sprinted out the room. Shame made it unbearable to breath. Regina felt so bad for ignoring the older woman but she was unable to speak, for fear of breaking down, once again. The way Regina felt about herself, no one could tell her that she wasn't the dumbest person in existence.

I can't stand myself right now!

Regina drove down the street dazed and confused. She was driving on sheer instinct alone, with her mind on everything but the road. It was an act of God that she wasn't involved in a car wreck. Regina had no clue where would wind up. But one thing she knew for sure, she didn't want to be alone. The state of mind she was in, being alone was the worst possible thing for Regina at this time. She feared what she *might* do. Suicide may have been an option and Regina was scared to death of that.

When Regina was allowed a moment of clarity, she pondered the thought of whose house she could possibly go to.

Lisa's hands are full caring for her mother and trying to tend to her own life. Danielle maybe working and possibly planning to spend time with her baby, Justin. Ugh! I don't know why I don't like him. Cynthia is probably doing, Lord knows what, with Lord knows who! I guess that leaves me no choice. I'm going to go by Tommy's house.

Tommy was Regina's ex-boyfriend. He was the reason behind both of them getting kicked out of college. They were inseparable before they wasted their parent's money and almost destroyed their lives. Tommy and Regina were one another's shadows. You couldn't see one without the other. Everyone complimented the young couple on how cute they looked together. Regina's parents even adored him, which was a real shocker to her, seeing that they rarely liked anyone. At times, Regina doubted that they even liked her.

Throughout high school, the only drug they experimented with was marijuana, never trying anything else. When most of their peers went from marijuana to primos, that's cocaine and marijuana mixed together, Regina and Tommy remained strictly weed smokers. They were teased and pressured by their friends into trying other drugs but they never gave in. The one day that Regina suggested they try a primo just to see how the high she would feel, Tommy scolded her so severely that she thought he was going to leave her. She felt so horrible afterwards, that she never thought about trying primos again.

Tommy swore he would never try anything stronger than marijuana. His two older brothers were stone cold crack heads and heroin addicts. Tommy couldn't stand seeing the pain they caused their mother. He developed a strong hatred for his brothers and all hardcore drugs.

As much weed as they both smoked, it was amazing that they ever graduated from high school with a 3.5 G.P.A. Regina and Tommy both received acceptance letters from every college they applied to. They both received scholarships and financial support from their parents. Their futures appeared to be bright and promising. All the two had to do, was enjoy the summer and prepare themselves for college in the fall, how difficult was that?

The summer went by without any troubles. Everything was set in place for their smooth transition from high school graduates to college freshmen.

The university they attended was located in northern California. They lived on campus and of course, Tommy and Regina spent most of their time together. Things *appeared* to be going well for the young starry-eyed couple. They took to college like naturals. All the drama that went hand and hand with college life, had no effect on Regina and Tommy. On holidays, they never dreaded driving back home to visit family and friends. They actually looked forward to seeing them. During the second month of the second semester, all hell broke loose in Tommy's life, spilling over into Regina's.

One early afternoon, she sat in her dorm room studying for her evening literature class when someone began knocking frantically at the door. A startled Regina rushed to the door, made sure it was locked before she asks,

"Who is it!" Her heart pounded in her chest. She hated how anxious she was.

"It's Tommy! Open up," he said sounding annoyed.

"Tommy!" Regina exclaimed. She quickly unlocked the door in 0.3 seconds. She tried to kiss his cheek, he avoided her like the plague and whisked by without saying a word. Tommy paced the floor like a madman.

Ugh! What's wrong with him? Highly offended by his dismissive actions, Regina closed the door and locked it. She walked across the floor and slowly took a seat on the bed, as if making any sudden movements would agitate him even more. A little guarded by his strange behavior, Regina asks, "What's going on, Tommy?" She sounded more scared, now, than nervous. Regina chastised herself inwardly. She couldn't stand showing signs of weakness in any situation.

"Shhhh!" Tommy hissed. "And make sure you locked the door," he said pointing wildly at her and the door.

"It is," Regina said. *Why is he acting like he's on America's Most Wanted!*

"Just make sure!" he snapped, which was something he really didn't ever do.

"Tommy, I locked the door after you came in. Are you going to tell me *why* you're freaking out like this? You're making me really uncomfortable, Tommy." He rubbed his face exasperatedly as he continued pacing the floor.

"I'm tired, baby," Tommy confessed. "This has gotten way too complicated. I can't do this anymore, Regina!" Instead of being relieved by his confession, Regina was more confused than ever.

Tired of what! He can't do what? Is he talking about school? "Oh! You're talking about school?" Regina said like she just solved the problem. "You know I got you!" she said confidently, as she tried to comfort him. "All you had to do is ask for help. We can hire a tutor," Regina chimed, excitedly reaching for his arm and Tommy yanked away from her.

"I'm not talking about school, damn baby! I don't *need* a tutor and I don't need tutoring!" Tommy yelled, causing the walls to vibrate. He stopped dead in his tracks and stared at her with angry red devilish eyes.

Regina had never been a victim of domestic violence and she didn't plan on becoming one now. The way Tommy was acting, putting hands on her, didn't seem too farfetched. She watched him closely while choosing her words carefully.

"Baby, I don't understand what you are talking about. Help me to understand, okay?" Tommy peered at Regina with eyes of flame. She wanted to bolt from the room and let him deal with his own damn problems. Regina had been told one too many stories about how some men will beat their girlfriends out of frustration. She felt that was a cowardice excuse for a man to put his hands on a woman. There have been countless times that she's been frustrated with life but she never took it out on Tommy or anyone else for that matter.

"There is nothing you or anyone can do to help me. I'm tired of trying."

"There are people who can help you, Tommy. You don't have to carry this by yourself."

91

"Don't you think I've tried to talk to people, Regina! Come on now, don't come at me like I'm stupid!" Now she's terrified.

Should I fear for my life? The thought flashed across her mind. Regina immediately stood to her feet and bolted to the door. She had no plans of dying tonight nor did her plans consist of killing anyone including, him. Tommy desperately reached for her arm before she could unlock the door. Regina pulled away and says, "One of us has to leave before something really bad happens." His facial expression softened.

"I'm sorry Gina." He drew her into his chest, holding her tightly. "Nothing is going to happen. I didn't mean to scare you, baby. You are all that I have. There's no way I could ever hurt you, please come here." Tommy took Regina by the hand and escorted her back to the bed. "Sit down." He sat next to her. Tommy's jaws were clenched tight and the vein in his forehead pulsated but Regina knew she wasn't in harm's way. Tommy gently held her face in the palms of his hands and kissed her softly on the lips and both sides of her neck.

Well dang! If he wanted sex, all he had to do was ask! Regina caressed his face, kissing him passionately but Tommy broke away.

"Wait a minute, baby." Tommy reached inside his pants pocket. Regina thought he was getting a condom.

Yup! It's going down! She took his chin and kissed him his lips. "Next time, just ask." Regina giggled with delight. "I'm more than willing to oblige you, Tommy." Now, he's looking confused.

"Okay," he said. Then he whipped out a little ziploc bag, dangling it in front of Regina's face. "You wanna try this?"

What?! "Huh?" She took the bag from his hand and looked at it closely. It appeared to be marijuana with a few tiny pieces of white rocks mixed in the weed. "Is this-," he cut her off.

"*Shhhhh!*" Tommy opened the bag and removed a rock, placing it in the palm of her hand. "This is rock cocaine. You take it and mix it with the marijuana to make a primo."

"Where did you get this?" Regina asked as she studied the white substance like it's a science project.

"I got it from someone in my dorm." She was thoroughly shocked that Tommy was even suggesting that they try crack cocaine. At the same time, Regina was also intrigued at the thought of trying a primo for the first time. She always wanted to try the concoction but never did because she feared how Tommy would react. The one-time Regina asked Tommy if he wanted to try the drug, he ripped into her like she was his enemy.

"I thought you were against hard drugs?" Regina was befuddled.

"Well, times have changed. Do you want to try it or not?" Tommy asked, like he was not for the games. "I mean, you don't have to, if you don't want to." Oh, boy did she *really* want to try it. Regina just didn't want him to know how excited she was about smoking a primo. Her best defense was to act as nonchalant as possible.

"I'll do it, *only* if *you* do it too."

"Are you sure?"

"Tommy, I'm a grown woman and I'm more than capable of making my own decisions."

"I know-I know, I just wanna make sure that you're cool with it, that's all."

If you don't spark it up and stop talking! was what Regina really wanted to say.

"Okay," Tommy mumbled as he dumped the contents of the ziploc bag on the nightstand and proceeded to roll up a primo. Moments later, he held up a perfectly rolled joint in between his fingers admiring his work. "Let's light it up." He sparked up the tree and an unusual smell hit Regina's nostrils within seconds. Tommy took two heavy hits, causing the fiery ambers to light up like a blaze. He held his breath making sure the toxic smoke filled his lungs to capacity.

Regina took the joint and mimicked Tommy's action. Once the smoke filled her lungs and circulated through her blood stream, Regina experienced a high like she never thought imaginable.

"*Ahhhhh!* Is this what I've been missing?" Regina said more so to the drugs, than to Tommy.

"I know, right! I feel so good!" He retrieved the joint from Regina and took two more hits, then passed it back to her. She hit it twice more, that's all she wrote. With that last hit, came instant arousal. Regina felt as though she was slipped a micky in the form of Spanish Fly. Tommy never looked so good, there were no words exchanged. Their clothes flew off at a record breaking speed. No area on their body was left undiscovered. They continued on in their passion filled lust extravaganza until the wee hours of the morning.

From the first hit of the primo, Regina was hooked until her college career came to a screeching halt. Needless to say, the inevitable was bound to happen. Once they became hooked on primos, school was no longer their top priority. She and Tommy indulged in nonstop drug use and sexcapades. They were smoking primos by the shipload and they needed more of the toxic mixture to attain their initial high. It wasn't enough for them to just get high from primos, they graduated to an even harder drug, like heroin.

Of course, neither were prepared for the terrible after effects of using heroin. Tommy and Regina quickly became desperate and thirsty like crack addicts. Their desire for the drug replaced all sound consciousness. And when the money ran out, the next thing up for sell, were their bodies. Fortunately, the partners in crime couldn't phantom the idea of demeaning themselves any more than they already had. After being put on one too many academic probations, they were finally expelled and sent packing, to take the long humiliating trip back home.

Both their parents were disappointed, ashamed and disgraced by their children' actions. Regina and Tommy were forbidden to have contact with one another ever again in life or their families threatened to disown them.

The sight of Regina sickened her parents. She was ignored and treated like the invisible woman. She was a ghost to them. Her mother looked at her in total disgust and lowered her eyes shaking her head like she couldn't believe Regina came from her womb. Her parents always told her that the weakest person on the face of the earth was a drug addict. They were repulsed by the very sight of her.

Finally, after a month of cruel and unusual punishment, Regina was shipped off to the south to live with relatives but not before her father told her how he felt about the choice she made.

"How could you be so damn stupid and get yourself kicked out of school! What possessed you to make such a foolish mistake! I don't know who I'm angrier with. You, or myself for believing that you could possibly amount to anything in life! *Drugs!* And you did them with a no-good son-of-a...!*"* he yelled with his face twisted in a grotesque mask of hatred. She shrinks back. "Drugs are for weak minded people!" her father bellowed with unadulterated disgust. After her father's verbal assassination, Regina felt as though she did not exist.

The move to the south was definitely a culture shock to Regina, however she eventually learned to adapt. When she returned to Los Angeles, almost a year later, Tommy was miraculously purged from her system.

Regina found herself driving through her old neighborhood noticing that it hadn't changed much within the last fifteen years. The majority of the residents in the community own their homes and they kept their property up quite nicely. She was always proud of her neighborhood. The high school still looked the same except for the tall black iron fence surrounding it resembling a penitentiary. The ominous iron bars weren't there when Regina attended

"The Wash House," *George Washington Preparatory High School. Really! I guess they're teaching them early to have a jail house mentality,* Regina thought bitterly to herself. She was agitated by the institutionalized systematic attack on our black youth. If it wasn't for the mishaps in her life, she might have become an activist to fight for the rights of all young Americans, particularly young blacks.

When Regina got to the corner of Denker Avenue and 109th street, she made a right turn driving down to the middle of the block, coasting to a stop in front of a pale blue house trimmed in white. Regina turned the car engine off and sat perfectly still as her mind was bombarded by every emotion imaginable. The feelings she thought she buried, suddenly resurfaced. Regina dropped her head down to the steering wheel not understanding how her life kept ending up in such a terrible rut!

"How did I manage to screw things up this time! God! Please help me!" Regina lifted her head as she wiped tears from her red swollen eyes while she tried to compose herself. "I should just drive away."

It was almost evening and the lights were dimly lit inside of Tommy's house. There didn't appear to be any movement going on.

"I don't even know if he still lives here! Why am I tripping!"
The more she tried to convince herself to leave, the more she wanted to get out the car and ring the doorbell.

Regina went to turn the key in the ignition but her hands froze and her mind drew a blank. She didn't know what to do. Tired of fighting herself she swung the car door open and leaped out before she changed her mind. Regina was thankful to God that no one noticed her. She knew her actions had been questionable since she parked in front of Tommy's house. She self-consciously gave herself a once-over and painstakingly drifted up the walkway.

When she was within a few feet of the porch, a strange foreboding feeling overtook Regina. Imagines of her taking her last and final steps to the gas chamber almost rendered her motionless. With every step, Regina told herself to run the hell away!

As she raised her finger to push the doorbell, the door opened and Regina practically jumped out of her skin. Her eyes were bucked open wide like she was looking at a ghost.

He still looks the same!

Regina couldn't believe how strikingly gorgeous Tommy was. He adorned her with a warm smile and she was reminded of the love they once shared. The memories brought back warm and gentle feelings. Every thought that was buried deep within her soul encroached its boundaries and came flooding through like a broken dam. At that very moment, Regina knew beyond a shadow of a doubt that she was still in love with him.

"I stood here waiting for you to get out the car," Tommy whispered seductively.

Damn...it's on.

HOPE DEFERRED MAKES THE HEART SICK

LISA

Ever since Lisa assumed full responsibility of caring for her mother, she had forgotten how it felt to have free time for herself. The days flew by while her personal business continued to mount up. Although, it was overwhelming at times, Lisa chose to follow God's commands and cast all her cares on Him, because He cares for her and loves her immensely. This was why she cares for her mother the way that she does.

When Lisa allowed herself to focus on the circumstances, anxiety stress and worries plagued her mind weighing heavy on her heart. When her mind became burden with doubts, she's reminded of Peter when he was moved by the troubled water and began sinking.

The sound of dishes clashing in the sink resonated throughout the house. Washing dishes for Lisa, was therapeutic. She used that time to reflect on life and all the trials and tribulations she endured.

Unfortunately, Lisa was not feeling tranquil at all today, she felt quite the opposite. Lisa was frustrated by the fact that she had been waiting a long time for God's promises to manifest in her life. It appeared that Lisa had more setbacks and satanic attacks than blessings from God. At least, that's *how she* saw it.

Lisa believed, whole heartedly, in the act of forgiving those who hurt her and loving those who seemed unlovable. She always

97

helped the needy and ignored the greedy; she desired to minister to people by her lifestyle and through her conversations, in her deeds, in her thoughts and in her actions. But Lisa's life still felt like it was on hold.

"When am I going to live my life, Lord! Every time I start something, it never gets finished. You say in Your word, that if I delight myself in You, You will give me the desires of my heart," *(Psalm 37:4),* "…You also said that hope deferred makes the heart sorrow…" *(Proverbs 13:12,* "Right now, God, I feel like my heart is sorrowful and my hope is deferred!" She wiped free flowing tears away, placed the dish in the drainer that she finished washing and picked up another. "I have been standing on Your promises and trusting in Your word for over *twenty years,* Father God, and nothing has changed! I've seen many fall by the way side. They talk the talk but choose not to follow You. They live their lives as though they don't *even* know You, while I have remained faithful to You, God! I don't have men *or women* in and out of my life nor am I shacked up with anyone. Your word is buried deep within my heart. I am not only a hearer of Your word, I am a doer of Your word. Others have taken Your word in vain, they toy with Your word like it's some sort of fairytale that they can dismiss or throw away at the drop of a dime. It appears that You are allowing them to get away Scott-free, while I long-suffer waiting on You! You constantly tell me to wait while others do as they please. I'm not trying to live a life opposite of You. All I want to do is what You have placed in my heart to do! When will You move for me God!! You have told me that I am Your queen, Your daughter but I continue to wait day in and day out on You!"

Lisa loosened her grip on the cup she was washing and dropped it back into the dirty dish water, causing it to splash onto her blouse. In a fit of anger, Lisa snatched the rubber gloves off her hands, slamming them down on the cabinet emphasizing her displeasure.

"God, I'm so tired of this!" Lisa pulled out a chair and plopped down in it. She laid her head on the table preparing to cry like she just lost her one of her dearest friends. Instead of crying tears of sorrow, a hearty laughter bubbled up in her soul. Lisa began to laugh out loud as she doubled over trying to catch her breath.

Whenever Lisa was inclined to have a pity party, God immediately came on the scene turning her sorrow into joy. He knew what sorrow and disappointment brought and that was bitterness.

She immediately felt God's warmth and love surrounding her like the sea. She couldn't help but to embrace and receive His everlasting love.

"I love You, Lord God with all my heart, I really do! I know You will never forsake me nor leave me. I just get frustrated at times, when I think about not being able to do what's in my heart." Tears fall from her eyes once again, but this time, they aren't tears of sorrow, they are tears of joy. "God please forgive me for my anxiousness and for being moved by what I see. Thank you, Lord! Praise You Father God!" She clapped her hands together, praising God for His love and mercy. "Thank You Father for Your faithfulness! Thank You for loving me and being my strength when I am weak and calming me down when I think too much of myself. Praise Your Heavenly name! You are more than worthy to be praised!"

Lisa stood to her feet and began to praise His majestic name. She looked to the ceiling and saw His glory cloud fill the place. He promised to never leave or forsake His children. God is with Lisa and with Him, she shall always remain.

That night, Lisa felt as though she slept on a cloud filled with God's love. There was nothing in this world that could ever separate her from His love nor does she want to be separated from His love.

God woke Lisa up at 3:20 AM to pray. After thirty minutes of praying and interceding she fell back to sleep. God woke her up once again and says,

"Don't be anxious my child. I heard your cries, my daughter and I have rescued you from all your troubles." Lisa fell asleep feeling God's love and comfort, knowing that she serves the true living God. *(The God who sees. Genesis 16:13. If God is for us who can be against us? Romans 8:31).*

Lisa was awakened by the metallic sound of her mother's walker hitting the marble kitchen floor. She stared at the alarm clock and was immediately annoyed.

"Why is she up so early!" she said out loud, irritated by her mother's lack of consideration.

"Lisa!" her mother called out. "Can I have some fruit?"

Are you serious! God! It's the same thing every morning! Lisa yanked the comforter over her head. Her first mind was to ignore her mother and hope that she would go back to bed. Lisa was filled with conviction. Moments later, she slid on her house shoes and went into the kitchen to help her mother get something to eat.

When Lisa walked into the kitchen she saw her mother bent over her walker, looking inside the refrigerator.

"I gave you fruit last night to eat for breakfast. What did you do with it?" Her mother closed the refrigerator door and turned to her daughter with a look of indifference on her face. She had an issue with being stubborn and defiant. Lisa had grown tired of telling her mother the same thing over and over again. The roles have now reversed, Lisa became the mother and the mother was now the child. At least with a child, you were given the ability to train them and raise them up in the proper way they should go. When you are dealing with an adult who elects to behave like a child it is far worse than dealing with an actual child.

"I already ate it this morning," her mother said sulking as she turned to walk back to her bedroom. Lisa tried her hardest not to walk in the flesh by not allowing her mother's childishness to upset her.

Lisa walked to the counter and pulled a banana from the bunch to give to her mother.

"Here." With the coordination of a five-year-old on a pair of roller skates her mother turned around gripping the walker like it was her life support. She walked up to her daughter and slowly took the piece of fruit from her hand. Her mother exited the kitchen without saying, 'thank you' or showing any kind of appreciation. "I told you about waking up so early eating fruit and drinking as much water as you do because it gives you the runs." Lisa knew her mother wasn't listening to a word she said. All Lisa could do was look up at the ceiling and thank God for patience.

There had been times it was apparent that her mother was allowing God to reestablish a relationship with Him. Just when Lisa was about to exhale and praise God for giving her mother a heart of flesh, she would quickly revert back to her old selfish ways...then it was back to the drawing board.

Lisa took a deep breath, slowly releasing it as she watched her mother walk back to her bedroom. "God, I know You didn't bring me this far to leave me." See, Lisa wasn't just standing and believing God for manifesting *her* blessings into her life, she was also standing and believing God for delivering her mother from all generational curses. Lisa knew this was one of the reasons, God chose her to care for her mother. God knew that Lisa would remain faithful, continuing to stand and wait on Him, as He delivered her mother from all the things that interfered with her relationship with Him.

Lisa's mother lived most, if not *all,* of her life in oppression and in fear. Stress and fear were the culprits that caused her to suffer a stroke, over a year ago. God's power was able to reach down and touch people while they are in dark despair. Lisa's mother always confessed to being a spirit filled Christian, although her actions spoke louder than her words, leaving others to question her true Christianity. There's no judging, Lisa was just analyzing things that didn't bear witness to her spirit.

Her mother routinely, boasted and bragged about the close walk she once had with Jesus Christ. She would say that she literally felt Jesus walking beside her. Now, that glorious relationship was covered up and dismantled. For *years,* Lisa's mother suffered for the mistake she made by choosing a man over God. Every decision she's made after her fall from grace, had been questionable and reflective of the wedge that she allowed to come between her and her God.

There was one thing Lisa will forever be thankful for and that was how God used her mother to pray for her when she was lost in sin and in total darkness. If it wasn't for her mother's prayers, she would have sunk deep in despair and depression and would have eventually died in her sins. The mercy God showed Lisa, would make her forever grateful unto God.

Lisa found herself arguing quite often with her mother about her lack of faith and trust in God. When God opened Lisa's spiritual eyes, He also began to tell her private things about certain people, including her mother, that no one else knew about. This is called the gift of discernment. Lisa was blinded to the truth when she was lost in sin. She always thought her mother was the holiest person on earth, *until* God opened her eyes to the *truth!* When the scales of sin were removed from Lisa's eyes, she was able to see that her mother was the total opposite of a true devout God fearing person. It was during an argument with her mother, was when things that were revealed to Lisa was confirmed. On that day, she learned something that she could never forget.

After dinner, the family was seated at the table engrossed in a conversation about their mother and how she used to be on fire for the Lord, that she came off like a fanatic. Their mother would have her daughters create signs to carry up and down the street witnessing to the multitudes about Jesus Christ. Of course, this act alone, was quite embarrassing to her children. Needless to say, their mother's choice of demonstrating her love for her Lord, seemed over the top. None of her daughters could deny that their mother's love for God was certainly real.

The discussion became heated as they reminisced about the passion their mother displayed and how now, it seemed to dwindle. If they knew what this argument would reveal, they probably would have avoided the discussion altogether.

"...you forced God on us!" Lisa said with undeniable hurt in her voice. "Every time we came to you for advice about *anything,* the only thing you'd say, is pray! Pray for this, pray for that! You drilled that into us all the *frig...gin'* time! And when you weren't cramming prayer down our throats, you tried to condemn us about gossiping! Sometimes, all we wanted was a shoulder to cry on or a show of support. We weren't always gossiping but you were too sanctimonious that you couldn't be a mother, everybody sins, except for you. Now, you walk around timid and fearful like you never knew God. After all these years, why are you acting like this!" Lisa's voice reflected years of confusion and disappointment from watching her mother go from a devout Christian, to a Christian on her way to hell, a backslider.

The room was engulfed in silence. Their mother lowered her eyes and stared at her hand. When she found the courage to speak Lisa and her siblings were blown away by the naked truth. In a low unsettling voice, their mother says,

"How do you know I wasn't always like this?" Her confession alone, flipped Lisa's wig. The person who single-handily preached God and Bible to them until they wanted to run away from God forever, finally revealed that she was a fraud. All these years, and she didn't believe anything that she told us! Wow! What a hypocrite!

How does one respond to such a heart stopping revelation? You can't. Being the God-fearing woman that Lisa is, the only options were to release and let go of the past and forgive her mother wholeheartedly. Lisa chose to forgive her for being overbearing and deceitful and she asked God to make Himself known in her mother's life.

Lisa knew there was a task ahead of her, in standing for her mother's total divine deliverance. As long as she kept her mind stayed on Jesus, Lisa would have nothing to be concerned about. God doesn't give us more than we can handle. He equipped us with all we need to do whatever, He leads us to do, no matter how it appeared. *For we walk by faith not by sight 2 Corinthians 5:7.*

The phone rang while Lisa relaxed on the sofa watching recorded episodes of her favorite reality show. She paused the TV and looked at the caller ID.

"Adult Center? What?" Lisa stalled for a moment, unsure as to why they were calling. She put the phone to her ear and says, "Hello?"

"Hello, may I speak to Lisa?" the young receptionist asked.

"This is Lisa," *please don't let this be...! Lord!* She hoped that nothing was wrong with her mother.

"Hello Lisa, this is Michelle from Greater Living Adult Care Center."

"Hello Michelle," she said reluctantly hoping for the best but expecting the worse. You never could tell with her mother.

"Hi Lisa, I'm calling because we haven't received your mother's doctor's release forms yet. In order for us to administer your mother's medication to her, we have to have the forms completely filled out by her doctor as soon as possible," the receptionist said in a professional tone.

Lisa became exhausted just being reminded of what she has to do but at the same time, she's relived knowing that it's a minor thing and nothing more.

"Oh! Her doctor hasn't faxed the paperwork yet?"

"No, he hasn't. Do you have any idea when he's going to fax it?"

"I spoke to the nurse yesterday. I asked them to fax the authorization form as soon as possible and she said they would. I'll call them and find out what happened."

"Okay, thank you, Lisa."

"Um, Michelle?"

"Yes." Lisa's mother was complaining about not being treated right at the adult center. She wanted to find out if the complaints are valid or if her mother's just fabricating stories in order not to go.

"My mother came home yesterday saying the chair she sits in is uncomfortable and it hurts her dislocated hip. She said when she asks for help to go to the restroom, no one is there to help her."

"Really!" Michelle seemed sincerely surprised.

"Yup, she said no one has been helping her for the last two days and that was on Monday, today is Wednesday."

"Oh! Well I'm not aware of this. Did she tell someone here at the center?"

"That's what I asked her and she said no." Now Lisa was agitated remembering the conversation she had with her mother, the day she came home with the complaint.

"Well, I can speak to the director about the matter. I'll have him to give you a call when he's available. Would you like that?"

"Sure, tell him to call me please. In the meantime, I'll call her doctor to find out what's going on with the authorization forms."

"Thank you, Lisa. Have a good day."

"You too." She hung the phone up and leaned her head against the sofa. "Lord, I thank You for giving me favor in the eyes of all man. I thank You, heavenly Father that there are no problems with the doctor's office faxing the forms over to the adult daycare center now Lord in Jesus name, Amen." Lisa looked at the cordless phone then at the wall clock. "It's 12:50." She picked up the remote control and pressed play. "The doctor will be going to lunch in ten minutes. I'll just call them after lunch."

When her mother was hospitalized after having a stroke, the only way they would release her was if she had someone to care for her 24hrs a day. Her speech was limited and her cognitive functions were damaged. Being released to go home alone, was not an option. Lisa meant it from her heart when she volunteered to take care of her mother, even though their relationship was and had been rocky the majority of her life. The thought of sending her to a nursing home was intolerable.

Although, Lisa was the sole caretaker for her mother, Lisa knew that she needed time to relax. What she wanted and what she *needed* was a *VACATION!* A nice vacation, would have her functioning on all eight cylinders, instead of two.

Lisa muted the commercial that just came on. Her mind was suddenly bombarded by all the things she had to do. "Father God, I know You know what's best for me and I know You will come through for me at the right time. One of Your favorites, King David, said I have been young and now I am old, yet I have never seen the righteous forsake or their children begging for bread. Thank You Jesus Christ. Amen." *(Psalm 37:25.)*

THE TRAP IS MADE OUT OF CARNALITY

DANIELLE

was finished with work for the day. She absolutely loved the freedom of being set free from obligations that came from the duties of being a junior executive.

Heads turned as she strutted down the hall like she's turned over a new leaf. Danielle noticed how people were looking at her with a new-found interest. Their stares were more intense than usual. She felt super energetic and excited about the possibilities of having a day of excitement and adventure in the City of the Angels.

When Danielle got off work, most days she felt like running for the hills, not being seen until the next work day but today was different. Her body was renewed as she felt energy pulsating through her veins. She couldn't help but to think this titillation had to do with the young lady she will be dining with tonight.

Danielle pressed the car's remote, jumped inside her ride, revved the engine and off she went. When the rubber hit the road, she turned on the CD player and Anita Baker's powerful voice sailed through the concert like sounding speakers. *Will You Be Mine,*

"Something has come over me, a feeling I can't explaaaiinn, the love and the lost are found again my broken heart it came to mend but it still seems though we are miles and miles apart..."

"Sing it Nita!" Danielle had no way of explaining the new-found happiness but she didn't want it to leave and she would do whatever it took to keep it.

Her cell phone rung and she turned the music down. Since there is a hands-free law in California, Danielle put her bluetooth on and grabbed her phone to see who was calling. She did not recognize the number, and unrecognized numbers usually went unanswered. But since she had been working on new ad campaigns, it served in her best interest to take the call anyway. It's not uncommon for clients to call from unlisted numbers. Danielle learned early in the game, that slipping or sleeping on the job could cause you to lose your job. Many people envied her position but if it's left up to her, there's no way in hell, they would ever get it.

"This is Danielle Stevens."

"Hello, lady." Danielle didn't recognize the voice on the other end of the line.

"Hello? How may I help you?" Were the wisest and safest words she could utter at that time.

"Wow, she's even professional away from the office," the voice teased.

Danielle was annoyed. She thought her question would prompt a satisfactory answer, instead they chose to remain anonymous.

"I'm sorry but may I ask whom I'm speaking to?" *Did I really have to ask that question?*

"And she's modest too! *Hmmmm,* is it too much to admit that my feelings are hurt because you don't who I am?"

Ding! "No." Danielle chuckled. Feeling relieved that she could finally put a face to the voice. "Your phone voice is quite different than your face-to-face voice, so *please,* there's no need to take it personal."

Felicia laughed. "You're *good.*"

"*Well,* I try," Danielle responded, mentally dusting off her shoulder. "So!" *Did I forget something?* "What's up?" Danielle was not one for beating around the bush, she liked to get straight to the point. Her pet peeve was procrastination, she hated it with a passion. *Ain't nobody got time for that!*

"I'm calling to find out if you're still going to accompany me to dinner this evening?"

You really want me to go that bad, huh? Danielle chose not to answer the question in a haste. Felicia's anticipation fed her growing interest like a drug, Danielle was turnt up! "My plans haven't changed." She believed she heard Felicia let out a sigh of relief.

"Good, well, that's all I wanted. I'm going to let you get off this phone." Pause. "Um," Felicia said as she paused again. Danielle's breathing rather rapidly as she listened intensely. It felt like Felicia wanted to ask her something. "Never mind, I'll let you go, talk to you later."

"Okay." Danielle hung the phone up with her curiosity turned up to a thousand percent. *What did she want to say?* "Oh well, closed mouths don't get fed. After a few drinks, Ms. Lady will become Tammy Talk-A-Lot with the quickness." She changed the CD to Jill Scott, whose beautiful voice serenaded her all the way home.

When she entered the house, she stripped out her clothes, ran a tub full of water to take a much-needed bath. Sometime during her bath, she fell asleep.

"It's 2:30!" Danielle exclaimed while jumping out of the tub. "I don't even remember falling asleep." Danielle yanked her towel from the holder to dry herself off. Then she put her robe on and walked out the bathroom. "*Oooh!* That felt so good! I Love it!"

The light blinked on the answering machine that sat on the nightstand next to the bed.

"Two calls? I didn't hear the phone ring once! I must have been really exhausted to fall asleep in the tub. I seriously need to cut back on my hours at work."

Danielle fell on top of the king size plush mattress. "This feels so wonderful." She turned over, reaching for the phone and it rang. "Who dis is!" Danielle looked at the caller ID. "Cynthia." She put the phone to her ear, "Hello?"

"Hello stranger, where have you been? I called you twice." Danielle stared at the answering machine like she expected some kind of confirmation.

"*Oh!* You called and left two messages?"

"Yes, Sherlock...I did. That's why I'm calling you back. Were you planning on calling me back?"

Wow! Why is she all extra! I guess she thinks I'm avoiding her. Really! "Okay! *Weeellll...*let's see why I didn't call you back. *Ummmm,* I just got home from a twelve-hour work day. I fell

108

asleep in the bathtub and we all know how dangerous that is, right? That should show you just how tired I am. Oh, by the way, did I mention just how *tired* I am? I've been extremely overloaded with work, clients and the new campaign ads. I would think that my *closest* friend would remember that I do have to create and produce *three*, not one, but *three brand new* campaign ads, for *three globally* recognized brands. Did I also mention, that I just got out the tub about ten minutes ago? It doesn't take a *scientist rocketest* to understand why I haven't called you back." Danielle hoped her explanation was enough for her overbearing friend.

"Excuse me! Don't you mean a *rocket scientist?* Anyway, you need to learn how to call people back, when they call *you.com.*"

Danielle dropped the phone to her side, already exhausted. Cynthia was making her feel comatose.

Not today-day! Of all days, please not today! She brought the phone back to her ear, feeling irritated. "Hello?"

"Hello? So, what's up?" Cynthia asked.

Is this a trick question? I mean, is there a right or wrong answer? "I'm just lying in bed trying to rest." As she waited for Cynthia's response, a thought of Felicia flashed through her mind, Danielle was instantly aroused.

When she began to entertain Felicia's carnal desires, Danielle unknowingly opened herself to receive a strong spirit of lust and inadvertently welcomed a spirit of bisexuality into her life, the two spirits are insatiable. They have an appetite that is out of this world. Lust spirits *do not* differentiate.

What Danielle didn't know was, she would have sexual thoughts for just about anyone that she came in contact with, whether they were a male or female. When a person was instantly attracted to someone and there was an uncontrollable sexual urge to be with that person, it was definitely the spirit of lust at work. The lust spirit drew individuals together, causing them to believe that it's a harmless 'natural attraction' or 'animal magnetism' between them, but it's most certainly not. Spirits are like magnets, they gravitate to one another. The persons may appear to be complete opposite but if both are housing the same unclean spirit or spirits they will inevitably become attracted to one another. The attraction will sometimes feel like a compulsion or obsession. You feel like that person is stuck in your brain. You're consumed with thoughts of them. When the two come together they become overly excited, faintish and nervous. The thought of being away from one another could possibly make one or both feel physically ill. Human power alone, cannot destroy the spirit of lust. It takes the power of Jesus Christ to be set free and delivered from lust. Our human strength and will-power will never overcome an evil spirit. This is why some are seldom successful at attempting to wean themselves from people and/or bad habits. God will *NEVER* make you feel enslaved to a person or thing. When you feel strong desires for a person or a thing and it feels like you have NO way of escape, IT IS NOT OF GOD! The awesome powerful BLOOD OF THE LAMB OF GOD is the ONLY power that can eradicate uncontrollable compulsions out of your life in its entirety. Everything else is a fluke and you are wasting your time.

(Luke 4:18 "The Spirit of the Lord is upon me, because he hath anointed me to preach the gospel to the poor; he hath sent me to heal the brokenhearted, <u>to preach deliverance to the captives,</u> and recovering of sight to the blind, to set at liberty them that are bruised, to preach the acceptable year of the Lord.")

Cynthia cleared her throat and asks,

"Why haven't I seen you?" Danielle was suddenly confused.

Why haven't you seen me? What, are we dating bow? "I just explained that to you, Cindy." Pause. Danielle looked at the time. It's ten minutes to 3 PM. *I really need to get some rest so I can go out tonight.* Danielle knew it wasn't cool to rush her friend off the phone but she was just about to take a nap before Cynthia called. Danielle cleared her throat and says, "Um-" Cynthia cut her off.

"What are you doing later on? I was thinking about dropping by this evening."

Man. "Oh! Okay, that sounds cool but-" Cynthia interrupted her off again, sounding annoyed.

"What? Do you have plans?"

"I'm sorry Cindy, I-" Danielle was interrupted once more.

"With who! Justin?" Cynthia words were laced with distain.

"No!" Danielle said not trying to hide her agitation. She was growing tired of Cynthia's insecurities when it came to him. "Is it always going to be like this Cynthia? You're gonna always make a crass remark about Justin?"

"I've been doing it for a year. Why is it a problem now?" Danielle asked, sounding hurt.

Danielle didn't have an answer for her because she didn't understand why she became so annoyed with Cynthia.

She is most definitely correct about that. Cynthia has always made snide remarks about him. Why am I tripping now? Anyway, I wish she just stay in her lane and get out of mine, please!

The answer to Danielle's dilemma was, a stronger emotional bond had been forged between them after they entertained sexual feelings for one another. The unnatural bond between them, made Cynthia overly sensitive and aggressive towards her.

"It's cool Cin, but no, I'm not going out with Justin tonight." Cynthia exhaled loudly into the phone. "I have a dinner/business date with one of my colleagues."

"Well, do you think you'll be coming back home, after dinner?" Danielle had no other plans, although she's not sure what will go down afterwards.

"I have no idea what I'll be doing after dinner but you know it's cool for you to come over. I'll call you when I get home, okay?"

"Good, I, I don't mean it like that. I mean, if you're not doing anything else, I would love to see you." Cynthia's heart was about to explode out of her chest. Danielle secretly wanted to see her too but she didn't know how to express it because she's feeling some kind of way. To try to ease the tension, Danielle made light of the subject by playing it off, not trying to sound overly excited about seeing her tonight.

"I'll make sure to save some energy for ya," Danielle said with a chuckle, Cynthia remained silent. Danielle certainly didn't get the outcome she expected. She usually got a laugh from Cynthia or a quick-witted retort but not tonight. This was when it became quite obvious that something strange was going on between them. Where it will go, Danielle didn't know but who's to say she wasn't interested in finding out. If she only knew what the enemy had planned, Danielle would be terrified.

"So..." Cynthia finally spoke, "...I'll see you later then, bye."

Danielle sat the phone down set the alarm clock for 4 PM. Before she dozed off to sleep, the conversation she just had with Cynthia played over in her mind. After ten minutes of reminiscing, Danielle was completely out.

While Danielle was fast asleep there was, a war taken place in the spiritual realm. The devil and his minions, were hard at work plotting Danielle's demise. The enemy wanted desperately for the three to enter into debauchery so he could obtain total access in their lives. He wanted to take their souls, ultimately destroying them for an eternity.

(Be sober, be vigilant; because your adversary the devil walks about like a roaring lion, seeking whom he may devour. 1Peter 5:8). NKJV.

THE WORD "NO" IS A CURSE TO A HEDONIST

In the meantime and between time, Cynthia was lying on the sofa wearing nothing but a red lace bra and matching panty's. She was trying to find something to do to occupy her time until she saw Danielle. The lust Cynthia exuded, was so potent that it could make a priest denounce his vows and turn to a life of sin. Cynthia became terribly aroused during her phone conversation with Danielle and full of anxiety.

"Who says you can't have fun by yourself?"

She reached underneath the sofa for a medium size black velvet case. The latch was still unattached from her last sexual encounter. Cynthia lifted the lid, revealing an array of naughty sex toys, including dildos in all shapes, sizes and colors. Cynthia prided herself on having an extensive sex toy collection for every kind of sexual desire one could imagine. Her motto was: "You can definitely have it your way." She reached for her favorite toy but stopped abruptly. "Why do it alone, when two is better than one?" Cynthia picked the phone up and dialed a number. The phone was answered on the second ring.

"Hello baby," the young seductive voice purred.

"*Heeeyyy!* How are you?" Cynthia asked, while unconsciously outlining her lips with the tip of the toy.

"I'm better now, that you've called. I haven't stopped thinking about you since last night."

"*Oooh,* really?" Cynthia asked teasingly.

"Really…are you thinking about me, too?"

"That's why I called." Pause. "Come over to my place." Pause. "Please." Every syllable was saturated in lust.

Cynthia was greeted by total silence from the other end of the line then, the phone went dead. She removed the phone from her ear and smiled. Cynthia sashayed across the living room to her bedroom to put on her matching robe. A half empty bottle of Jack Daniels sat near her bed.

"It's never a bad time for some liquid sunshine." Cynthia confiscated the bottle and headed to the bar taking two small glasses from the shelf, filling, one with ice. "I take mine straight." As she poured the liquor in the glasses the doorbell chimed. Cynthia looked at the clock on the wall. "Perfect timing."

She walked to the door with a purpose of obtaining the highest degree of sexual pleasure her body could handle.

(They will be traitors. They will be reckless and conceited. They will love pleasure rather than God. 2 Timothy 3:4).

Cynthia removed the chain from the door and opened it to find the beautiful Lori, standing before her wearing a black trench coat and red stilettos. Cynthia licked her lips like a wino after he took a swig of alcohol.

"Come in baby." She moved to the side, as Lori walked passed, taking in every square inch of her. Lori saw desire in Cynthia's eyes and that made her smile with satisfaction.

She walked a few steps ahead of Cynthia and with her back still facing her, Lori let her trench coat fall slowly to the floor revealing her sexy nude body. Cynthia slammed the door shut, while taking Lori by the arm, swirling her around to face her. Cynthia's breathing sounded raspy, she was speechless.

I don't recall her body looking this good last night! Cynthia was so captivated by Lori's essence that she forgot about the drinks she prepared for their consumption. Cynthia took Lori's hand leading her to the living room where she laid her down on the plush carpet next to the opened black velvet case. Lori was thoroughly impressed by her collection of adult toys.

The buffet of sexual carnal desires was open and there was no set time for it to close. Man's selfish desires often spoke louder than the voice of God. It was up to that individual to choose who they will listen to.

("Being filled with all unrighteousness wickedness, greed, evil; full of envy, murder, strife, deceit, malice; they are gossips,

slanderers, haters of God, insolent, arrogant, boastful, inventors of evil, disobedient to parents, without understanding, untrustworthy, unloving, unmerciful; and although they know the ordinance of God, that those who practice such things are worthy of death, they not only do the same, but also give hearty approval to those who practice them." Romans 1:29-32). (And if it seems evil to you to serve the LORD, choose for yourselves this day whom you will serve, whether the gods which your fathers served that were on the other side of the River, or the gods of the Amorites, in whose land you dwell. But as for me and my house, we will serve the LORD. Joshua 24:15).

BELLS AND SIRENS

The alarm clock buzzed, waking Danielle up from a tranquil sleep. It's been a long time since she's gotten any real rest. But the nap was just a taste of what her body and mind needed.

"OMG!" Danielle exclaimed. *"I am soooo* in love with sleep right now!" She rubbed her eyes and climbed out of bed. "Let's see, let's see."

Danielle went to her walk-in closet, opening the massive double doors revealing a plethora of designers. Every name brand that you could think of, it's a possibility she owns it. Danielle's closet was the epitome of every woman's dream; Prada, Vera Wang, Christian Dior, Gucci, Burberry, Pierre Balman, Dolce & Gabbana, Donna Karan, Armani, Oscar de la Renta, Valentino, just to name a few.

Tonight, Danielle was going for a more casual sophisticated look. She imagined how she'd look in various ensembles as she carefully scrutinized the expensive clothing hanging in front of her.

A peasant blouse with a pair of tight jeans and my mesh Jimmy Choo sandals?

Danielle took a moment to envision how she would look rocking her selection.

I'm feeling it.

Danielle, then chose a magenta pink peasant blouse, a pair of brand new white J Brand close fitting jeans and the cherry on top of the sundae was her magenta pink mesh Jimmy Choo sandals and a matching mesh clutch bag.

"Whoop there it is! I did that!" Danielle glanced at the clock, it was 4:30 PM. "Okay! I need to put a rush on it so that I can *at least* be ready on time!" In one move her robe was off. Her next decision was deciding whether to wear panty's or a pair of thongs.

She strutted over to her chest of drawers, opened the top drawer and selected a pair of white thongs.

116

"This is what I wear when I want to avoid wearing panty's but I feel like I just gotta wear *sumtin!*" Danielle learned that it was easier keeping her panty's and thongs separated in different drawers. Her thongs occupied the top drawer because she wears them the most. Her bikini panties were in the second drawer. She only wore those when she's not in the mood to wear thongs. The third drawer was specifically for her monthly visitor, her granny panties.

Danielle stood in front of the full-length mirror modeling her thongs.

"With the right pair of thongs, you can *never* go wrong!" She twirled around in the mirror making sure they looked right. Danielle checked the clock once more. "*Ohhhh!* It's ten minutes to five! The car should be here any minute and traffic in L.A. sucks!"

Danielle stepped into high gear. The car service called her a few minutes later. She retrieved her clutch bag, house keys and her black leather waist length jacket.

"I'll be there in a few minutes," she said into the phone. Danielle did a quick once-over in the mirror as she exits the house.

Felicia made quite an impression on Danielle by sending a black stretched Hummer limousine to pick her up. A tall handsome male driver stood near the rear of the vehicle.

"How do you do madam?" He tilted his hat in Danielle's direction and took a bow.

"I'm fine," she said with a smile. The driver opened the door revealing sheer elegance. The inside of the limo was fabulous! He extended his hand to assist her into the limousine. "Thank you, kindly." The driver closed the door, moments later, Danielle heard the roaring of the engine, while the humming from the air conditioner buzzed lightly in her ears.

"Are there any stops you'd like to make before we arrive to your destination?" the driver asked over the intercom system.

Danielle pressed the intercom button located in the middle console where she was seated and says, "No thank you. We can proceed to the restaurant." Their destination was an upscale Italian restaurant located on Melrose Avenue. Danielle lives in Culver City, she wasn't too far from the restaurant's location. Her head was spinning from how amazing the Hummer was.

"She did that!" Danielle said in reference to Felicia's excellent taste. The Hummer could seat up to twenty-five to thirty people comfortably. It had a fascinating wet bar that could almost rival Danielle's bar and there were two tall see-through cylinders on either side of the bar filled with bubbling water. A light blue light shined through each cylinder. Of course, the bar was fully stocked.

Danielle's nervous were on edge. She required some kind of liquid joy to loosen up the kinks. Danielle took two shots of vodka and one shot of cranberry juice on the rocks.

"Now, that's how you do it." She brought the glass to eye-level to examine it. Then, she parted her lips to take a nice long sip from her cocktail. Danielle leaned back in her seat to get comfortable while looking through the large moon roof located just above her head. She was mesmerized by the rows of decorative lights aligning the ceiling, adding a certain ambience to the interior, making it aesthetically pleasing, and the Bose sound system made the music sound like heaven. Heavy metal music could have been pumping through the speakers sounding so good that even a dog would have fallen asleep listening to it.

Danielle had gotten so relaxed during the ride to the restaurant to meet Felicia, that she wasn't even paying attention to the time. For a moment, she actually forgot she was inside of a limo and not in the cozy confinements of her living room.

When the smooth driven vehicle came to a complete stop, Danielle looked through the darkly tinted windows to see where they were. They were parked directly in front of the posh restaurant. The driver opened the door and extended his glove covered hand to assist Danielle.

"I hope you have a joyous evening, Madam."

"I certainly will, and thank you."

The sidewalk in front of the Italian restaurant was filled with pedestrians, who were happily walking to various places. Danielle could feel an air of electricity in the air that made a person feel like the world *was* a beautiful place and anything was possible.

Danielle felt unusually light as she strutted inside the restaurant. The mairte'd led her to the table where the first party member was awaiting her arrival. Felicia was just about to stand up but she quickly caught herself and remained seated as she greeted Danielle with a sexy smile.

Was she about to stand up for me! Wow! That has to be embarrassing!

Felicia lowered her head, feeling shamed by the mishap. Danielle's knees began to buckle and her heart was pounding so erratically that it felt like it was about to burst out of her throat! Watching Felicia as she sat there looking so beautiful, Danielle became overly anxious. She held onto the maître'd arm with a vice like grip just to keep from slipping to the floor. Danielle managed a weak smile.

I don't believe this! Why am I so nervous? I cause people to be nervous! The maitre'd pulled out Danielle's chair for her. "Thank you kindly."

"You're welcome. Would the lady like a menu?"

"Yes, I would." He gave Danielle a menu and she cleverly used it as a convenient distraction to avoid Felicia's piercing stare.

"May I refresh your glass of water?" he asked both ladies.

"No, thank you," Felicia responded.

"I'm fine," Danielle told the Maitre'd.

"Thank you, ladies." He bowed before Danielle and Felica and quickly left their table.

The minute he was gone, Danielle wished he stayed a bit longer. She needed to calm down. Danielle knew she couldn't hide behind the menu all night, looking like a moron. She took in a deep breath.

Suck it up Danni and stop acting like a silly sixteen-year-old girl on her first date. Date!? Could this possibly be an elaborate hook-up? Wait a minute! Shut the damn front door! Is this a...!

Danielle sat the menu down looking directly at Felicia as she took a sip from her glass of water, their eyes locked. Danielle's imagination was on autopilot, as she undressed Felicia with her eyes.

Felicia dipped her index finger into the water and seductively stuck her finger into her mouth. Danielle instantly felt something leap inside her, showering her body with intoxicating feelings of intense sexual arousal. She sat erect in the chair as Felicia pulled her into her mental seduction. Danielle was stupefied. The spell was broken when Felicia finally opened her mouth to speak,

"*Soooooo,* how was your day?" The words carried their own intensity.

Danielle choked. She could have sworn she heard Felicia say, '*How comfortable is your bed?*' Maybe, Danielle misinterpreted what Felica said because she couldn't get over how beautiful Felicia was.

The soft peach color batwing sleeve cashmere sweater fit Felicia perfectly. A modest diamond necklace hung daintily around her neck. The way Felicia's matching shaped diamond chandler earrings danced with every slight movement of her head, was indeed hypnotizing. Her soft lips were covered with a thin layer of lip gloss making them look even more sensual. What radiated from Felicia made her appear irresistible.

Danielle found herself slipping deeper into an abyss of strong attraction for this woman, leaving her powerless to fight Felicia's mental persuasions. When Danielle tried to resist Felicia's charms, she found herself tumbling head-first into Felicia's pool of carnal desires, even quicker. Danielle never experienced lust like this before; lust that was so damn powerful, that it engulfed her, taking her captive. Danielle couldn't recall ever feeling this way about Justin or any man, for that matter.

The attraction brewing between Felicia and Danielle, was unnaturally strong. That's what terrified Danielle and intrigued her at the same time.

My God! How am I going to get through this dinner! Danielle sucked in a sharp breath, before answering Felicia's question about her day. "Well, besides work, my day went rather nicely," Danielle said, giggling like a school girl. *You gotta be kidding me, for crying out loud!* She couldn't believe how she was behaving. *I'm carrying on like a giddy fifteen-year-old!* Danielle outwardly shook her head in disapproval of her interactions with her gorgeous dinner date. Felicia noticed her shaking her head.

"What's that all about?"

"What's what, all about?"

"You were shaking your head, why?"

Is it time for a confession session? I think not. "Oh! It's nothing. I was just thinking about something a friend said to me." Felicia did not miss a beat.

"Tell me, I mean, I'd like to hear about it, if you don't mind." A sheepish look spread across her face. Felicia knew she was stepping over the line but it didn't matter. She was use to being the aggressor and getting what she wanted. And what Felicia wanted, was sitting in front of her. Danielle gave her a knowing look.

"Are you sure, you wanna go there?" Felicia smiled.

"I'm sorry, but where am I trying to go?" Felicia asked daringly while she stared at Danielle, knowing that Danielle was not bold enough to say what she meant. "I don't mean to pry, if that's what you're referring to?" Danielle smirked.

"Are you sure?" It's her turn to tease.

"Oh, I'm very sure, unless...you want me to." Silence. Both were lost in the trap they set for one another. Danielle cleared her throat.

"You weren't prying, like I said, it was nothing. It was just a little something shared between friends." Felicia flinched. Danielle was shocked by her visible display of hyper-sensitivity. Her last remark wasn't intended to make her feel insecure. With a puppy dog look on Felicia's face she says,

"I'd like to be your *friend*," a strong emphasis on the word "friend." Felicia demonstrated her flare for the theatrics, when she feigned innocence, by laying her head-on top of her hands while playfully pouting her lips.

You don't want to just, be friends, Danielle said to herself. Her thoughts were interrupted when Felicia asks,

"So, tell me, do you think I have a shot at becoming one of your *close* friends?" Felicia reached across the table to caress Danielle's hand. Danielle allowed her hand to be held for a moment before she politely reclaimed it. Danielle was far from being wet behind the ears.

I don't discriminate. If she wants these goodies, she's going to have to work for it just like any man. Danielle tugged at her ear lobe licking her lips seductively and says, "Let's order." Casting

121

her eyes downward, she then shot Felicia a sexy look and says, "I'm down to try *anything,* on the menu." Danielle hoped that Felicia interpreted what she *didn't* say. Now, it was time for Felicia to be mesmerized. She pretended to be focused on her menu but actually, she was really studying Danielle, her dinner date. *Didn't think I could flip it on ya like that, huh?*

Felicia smiled at her temptress, then she picked up her menu and says "*Mmmm,* do you know *for sure* what you are having?"

"Everything looks so good but I think I'll pass on having my *usual* selection and try something, *new."* Danielle's response carried serious undertones. Felicia pulled down the menu, peering over the top, looking directly at Danielle who was already staring at her.

"*Hmmm,* I'm sure that *whatever* you *decide, will be good.* Maybe even, better than good...I know that for a fact." Felicia's message was loud and clear.

The waiter approached the table interrupting their mental foreplay. "What are you lovely ladies having this evening?"

"I'd like the baked pasta romana with chicken. And will you please tell the chef to make sure my pasta isn't al dente?"

"Ohhh! Al denta! You speak Italian, no?" Danielle blushed.

"Only when I order Italian food." She smiled. He nodded his head as he wrote down her order.

"Your wish is my command."

"Also, will you bring me a side of melted butter with two slices of lime?" Danielle gave the waiter her menu.

"Very well," he said as he nodded to Felicia. "And you, Madam?"

"Romana chicken sounds lovely but sir, I'll have your grilled *shrimp...*" Felicia added with a wink and a smile at Danielle, "...caprese with an extra side of fresh basil tomato grilled garlic and butter sauce."

"Excellent choice! Shrimp caprese..." the waiter did the traditional Italian display, of kissing his fingertips showing his enthusiasm, "...excellente! And your choice of wine, Madam?" Felicia scanned the wine list but decided to ask the waiter for the restaurant's recommendations.

"How 'bout you bring us a bottle of your finest selection." He smiled excitedly.

"Certainly, madam. I'll bring you a bottle of Amarone! It's very exquisite!" The waiter kissed the tips of his fingers again. "Very well, I'll be back with your wine, ladies." He took their menus and spun around on his heels, leaving as quickly as he came.

There was nothing between the two but space and opportunity. They eyed each other teasingly, waiting for one to break the silence. Danielle took the initiative.

"I should have asked him to bring some more bread, I'm starving." Felicia searched the restaurant looking for the waiter. "It's okay, I don't want to spoil my appetite. I'm not one of those eaters whose eyes are bigger than their stomach." Felicia arched her eyebrows wondering if there was an underlining meaning to what she said. Danielle gave her a puzzling look. "Don't worry, if I have something to say, I'll say it to you directly. I don't do hidden messages." *I do. But you don't need to know that.* Felicia let a small stream of air escape through her lips.

"Good, because that went over this sista's head." They both laughed. Felicia reached across the table and drew circles on the top of Danielle's hand with the tip of her finger. "So, Danielle Stevens, tell me a little something about yourself." Danielle slowly sipped her water and says,

"Let's see, some people say I'm a private person." She shrugged her shoulders and looked off in a distance. "I guess, that's because I don't go around blabbing my business to everybody. I always remembered what my mother use to say." Danielle grew silent, as she watched Felicia with a mixture of emotions.

"What did your mother use to say?"

"My mother use to always say, that only foolish women put their business in the streets."

"Sounds like a wise woman."

"That she is, I've learned a lil sumtin from her." Danielle chuckled.

"Oh yeah? What else have you learned?"

"I know that a person has to be very special *to me,* in order for me to share intimate details about myself to them." Keeping her eyes glued on Felicia, Danielle took a slice of lemon wedge from her glass and seductively squeezed lemon juice on her tongue. Felicia broke eye contact and cleared her throat. She couldn't handle the teasing.

"That's-that's quite interesting. I'm kinda like that myself, that's why I keep my circle tight. It consists of *only* the sharpest and sexiest women, I mean!" Felicia said, stumbling to clean up her second mistake.

No! You said exactly what you meant. Danielle laughed to herself. *Why does she keep busting herself out like this?*

"I meant to say, that I like having the sharpest, sexiest people in my circle, who I can trust. *And,* that number is small because there aren't too many people that I trust. *But* when I do trust someone, that person *should* feel extremely privileged." Danielle offered a sexy smile. She knew Felicia's last statement was directed towards her.

"I see, so are you saying that I-" Danielle was cut off by the waiter reappearing with a bottle of wine, holding it up for their approval. Felicia motioned for the waiter to continue. He expertly removed the cork and placed two chilled wine glasses in front of them. Danielle and Felicia were fixated on the lovely glasses as they watched the waiter fill the expensive flutes with the red liquid.

"It looks delicious," Felicia said as she picked up the glass, sniffed it, took a sip, swirled it around in her mouth and spat it into the spit bucket. "Just as I said, it's delicious!" The waited offered Danielle a glass of wine to test. She held up her hand to stop him.

"I'll take her word for it. The lady appears to have *superb* taste." Felicia blushed.

"That, I do."

"Okay, if there is nothing else, your dinner should be here shortly."

"Thank you," was said in unison. Danielle sipped the wine.

"*Mmmm!* It *is* delicious! Smooth and sweet, just like I like it." Felicia couldn't resist. With an overdose of lasciviousness, she says,

"Really? *Is* that how you like it?"

Danielle leaned back in her chair, studying Felicia like she was lying on an examination table getting ready to be dissected. "I'll tell you what, how bout *I* let *you* get to know what I like and then *you* can tell *me,* what I like. How do you like that?"

"Hmmm, that sounds like an adventure I will never grow tired of." They both laughed.

"You sure won't." Danielle took on a more serious tone, "How many business meetings do you stand-in for your boss on a monthly basis?"

"Wow, it has gotten to the point where I've lost count."

"That many times?"

"Yes, that many times."

"Tell me this…?"

"Tell you what?" Felicia sipped her wine, making sure to keep eyes on Danielle.

"How many sharp sexy people do you tend to extract from these meetings, hoping to add to your *inner* circle?" Felicia bursts out laughing spraying wine out her mouth, redecorating the table cloth with red droplets.

"You're too funny!" Felicia said in between wiping her mouth and the table cloth with a napkin. Danielle watched humorously.

"I'm not trying to be funny at all. I just want to find out if this is your get down. You know, taking women to dinner and captivating them with your charm?" All jokes aside. They stared at one another hoping to see, clearly, what the other's intentions were.

"F.Y.I., I don't do this very often. It's only when I feel a deep…" she watched Danielle carefully to gauge her reaction before she spoke candidly, "…*connection* with a person, that I'll even take the time to consider inviting them into my *inner* circle. Does that satisfy your inquiring mind?"

"*Ummm,* I'm going to have to let *you* get to know *me* for yourself. That way, *you'll* be able to answer your own question." Felicia laughed.

"I walked right into that one, huh?"

125

"Yes...yes, you did." The waiter and a helper appeared with their food. *Right on time! I was about to start nibbling on this table cloth.*

"Ladies, would you like your water and wine glasses refreshed?"

"I would like more water please," Danielle said.

"So, would I," Felicia added. The waiter walked away and returned with an exquisite silver pitcher of water.

"Is there anything else?" he asked after filling their glasses to the rim.

"No, we're fine," Felicia said. Danielle couldn't answer because her mouth was full of food. Felicia laughed. "You weren't kidding when you said you were hungry." Danielle was seriously chowing down on the food in her mouth. She took a sip of water and says,

"*Mmmm, mmm!* This is *sooo* good, this *chicken!*" Danielle put another piece of scrumptious chicken into her mouth, taking her sweet time as the savory morsels caressed each taste bud.

"I'm glad you like it." Danielle examined Felicia's plate.

"How's *your shrimp?*" she asked with a hint of salaciousness. Felicia picked up a shrimp, opened her mouth, stuck out her tongue and enticingly placed the crustacean on the tip of her tongue. Danielle sat motionless, in total suspense as she watched Felicia's every move.

"It's just like *I* like it...*fresh* and very tasteful."

"Sounds delish."

"It is."

The two ladies continued eating and sharing endless soft-core overtones with one another, building an eagerness that couldn't be contained.

Danielle rubbed her stomach feeling satisfied. The waiter approached their table with bill in hand. Before he laid the check on the table Felicia handed him a credit card.

"Grazie madam! I'll be back with the receipt." Moments later, he returned with the receipt and Felicia's credit card.

"Thank you," Felicia said as both stood, while the waiter rushed to assist the ladies out of their chairs.

"You're welcome, and please come again."

"Have a good night, Garçon," Felicia said to the waiter as they prepared to exit the restaurant.

"You too, as well, Madam."

Danielle stole the opportunity and allowed her dinner date to walk ahead of her, so she could enjoy the tantalizing view from behind. Needless to say, Danielle was enthralled by the way Felicia's peach colored flare skirt caressed her midsection flowing out, and hanging just above Felicia's ankles.

I can imagine how she looks naked.

The night air wrapped around Danielle as she stepped out the restaurant, leaving her wanting more. She didn't want the night to end but she remembered her plans with Cynthia.

Why did I do that to myself! I really don't want to go home right now. But if I don't keep my word, Cynthia will never let me live it down. Man!

Once they were inside the limo, Felicia noticed the somber look on Danielle's face.

"Why are you frowning?" Her deposition changed rather drastically, from the time they stepped out the restaurant and into the limo. Felicia wanted to make *sure* that *she* wasn't the reason behind the sudden change.

"Oh, it's nothing," Danielle said as she sat next to Felicia. "It's just such a lovely night, it's a shame it has to come to an end." Electricity encircled the ladies as they sat side by side in the dimly lit vehicle. They allowed the silence to overtake them, only listening to the rhythmic sounds of the tires hitting the road and the smooth romantic sounds of Jagged Edge's, Remedy, as it played softly in the background. Felicia lightly brushed Danielle's upper arm, summoning her attention.

"It doesn't have to end, you know, not if you don't want it to." The quietness that filled the limo's interior was deafening. It was hardly difficult to read the message that their eyes revealed but their mouths dared to say.

Felicia was the first to drop her gaze. The desire to kiss Danielle was undeniably intense! Felicia couldn't find the words to say how she felt at that moment. She decided to remain silent and let J.E. say it for her,

"...girl, it's you I want and it's you I need, girl I got the remedy. If you feel it, girl I got the key, remedy to your body..." Felicia slowly raised her head, daring to look at Danielle, who was already watching her intently.

"Look...," Felicia said, barely above a whisper. Danielle nodded her head letting Felicia know that she was listening, "...I invited you out on false pretenses...," she stopped speaking, giving Danielle room to protest if she wanted to. When she didn't, Felicia continued, "When I first laid eyes on you, I wanted you. If you only knew how hard it was for me to contain myself this afternoon when we were in the conference room, in the restaurant and right now."

Danielle turned away, glancing outside the window. She needed to focus on something else, other than the beautiful desirous creature sitting, literally millimeters away from her. Danielle knew her actions would probably give Felicia the wrong impression but she wasn't as bold, nor as carefree as Felicia.

I feel the same way, and how can I tell you that! It's taking a lot of restraint just to keep from kissing you.

Felicia must have felt what Danielle was thinking. She gently turned Danielle's face back to her and with her voice barely above a whisper Felicia says,

"I would love to kiss your lips." The urge building between them, begged to be satisfied! Felicia added, "Please?" When Danielle didn't protest, she took her nonresistance as a greenlight by slowly leaning in, trying her best to savor the moment. Felicia placed her lips onto Danielle's lips and kissed her like she would never have that chance again. Felicia's heart began to race and her breathing quickened. *Mmmmm, just as I imagined!* She unreluctantly withdrew just enough to read Danielle's face. When she saw no signs of opposition, Felicia poured out every ounce of her passion onto Danielle's lips.

"Excuse me ladies," the driver's voice broke through the intercom system, piercing the heavy-laden lust filled atmosphere, "...do you need anything?" If he hadn't interrupted their playtime, there's *no* telling *how* far they would have gone.

Startled, Danielle jumped back in her seat and tried to straighten her clothes. Felicia put her annoyance by the diver's interruption on display by saying,

"No! We're fine, and no more interruptions until we've arrived at Ms. Stevens' residence, please."

"Yes, Mame."

Felicia knew there might be a challenge attempting to get Danielle back in the mood but she hadn't gotten where she was by giving up so easily. She leaned over and kissed Danielle's neck. But before Felicia could go any further, Danielle pressed her hand against Felicia's chest, signaling for her to slowdown.

"What's wrong?" Felicia asked.

I have never been with a woman before and this is scaring the ish outta me! "This is so new to me, Felicia. I…I don't-" She put her finger against Danielle's lips.

"Shhhhh." Felicia laughed. "I figured that out a *looonngg* time ago, honey. Don't worry, I'll show you what to do. Can I, show you what to do, please?" At first, Felicia's kisses started off soft but within seconds, those sweet sublet kisses turned ferocious. Danielle was going delirious!

What in the world is happening to me!

Felicia made a bold move by unbuttoning Danielle's blouse to explore her breast. Her mind screamed for Felicia to stop but her body betrayed her, it wanted more. Danielle feared they would be stripped down to nothing if they didn't stop! She found the strength from somewhere deep inside and pushed Felicia away from her, once again. This time, when Danielle denied Felicia's last attempt at getting her undressed, it was done with much stronger conviction.

"What's wrong, baby!" Felicia asked breathlessly. "Are you okay?"

"I'm fine," Danielle's voice was strained, exposing how sexually frustrated she was. Her body yearned to be touched and caressed by Felicia but it's going too damn fast! If this was going to go down, Danielle *had* to be in control! She'd be damned, if she allowed herself to be left wide open, acting desperate like a drug feign. What scared Danielle the most was, they haven't even *done anything,* yet and she's already feeling thirsty.

"Wa-*waaait* a minute. I'm pretty sure you have no problem with snatching it up when it comes to what you want but I don't want this to be a booty call. I aint into getting turned out in the backseat of a car and getting dropped off on the corner like a hoe." Felicia dropped her head trying to suppress a laugh. She was flattered.

"Wow, that's how you feel? I mean, I am truly flattered but I wouldn't drop you on the corner like a hoe. I'd, at least drop you off at your front door. I mean, can a girl get *some* kind of credit?" Danielle stared at Felicia through slanted eyes, but she failed to hold back the burst of laughter threatening to explode from behind her throat. "I'm only kidding," Felicia said, while she laughed along with Danielle. "But seriously," she lightly touched Danielle's inner thigh, commanding her earnest attention. Felicia's touch sent shivers down Danielle's spine but she fought to suppress the obvious hold Felicia was beginning to have on her, "…although, I don't bedhop but *whomever* I'm with, gets *all* of me. And I don't play games *but* I definitely feel where you're coming from, so yes, let's slow down." Felicia stamped Danielle's hand with a kiss. "Besides, the longer we wait, the better the anticipation will be. Anticipation, equals intensity." Felicia demonstrated just what she meant by kissing Danielle passionately, her guards fell down, again. Of course, Felicia tried once more, to undress Danielle. She almost succeeded, until reality kicked in.

I gotta get out of this car before she has me bringing her breakfast in bed and signing over the deed to my house! The driver announced their arrival,

"We're at Ms. Stevens' residence."

Thank God!

Danielle straightened out her clothes faster than lightening, before rolling down the window informing the security guard, at her gated community, to open the gate. Five minutes later, the car door opened and Danielle was ready to leap out in one single-bound. Felicia couldn't move fast enough to keep up with her. When she finally caught up to Danielle, she reached out to grab her sleeve.

"Lord Jesus, where's the fire!" Felicia joked as she tried to catch her breath. Danielle reluctantly, turned to face Felicia but her instincts told her to run like the wind. "You got me jogging out here! And, I don't know if you've noticed but I'm not quite dressed to be doing the fifty-yard dash." Felicia pointed to her attire, while doing a curtsy. Danielle was on an emotional roller coaster, indeed. She's confused about her *new* feelings for her new-found friend.

"Felicia, you know, what you're doing."

"Huh?" Felicia asked, defensively. Danielle rolled her eyes out of frustration. "Are you implying that I'm trying to run-game on you?"

"Noooo." Danielle put her hands-on Felicia's shoulders endearingly. "That is not what I am saying at *all. But,* what *I am* saying is, what you exude, is damn near impossible to fight! I'm fighting tooth and nail not to give into you." A sexy smile spreads across Felicia's face. She used Danielle's confession as a ploy to try to get close to her again but Danielle was too quick on the draw. She pulled away from Felicia's grasp before she could even lay hands on Danielle. Felicia's hurtful feelings came to surface.

"My animal-like magnetism doesn't seem to be working now," Felicia admitted solemnly. Danielle kissed Felicia's finger tips and says,

"It's not working because I have the antidote." She turned away and walked to her door, leaving Felicia behind to wonder about all the possibilities of how she could be granted an invitation into Danielle's bed.

"You have the antidote?" Felicia yelled the question to Danielle's back.

"That's right," Danielle threw over her shoulder, refusing to cast eyes on Felicia for fear of giving into her lustful, irresistible demands.

"Do you mind if I ask what your antidote is?" Felicia asked, smiling devilishly. She wasn't giving up so easy. Danielle boldly turned to face her temptation and says,

"Self-control, baby." With that said, she opened her front door and walked in the house. All Felicia could do was laugh out loud to herself as she went back to the car with thoughts of their brief but hot make out session.

OLD CONNECTIONS ARE HARD TO BREAK

Tommy shut the door behind Regina with his eyes still fixated her. He stared at Regina causing her to be extremely uncomfortable.

"Well, are you going to say something or just keep watching me like I'm a ghost?" Tommy blushed and held Regina's hand, leading her to the sofa.

"Can you blame me?" he asked excitedly. "I haven't seen you since our junior year in *college!"* The realization of how long they've been a part made, him lightheaded. "And you're still beautiful." Tommy's mere words touched her heart.

Regina gazed into her ex-lover's eyes remembering how it was when they shared their lives together. She's trying to process it all. It's been years since she stepped foot inside this house.

Nothing has changed. It looks the same! They still have the same ole furniture! Regina remembered the day his mother bought the floral sofa they were sitting on, now. The shelf that stored Tommy's athletic trophies sat in the same exact place, right next to the window by the front door. Although, the carpet was a bit worn from years of traffic, it still looked good. *They don't make carpet like this anymore.*

Tommy touched Regina's chin, gently bringing her face close to his.

"Hey, where are you?"

She instantly snapped back to the here and now, struggling with feelings of guilt about their quaint reunion. Although, Regina was enjoying reminiscing about the old times, unfortunately that's not what she came there for. The old memories have only added to the hurt and pain that was boiling over in her soul. All Regina wanted to do was get high, and maybe even get high with him. The problem Regina faced was, she had bought weed from the same person for years. She wouldn't know *how* to find a dope spot if her life depended on it. This was where Tommy came in. Regina secretly hoped he was still getting high or at least knew where she could score dope without encountering problems. Yes, she wanted to get high but it wasn't worth going to jail.

"I'm here. I was just thinking…"

"About what? Me, I hope."

"I'm thinking about everything." She took a deep breath. "Tommy, it's been years."

"Too many years," Tommy said with endearment. Regina could still tell that he still loved her. Seeing his heart exposed, only overwhelmed her with conviction.

Here I am, trying to get high with this man and he's still in love with me! I'm a piece of work! Regina was still, very much in love with Tommy, too but at this point in her life, she didn't want any emotional ties. The only thing she wanted to do, was get high. Regina wanted to get so high that she could run away and hide from *all* the misery she harbored. Finding out that Tommy still loved her, just made the situation a little more complicated.

Regina jumped to her feet preparing to leave and never look back. Tommy had the reflex of a panther. He grabbed her by the arm, pleading with his eyes.

"What's wrong!"

"I should not have come here. I, I got to go." Regina tried prying her arm from his vice grip but he wouldn't let go.

"I'm not trying to lose you again, Regina!" A mixture of emotions showed in Tommy's eyes. The fear that Regina saw alarmed her. She knew all too well what fear could do.

"Tommy, please don't do this!" He was confused and did not understand why she's refusing his love.

Isn't it obvious that I still love her! "What Regina! What am I doing that is making you want to leave me, again? I still love you!"

"I know, and I feel horrible about it! Please! Please, let go of me Tommy!" The walls were closing in, Regina felt claustrophobic. *I need to get out of here! Telling him the real reason I'm here, would only kill him,* she rationalized.

"Stop! Will you stop fighting me, Regina! I love you!" Tommy took her into his arms holding her tightly. At first Regina didn't resist until she felt his heart pounding against her chest. She tried to pull away but he was too strong. Tommy held onto her for dear life.

"Tommy! *Please.*" Regina collapsed in his arms, howling like a wounded animal.

"It's okay, baby, let it out. I'm here...Tommy's here for my baby." Regina balled up her fist and pounded against his chest.

"I'm sorry! I'm so sorry, Tommy!" she cried out.

"It's all right, don't be sorry. You didn't do anything wrong."

Yes! Yes, I did. "Please stop," Regina said between heart wrenching tears. Hear crying only made Tommy comfort her even more and she cried harder. Regina wasn't able to take anymore of Tommy's raw affection, so she blurted out, "I only came here to get high, dammit!" Regina held her breath waiting for the explosion. "I want...I wanted us to get high together!"

"That's it!" Tommy asked incredulously while he looked down at her tear stained-face. She turned away too ashamed. "Regina?" She refused to look at him. "Please Regina, look at me." She reluctantly faced Tommy. "I got you baby. I owe you for everything." She tried to look away again. "No! Look at me," Tommy pleaded, Regina did as he asked. "You were always with me, even until the end. I'll never forget that, never." She was astonished. Regina couldn't believe that he wasn't going to toss her out on her ass for just admitting that all she wanted to do was get high.

"What?" Regina asked stunned. She's not sure that she heard him correctly.

"I said, I got you." Tommy felt around in his pants pocket and pulled out a small ziploc bag containing two pieces of white rocks. He held them up to her eyes. At first look, Regina didn't know what it was until she took a closer examination. She removed the bag from his hand.

"Is this crack cocaine!" Regina asked excitedly.

"Baby, I promise, if you thought primos were something, you aint never felt a high like this. It'll make you feel like, *ooh wheee!"* Tommy excited his self by his own description of how good the high felt. He produced a pipe from out of nowhere and suddenly jumped to his feet, telling Regina to follow him.

Without question, Regina allowed her ex to lead her through a door that separated the living room from the hallway. Three bedrooms were attached to the hall. They walked pass a room to their immediate left with the door closed. As they continued down the short narrow hallway, they passed a second bedroom which was Tommy's mother's room and the door was open. For some strange reason, Regina wanted to take a closer inspection of his mother's room but that would be inappropriate. Physical darkness greeted Regina, along with a thick musty smell and the sever sadness emanating from the room was overwhelming.

God, that room feels so sad! I wish he'd crack open a window and open a few blinds, Regina said to herself. She wouldn't dare share her thoughts with Timmy. Well, at least not until she got high. The third door, Tommy's room, was partially open. Regina braced herself before they entered the room, not knowing *what* to expect. *He lives in his mother's house and he does drugs, go figure.*

Tommy gently pushed the door open and to Regina's surprise, his room was spotless! A small twin size bed sat to the left of the room, neatly made up with the corners of a new comforter tucked perfectly underneath the mattress. Next to the window, sat a medium size lounge chair. Faux wooden blinds hung over the two windows. Regina could see inside the closet because the door was ajar. Tommy's shoes were sitting in perfect alignment on the floor with his clothes hanging flawlessly on hangers. A chest of drawers sat in the corner with a collection of his smell-good on top. Regina felt real silly for assuming his room would be in shambles, unfit for a dog to sleep in. Tommy must have caught the sheer look of amazement on Regina's face as she sat on his bed.

"What?" He snickered. "You thought my room was gonna look like slobs-r-us.com?" All she could do was laugh. To tell it to you plainly, Regina expected not to be able to sit on *anything* in his room, comfortably, without feeling like something was crawling on her.

"Guilty as charged," Regina said as she hung her head to the floor. The color of his carpet suddenly became interesting to her. Regina raised her head up with a weak smile on her face, "I'm sorry. I-"

"*Shhhh*...no need to explain." Tommy stood up from the bed and closed the door. Now, Regina was nervous.

I hope he's not trying to get me high so he can get some. Tommy didn't say a word as he stood directly in front of Regina, using his knee to pry open her legs. *See! I knew I shouldn't have come in here! Why you can't just kick it with a man without him thinking you gon' give it up!* Regina worked herself up into a frenzy. "Tom-" she opened her mouth to protest but Tommy silenced her by kneeling down between her legs, sitting the rock on her left knee and a lighter on the other.

He finally looked at her grinning from ear to ear, because he knew what she assumed. Tommy picked up the pipe, took a deep breath and blew into the opening, trying to remove the excess residue. He placed the rock into the pipe and turned the mouthpiece towards Regina. This was all foreign to her.

"You want me to go first?" Regina asked nervously. For some strange reason, she felt overly cautions. Suddenly, Regina didn't want to smoke dope with Tommy anymore. However, feelings of despair outweighed the warnings. She snatched the pipe from Tommy's long fingers, fearing that if she hesitated any longer, she wouldn't do it.

Regina looked into Tommy's eyes before she took the first hit of the potent vapor and she could have sworn she saw a subtle smirk appear on his face. Tommy's eyes, once filled with warmth, quickly turned black as coal and cold as ice. Regina immediately felt intense regret and tremendous fear in the pit of her gut. The temperature in the room seemed to drop a few degrees.

Oh Lord! What is happening! Even after that harsh warning, Regina still wrapped her lips firmly around the stem and inhaled.

The effects of the drug were instantaneous. It started at the crown of her head and flowed to the soles of her feet. The feelings were equivalent to how it felt when she experienced her first orgasm but more intense.

Regina's arms fell to her side, her head was too heavy to hold and her eyes rolled to the back of her head as she fell backwards on the bed.

"Oh, oh! Oooh!" she mumbled. *What is* this feeling! It feels *soooooo, sooooo, goooood!*

Regina just opened the door and allowed a more dominate drug abuse spirit to enter her life. Its mission was to have her totally dependent on drugs, ultimately causing her demise.

INTERCESSION IS A PRIVATE CONVERSATION WITH GOD

LISA

had just gotten into bed from a long day's work and was fast asleep. She's been running around all day taking care of business for herself and her mother. Lisa went to the doctor with her mother for one of her bi-weekly visits.

It was now, 9:30 PM. Lisa woke up coughing violently. Coughing was one of the many ways God used to wake her up to pray. She removed the covers from her and sat on the edge of the bed, then she took a sip of water to soothe her throat.

"Yes Lord?" Lisa immediately heard,

Intercede. She dropped to her knees, leaning on the side of the bed and began interceding. The urgency in her spirit grew stronger by the second.

"Father God! My spirit is so heavy! What is going on?" He responded to her inquiry with heaviness in her spirit. God was letting her know that the matter was serious. He needed her to continue to pray.

(Finally, my brethren, be strong in the Lord and in the power of His might. Put on the whole armor of God, that you may be able to stand against the wiles of the devil. For we do not wrestle against flesh and blood, but against principalities, against powers, against the rulers of the darkness of this age, against spiritual hosts of wickedness in the heavenly places. Therefore, take up the whole armor of God, that you may be able to withstand in the evil day, and having done all, to stand. Stand therefore, having girded your waist with truth, having put on the breastplate of righteousness, and having shod your feet with the

139

preparation of the gospel of peace; above all, taking the shield of faith with which you will be able to quench all the fiery darts of the wicked one. And take the helmet of salvation, and the sword of the Spirit, which is the word of God; praying always with all prayer and supplication in the Spirit, being watchful to this end with all perseverance and supplication for all the saints. Ephesians 6:10-18 KNJV.)

Lisa chose not to look at the clock during intercession. She didn't want to feel like she was putting God on a time schedule. Lisa was earnestly committed to praying for whomever God had her to pray for, as though she was praying for herself. For all she knew, she *might* have praying for herself. The devil roamed around seeking whom he may devour but the desires of the wicked aren't granted.

(Do not grant, O LORD, the desires of the wicked; Do not further his wicked scheme, Lest, they be exalted. Selah. Psalms 140:8 NKJV).

About an hour passed when Lisa was released to go back to sleep. Although her body was resting, her spirit remained active, alert and still communicating with God.

There is *absolutely* nothing hidden from God. Our hearts are always laid open before Him. His eyes are on His children, especially those who have strayed away. The enemy wants nothing more than to take their souls but God will not grant the desires of the wicked. God has His prayer warriors' alert and meticulously positioned *all* around the globe interceding for those who are in need of prayer, day and night.

The devil had all three of Lisa's friends in his grasp and he's playing for keeps. God will reveal to Lisa in due time, about her friends. When God decides to make known the devil's plans to try to destroy their souls, it will be time for them to *choose who* they will serve. Almighty God, The Everlasting Father or the god of this world.

ONCE THAT LINE IS CROSSED

DANIELLE

opened the door to her townhouse in record breaking speed. As fast as she opened the door, you would have thought a serial killer was after her. Danielle stepped over the threshold, slammed the door shut and leaned against it, exhausted.

"Good grief!" The contents of her hands fell to the floor. "I need a stiff drink."

Danielle walked, half trotted to the bar. This situation called for the darker liquor. It didn't even matter what *kind* of liquor it was, just as long as it's dark.

"And the night isn't over, yet. I'ma need a triple shot to get through this." Danielle neglected the glass, picked up the bottle chugging down a big swig. Then she picked up a glass, sat it on the bar and filled it to the top, almost spilling over rim. Trying to be modest, Danielle returned the bottle to the shelf.

"Who am I kidding! This bottle will be polished off within the next hour." She removed the bottle from the shelf, sitting it back on the bar for easy access.

The clock read 8:59 PM. With glass in hand she went to the answering machine to check her messages. The LED screen flashed the number, two. "Oh my! I have three messages." She took another swig of liquor before pressing play. *Beep.* The automated voice says;

"First message, sent today at 7:51 PM. Beep;

"Hey baby, it's Justin..." Danielle covered her mouth with her hand. Hearing Justin's voice made her a little emotional. She realized how much she missed him.

"Ahhhh, suga bear! When are you coming to see your baby?" Danielle said, slurring her words. Yup, the liquor was certainly at work, doing what it's intended to do...she was drunk. Justin's message continued,

"...call me, baby. Maybe, we can get together tomorrow night or tonight, depending on how much you miss me! I hope you miss me a helluva lot! Talk to you later, baby." Beep.

"End of first message."

"Why didn't you call me earlier?" Danielle said out loud to the answering machine. She wanted to call him back but then he's going to want to come over. Tonight, was definitely not the night for a visit from Justin. *Beep.*

"Second message sent today at 8:00 PM." Beep.

"It's Cynthia, I'm just checking to see if you're back. It's 8 o'clock, I'll call you at 9." Beep.

"End of second message."

Danielle looked at her watch, it's 9:01 PM. "Humph, maybe she's not coming over. *Shooooo!* I ain't trippin!" Danielle took a sip of liquor and felt her inhibitions begin to slowly fade away. At the level of intoxication, Danielle was now experiencing, things she normally viewed as *wrong,* really didn't seem all that *wrong* to her any longer.

The phone rang and she stared at it like she didn't know what to do. She decided to let the machine answer it.

"Hello gorgeous...," Danielle immediately recognized the caller, it was Felicia. Hearing her sexy voice again, excited Danielle to the core, causing lustful desires to run rampant through her with vengeance, *"...I know I just left your presence but I just can't stop thinking about how I felt when I was with you, tonight. And...,"* the message continued with Felicia expressing how she felt about Danielle and candidly sharing the things she wanted to do to her. Danielle was in a state of frenzy after listening to Felicia's graphic but welcomed confession, *"...I'm sorry for taking up your time. I*

really enjoyed our night together. I hope to see you soon, good night." Beep.

Danielle reached for the phone but she stopped herself before she could press redial. She quickly placed the phone back on the base and yanked her hand away like the phone transformed into a poisonous viper. Danielle shook her head and finger at the phone, reminding herself why she could not trust Felicia.

"Uh-uh! It's like I said Ms. Lady! You know what the hell you're doing!"

The doorbell chimed. Danielle pranced to the door yanking, it open, startling Cynthia. Danielle laughed.

"Caught you slipping, huh!" She turned on her heels, heading straight to the bar to refresh her drink.

"I see somebody started partying without me." Cynthia closed the door and made her way to the sofa, taking a seat while keeping her eyes on Danielle.

"Baby, this ain't no party. This is a regular night for moi," Danielle said as she sauntered to the sofa with one hand wrapped around a bottle of Jack Daniels and the other hand was holding a glass.

"Can I have a drink?" Cynthia's question was loaded with underlining meanings. Danielle pointed to the bar.

"Help yourself, you know where it is. You probably know my bar better than I do. Lawd knows, you've taken enough liquor from it to open up your own liqua stow." Cynthia laughed and says,

"I know where it is but I *want* some of *yours."* The look in her best friend's eyes was unmistakable. Cynthia wanted something all right, but it wasn't liquor.

Cynthia's partial disclosure caused Danielle to stop in midair as she brought the liquor bottle up to her lips. She held the bottle out with one hand and motioned to Cynthia with her finger, to come and get it. The alcohol was readily at work in Danielle, causing her to feel unguarded and sexually unrestrained. Apprehension was a thing of the past.

Cynthia slowly made her way over to her inebriated friend and stood in front of her. Danielle made herself more comfortable,

143

leaning back against the sofa with the liquor bottle sitting between her warm thighs. She willingly surrendered to the lust within.

Cynthia circled the mouth of the bottle with the tip of her finger. She then dragged her fingers along the side of the bottle and seductively removed it from between Danielle's thighs. Cynthia proceeded to bring the bottle up to her lips, guzzling most of the liquor down like it was water.

Danielle sat in silence as she watched her daring friend with a mixture of carnal emotions. Cynthia handed the nearly empty bottle back to Danielle, then she's pulled down to the floor on her knees in front of Danielle by an unseen force. They were drawn into one another by a surge of lust so potent that it was definitely unnatural. Their limbs were entangled as they craved pleasure that they anticipated receiving from the other member. Their desires crossed all boundaries. The door was open and there was no turning back.

INSTEAD OF RUNNING

REGINA

opened her eyes to see Tommy's handsome face, within inches of hers. Granted, it took a few seconds to process where she was. When memories began to resurface, the reality she had to face was, Regina's still in love with this man. Those facts were quickly overshadowed by images of her smoking crack, along with the sensations of the drug, causing every cell in her body to jump with anticipation. Regina smiled and says,

"More please." Tommy returned a wicked smile and says,

"Your wish, is my every command." He stared at Regina as though he was peering into her soul, ready to ravish her. At that moment, Regina felt the awakening of something inside her that laid dormant for years. Her heart pounded loudly behind her rib cage. The area below her waist tingled and swelled with blood, bringing it to life. Their mouths pressed against one another, desperately searching for the familiarity they once shared. What was once familiar, was recognized again. There was nothing on this earth that would bring more pleasure than what they were experiencing now. That is, until their desire for one another dwindled and the *lust* for drugs commanded their immediate attention.

Regina was lying in Tommy's arms thinking about the future. But, as far as she could see, there *was* no future. You would think that Regina would be thinking about their passionate love making, although it was far better than what she remembered. But no, she wasn't entertaining the physical intimacy they just shared. Regina's mind was solely focused on the high she experienced a short time ago. She wanted more of that high, but with her short pockets, she'd have to just settle for nourishing memories of how it *felt* to get high.

How am I going to make this work? Regina's subtle movements awakened Tommy. He leaned over and kissed her on the cheek.

"What's up, baby? You all right?"

"I'm fine, but I'll feel a lot better if I could get another hit of that *ooh weeee!*" Regina didn't bother to beat around the bush. Everybody knows, that closed mouths don't get fed. She was gonna get fed, right here and right now. She looked up to read Tommy's face and what she saw was a mixture of disappointment, confusion and excitement. Tommy expected another round of making love and wanting his ego stroked.

Ain't that about a b---h! I put it down and all she can think about is getting high! What da hell? I do wanna get high but damn! Tommy felt shot down but what could he do? He awakened the dragon, now he must keep it fed.

He leaned over her and searched through his pants pocket for something. A short time later, Tommy fished out another ziploc bag containing a rock that was much larger than the one they smoked earlier. Regina's eyes bucked wide open, like she won the mega lottery.

Oh! I'm tryna get turnt up and he's holding out on me? Can't trust nobody! Now I gotta keep my eye on you, boo! She anxiously sat up in bed waiting for him to hit her off. Tommy laughed at how hyped she was acting. He put the rock inside of the pipe and gave it to Regina but he held onto the lighter. She looked at Tommy questionably.

"I'll fire it up," he said with a smirk. "You're so turnt up, you might need a steady hand to hold the lighter for you."

Strike two! Tommy earned *strike one*, when he introduced Regina to the hardcore drug during her vulnerable state. She looked at him sideways as she put the pipe in her mouth. The same excitement one experienced when they were sexually aroused, was what Regina felt as she waited for Tommy to light the pipe.

She took a hard pull, allowing the smoke to expand within her lungs until it felt like they were going to explode. Sounding like air escaping from a balloon, Regina released a heavy stream of smoke from her mouth. Tommy watched in delight as her body shivered and convulsed. The drug was so strong that she couldn't contain it. Regina collapsed on the bed, letting the drug have full control of her body. The hit she just had, was way more powerful than the first.

"Lawd, have mercy," Regina mumbled.

"Feels good huh, baby?" Tommy said as he planted voracious kisses all over her body. Between his kisses and the effects of the cocaine in her system, Regina was lost in total ecstasy.

It's sad to say, that Regina temporarily forgot that nothing was free. She would have to pay a steep price for indulging in carnal pleasures. Her life will soon spiral out of control, straight into degradation. When Regina reaches that point, only the awesome power of God will bring her through.

It was a week later and Regina had never left Tommy's room, all the while craving drugs, getting high oblivious to the functioning world outside. She hadn't bathe, combed her hair nor had she eaten much of anything since the first day of her arrival. Their days and nights were spent in total debauchery, getting high and having sex. There's no room for anything else. To be quite honest, Regina really wasn't interested in the "sex part." She was more focused on the "getting high part." All she wanted to do was, get high and stay high, numbing her mind to reality.

Regina was in the mist of smoking the last rock as Tommy watched her with fear and strong apprehension. When she finished with the last hit she asks irritably,

"Why are you looking at me like that?" Regina's eyes were bucked out, shifting back and forth between the bedroom door and Tommy. Her paranoia was ever increasing.

"Nothing, I-I was just thinking...*uuumm*-" Regina cut him off,

"You were thinking? Tell me what were you thinking about, Tommy!" He fidgeted with his pants leg, looking around the room that was once decent, now looked like a pig-sty and smelled even worse. Their combined body odors were atrocious and they weren't bothered by it in the least!

"What!" she barked.

"I, we, *ummmm,* that was our last one, baby." Tommy quickly looked away and lowered his head. He didn't want to tell her they were out of drugs because he feared she would leave him faster than an infant's heartbeat. He had grown attached to Regina. Tommy's all alone since his mother died. Choosing to live a life filled with drugs and criminal activities alienated his family members. No one wanted anything to do with him and the majority of his family didn't attend his mother's funeral.

On many nights, Tommy laid awake tormented by the heartache he knew he caused his mother. Although, he's not ready to admit it, Tommy knew that he was the reason why she died an early death. Tommy caused his mother to die from a broken heart. She was so stressed out by the dangerous lifestyle he chose to live that she'd go for days on end without eating or sleeping. When she didn't eat, she wouldn't take her medication for high blood pressure. And having one heartbreak too many, his mother finally succumbed to a heart attack, dying instantly. Tommy never forgave himself for being the cause of his mother's death and destroying his family. Needless to say, the drug binge with Regina, was a welcoming distraction.

"What do you mean, Tommy!" she screamed from the top of her lungs. Regina jumped up from the bed, pacing the floor furiously. "Okay, okay…Tommy, I gave you my gold watch. I know you got *at least* fifty dollars for it. What! Where did…?" Her eyes finished the question.

"Baby, look," Tommy stood up and walked closer to her. Regina intentionally blew her hot funky breath in his face and rolled her eyes showing hot contempt. She was seriously not feeling Tommy right now. All that mattered to Regina, was keeping a continuous supply of drugs. "Listen!" He placed his baseball sized mitten hands on both of her shoulders and shook her forcibly. Tommy made sure he had her full attention. "Fifty dollars is not a lot, Regina. We can smoke that in one sitting, and we have!" She raised her arms pushing his hands away from her.

"It was enough to get *you* high, wasn't it!" Regina stormed away and plopped down on the edge of the bed, with arms folded glaring at him.

"Baby," Tommy said as he fell to his knees in front of her knowing it's a risky position to be in. Regina could easily smack him in the face as mad as she was. "Baby…listen," she angrily turned away, "...come on, don't be that way. You know I didn't mean it."

"Uh-huh," Regina said as she rolled her eyes so hard that Tommy thought her eyelids would be sealed shut.

"Listen Gina, all I meant was, fifty dollars can go fast, that's it!" He studied her face, searching for understanding. When he saw none, he dropped his head in defeat. Regina saw how deflated Tommy was by her dismissive attitude. Her facial expression began to soften, she understood. He looked up and kissed her lips. "You all right, baby?" he asked as he stroked her hair. "For a minute, I thought you were gonna kill me or something." Regina tried to hold back but she let out a laugh, in spite of herself.

"Shut up," she said pouting. "Forget you for making me laugh and I really want to be mad at you right now."

"I know baby but like I said, when you first came here, I got you. I have a few things I can sell to make some money, okay?" Regina nodded her head but kept her eyes trained to the floor. "Don't worry."

He tried to reassure Regina but she knew there wasn't much left around the house that he could sell to get more money for dope. Regina knew this because she went snooping through the house a few times when Tommy left to cop more dope. You could blame her nosiness on curiosity, she let it get the best of her. They had been a part for years and naturally Regina wondered what her ex had been up all this time.

The inspection began in Tommy's room. After taking her time looking through his things with a fine-tooth comb, she decided it was time to inspect into his mother's room. When Regina entered the woman's room, she wondered *why* the hell she never asked Tommy about her!

It's a damn shame how one-track minded you can be, Regina.
She was the mother you never had. Where is she?

The blinds were drawn. There's not much light in the room but she could still see enough to make her way around the medium size bedroom. The stale air and musty smell was overwhelming. She wanted desperately to crack a window open so the air could circulate. Regina's afraid she'll get caught by Tommy if he made it back sooner than expected. She had to perform a very quick eye-spy job. Regina walked pass the neatly made up bed and smiled.

"I know this is Tommy's work," Regina said, smiling as she walked pass the neatly made up bed. She chuckled.

Experience taught Regina that if she wanted to learn more about a woman, she should see out how she arranged the top of her dresser. Regina nervously made her way to the older woman's dresser, while fighting bouts of guilt, for being somewhere she had no right to be. Choosing to ignore all cautions, Regina continued to examine the contents scattered on top of the dresser with no regard for privacy. Her eyes immediately fell upon a few gold chains and several rings lying next to an obituary. A chill travelled through her body, followed by her throat tightening, making it difficult to swallow.

Regina hesitantly picked up the obit as an involuntary shudder racked her core. She had to secure a firm grip on the side of the dresser to try to stable her legs. Regina covered her mouth trying to stifle the sound of her crying. Tears fell from her eyes. Regina loved Tommy's mother as though she was her very own birth mother. She never knew a mother could be so loving and understanding like Ms. Richards.

There was always a tremendous amount of warmth in their home. Of course, there were family problems but what family didn't have problems? When Tommy's father was killed in a fatal car accident, he was hit by a drunk driver, Ms. Richards tried her best to make up for the love that Tommy would no longer receive from his father. Her love alone, was not enough. Unfortunately, the void that was left in Tommy's soul, stemming from his father's death couldn't be filled by his mother.

When the numbness finally wore off from Regina being shocked by finding out that Tommy's mother passed away, she tried to carefully place the obituary exactly where it was, so he wouldn't suspect a thing. Regina wished she never stepped foot inside the room. Other than a few pieces of jewelry lying on the dresser, there was really nothing else of value. Tommy probably pawned most of his mother's possessions long before Regina entered the picture.

Since the day that Regina called herself playing, I-Spy, she self-consciously kept a mental note of their spending. From her calculations, there was less than twenty dollars between the two of them. Regina unfolded her arms and rested her hands on his shoulders.

"Tommy, there's not too much of anything left here that we can sell." He lowered his head in shame. In no way, was Regina trying to be cruel, she needed Tommy to face facts. "We have to come up with a plan to get more money."

"Baby, I said, I got this." Tommy looked at her with pseudo confidence. Regina elected not to derail his hope.

"Okay, Tommy, you got this." With that said, he hastily stood to his feet, walked to the closet and reached up to the top shelf. Tommy stepped out the closet, concealing something in his hand, all the while avoiding Regina's eyes. He immediately put his clothes and shoes on. When Tommy looked at Regina, she saw worry in his eyes.

"I'll be back."

"What are you going to do, Tommy?" she asked nervously.

"I got chu, Gina."

"But wha-" Tommy cut Regina off.

"I'll be back." He didn't give Regina a chance to respond before he swiftly turned to open the bedroom door. "If anybody knocks on the door, do not open it," Tommy bellowed out as he marched down the hallway.

"Tommy!" Regina exclaimed.

"I'll be back!" Seconds later, Regina heard the front door slam shut. Truth be told, Regina wasn't too concerned about Tommy's well-being. What she was really anxious about, was him making it back *safely* with *more* drugs. Regina wanted to resume her crack-fest without any troubles. She was changing. Regina had become coldhearted and selfish. She had no desire to turn away from the darkness that she so willingly embraced.

Until a person has a strong desire or conviction to turn from their carnal desires, there is absolutely nothing anyone can do to stop them. Prayer is the key! God will intervene because of the prayers that a person sends out for a loved one. God will not do anything against a person's sovereign will. Angels, demons nor the devil can act against someone's sovereign will. (*Sovereign* – *possessed of supreme power <a sovereign ruler> unlimited in extent: absolute – © 2011 Merriam-Webster, Inc.)* When we hear about people committing the most heinous, diabolical acts, we always wonder why. These people are more than likely led by demonic forces that have been *given* authority, by that person, to operate through them.

A SOLIDER MUST STAY READY FOR BATTLE

LISA

found herself travailing more in the spirit since she last attended church with her friends. Every day and night she felt Holy Spirit urging her to intercede. Natural instinct caused her to become alarmed.

God said, in His Holy Word, that The Holy Spirit is a great Comforter. *(John 16:7 Nevertheless I tell you the truth; It is expedient for you that I go away: for if I go not away, the Comforter will not come unto you; but if I depart, I will send him unto you. NKJV).*

The Holy Spirit proved Himself to be just that by bringing comfort to her spirit. Her Heavenly Father, let her know that there was absolutely nothing to be concerned about. It was all in God's loving hands.

Lisa was standing at the sink washing the last dish when she felt something stirring in her spirit. It was so powerful that her body doubled over the sink. Regina clenched her mid-section with one hand and tried to steady herself with the other hand, by holding onto the edge of the sink. She felt a momentary surge of fear rush through her, causing her heart to pound uncontrollably.

"Lord God! What is going on!" Lisa mustered up the strength to ask. The fear subsided and she immediately felt a calmness spread throughout her body, filling her with an abundance of peace. "Father? What do you want me to do?" Lisa heard a subtle voice say,

"Intercede." Lisa was a strong warrior for Jesus Christ. Lisa quickly did as instructed, without delay. She went into her

153

bedroom and laid down prostrate on the floor, going into deep travailing.

FORBIDDEN FRUIT TASTE SO GOOD

...choosing rather to suffer affliction with the people of God than to enjoy the passing pleasures of sin. Hebrews 11:25, NKJV

Good lawd, my head hurts!

Every time Danielle attempted to focus her eyes, the worse her head pounded. It felt like a damned punishment! She held her head, hoping for instant relief! Images of her cranium exploding, ransacked her mind.

"Damn, my head is hurting!" Danielle stretched out her arms and unknowing rubbed against something solid. *What the what!*

She instantly turned to look at *whatever* or *whoever,* was taking up space in her bed. The blood drained from her face when she saw the answer to her question.

"What in da world!" For a second, Danielle thought her eyes were deceiving her. But when she realized that what she was staring at was not a figment of her imagination. Danielle thought she was going to faint. Her voice was caught in the back of her throat. The only sound that escaped from her mouth, were a series of grunts. Her *best* friend was lying beside her, naked as hell! Danielle begrudgingly, dared herself to look down at her *own* anatomy. She almost scared herself to death when she discovered

155

that she *too,* was naked! "What in God's name, did we do!" she whispered.

Her movements stirred Cynthia out of sleep. She looked over at Danielle with a big cheesy smile on her face, needless to say, Cynthia was feeling quite lovely. The smile quickly faded to black when she saw her friend looking at her like she was a three-headed beast.

Why is she looking at me like that? "Well, good morning to you precious," Cynthia said, trying to break the awkward silence. Danielle was stuck, she couldn't say a word. "Hey, Danni? What's going on?"

Danielle responded with a gag reflex. She cupped both hands to her mouth, dashed out of bed, ran to the bathroom and slammed the door shut. Danielle was propelled to the floor by the forceful urge of wanting to throw-up. She gripped both sides of the porcelain throne, preparing herself for the explosion but nothing came out. Danielle coughed, gagged and salivated heavily for a while longer. When she felt that her stomach was calmed down enough, she turned on the faucet to splash cold water on her face.

When Danielle opened the door to see Cynthia sitting on the bed, still naked, staring at her, Danielle's knees began to tremble as she broke out in a cold sweat. She quickly turned away to study her reflection in the mirror.

I can't believe this! What am I going to do? Danielle had no answers. All she could do was leave out the bathroom, feeling defeated. Danielle plopped down on the edge of the bed, holding her head in her hands. "My God!" she muttered.

"Danni?" Danielle couldn't say one word. "Really, Danni? So, you're gonna act like I'm not even here?" Cynthia felt like the rug was pulled from beneath her. She foolishly thought Danielle would feel as good as she did. *Humph, fat chance.* Danielle finally found the strength to speak.

"Cynthia, I seriously don't have anything to say." Pause. "Are you aware of what happened between us!" The magnitude of the situation weighed Danielle down. She didn't really want to acknowledge what took place between them, although she wanted Cynthia to understand how she felt.

156

Cynthia tried to process how Danielle may be feeling but it was an impossible task. Her once, ecstatic moment was ruined! Now that she conquered her conquest, what was supposed to be a celebration, turned into grief.

"I, I-" Cynthia trailed off and reached out to touch Danielle's leg but on second thought, she retracted her hand. *I'm pretty sure, she doesn't want me touching her right now.* Cynthia knew that Danielle was too ashamed to face her and she didn't want to make the situation more uncomfortable than it already was.

"I, I don't know, Cynthia."

When emotions weren't involved, Cynthia was a pro. She would have her fun with whomever she pleased and when it was over, it was over. Sometimes, Cynthia would leave her partners with not so much as a, 'thank you' or 'see you around.' No emotional attachments was, how she liked it but she didn't have the luxury of being that way, now. Cynthia was being forced to feel *everything* that a person may possibly feel, when the one they care for was in deep pain. Cynthia utterly despised the position she was crammed in.

Anger rapidly replaced sympathy, Cynthia wanted to tell Danielle off! She wanted to tell her to grow the hell up and deal with it. After those harsh words, she'd collect her belongings and walk out the door. But Cynthia knew she couldn't behave so coldly towards her best friend.

Man! I forgot how it is when it's your first time. That was her weak attempt at trying to brush off Danielle's reaction to what took place last night.

Danielle suddenly spun around to face Cynthia, causing her to physically jump backwards, due to the appearance of Danielle's countenance. Her eyes were puffy blood shot red from all the crying she did this morning and from the liquor she consumed last night. Danielle resembled a lost little girl who didn't know where to go or where to turn. Cynthia's heart ached. She wanted so badly to apologize to her dear friend and tell her that she regretted what happened.

"Cindy," Cynthia held her breath not knowing what she's about to hear, "...I, I don't know what-" Danielle waved her hands frantically in the air as she struggled for the right thing to say, "...I mean, *how* do you expect me to feel, Cindy? At this point, I don't know what to feel!" Tears welled up in Cynthia's eyes but she quickly wiped them away. Danielle turned away to compose herself. Cynthia wanted to yell,

I don't know either! but her pride got in the way. Instead of making that confession, Cynthia wrapped a sheet around her naked body, then she sat next to her friend and covered her exposed body with a comforter. "Danni, baby, let's not go there, sweetheart." Cynthia moved a strand of hair from Danielle's brow. "Okay? Let's just be easy and not blow anything out of proportion. We haven't *done anything* wrong!" Cynthia emphasized passionately. "Listen Danni, I don't regret *one* moment that I've spent with you. Let's just embrace this and see where it goes, all right?" Danielle considered what her friend said.

I don't know, maybe I am acting a little over the top. After all, I really don't think we did anything wrong, no one was hurt. It might be hard to admit it right now but I really, I mean I really, enjoyed being with her more than I expected, Danielle said to herself.

It's sad to say, that they both were not thinking in their right frame of mind. They were being manipulated into believing that having sex together was not wrong. When there's a need to convince yourself that you are doing the right thing, most likely it's not the right thing. There is an ongoing battle between the carnal mind and our spirit man.

(For out of the heart proceed evil thoughts, murders, adulteries, fornications, thefts, false witness, blasphemies. Matthew 15:19 NKJV.) (We must fight to keep the flesh under our feet so that we live our lives just as our Lord and Savior Jesus Christ lived. For we do not have a High Priest who cannot sympathize with our weaknesses, but was in all points tempted as we are, yet without sin. Hebrews 4:15 NKJV).

"Are you cool with that?" Cynthia asked. There's a twinkle of delight in Danielle's eyes as she thought about the possibilities of what the outcome of this strange, yet tantalizing situation could be. Danielle nodded her head, "yes."

I mean, that's the least I can do after the crazy emotional roller coaster ride I put us on this morning.

Danielle leaned in and sealed the deal with a tender kiss. Cynthia was ecstatic! The morning started off in total chaos but it ended in pure bliss.

Cynthia stared in Danielle's eyes searching for any signs of uncertainty. She wanted to return Danielle's kiss but she feared rejection. Throwing caution in the wind, Cynthia decided to test the waters, once again. She moved closer to Danielle, gently removing the comforter away to expose her bare breast. Cynthia then, commenced to kissing Danielle in a way that was surprising to them both. All of their reservations were gone.

They thought that because they have been friends for so long, their friendship could be added to their intimate relationship and everything would come together, perfectly. Wrong! Now that she and Cynthia were firmly in the enemy's trap, he would cause rapid deterioration and much chaos in their lives that is designed to take them out. They have given the devil ALL rights to terrorize their lives. It will be the earnest prayers of a strong God fearing believer and God's mercy and grace that will destroy the shackles of sin and set them free.

Cynthia loved the feel of the hot water streaming down her body. She still could not believe what she did! Making love to Danielle felt surreal. Just thinking about it made her excited all over again.

"Wow! I can't believe it finally happened," Cynthia said smiling to herself. "It took all these years!" She's always wondered how it would be to hook up with her best friend. Never in her wildest dreams could she imagine it would make her feel this good. Happiness seemed so unattainable, like a ridiculous fairytale. Now, it's here and Cynthia hoped it was here to stay.

Danielle didn't wake up until Cynthia left at 6 o'clock that evening. After showering, she felt like a million bucks. She wrapped a towel around her body and strutted out the bathroom like a proud peacock. Danielle felt so light and carefree as she danced around the room humming the words to Evelyn *Champagne* King's song, "Kisses Don't Lie." When Champagne's song ended, she began singing Keith Washington's song, "When You Love Somebody."

Danielle slid a t-shirt over her head then she stopped in midair, stunned.

Is this how being in love makes you feel! "Am I in love! Am I in love with Cynthia?" Her knees felt weak, like they could no longer support the weight of her body. She sat down on the edge of the bed. "OMG!" Danielle's mind drew a blank and her head was spinning like crazy. "Focus Danielle, focus!" She had to get up and move around to get the blood circulating.

Danielle went to the dresser and searched for a pair of sweat pants to wear. Then she retrieved her cell phone from the nightstand. It was Saturday, Monday would begin her one-week vacation. The fact that she was on a vacation did nothing to deter her staff from calling.

With her electronic leash in hand, Danielle exited the bedroom, going into the living room to sprawl out on the sofa and watch mindless television. Watching TV with nothing to do was a luxury Danielle hadn't been able to afford for some time now.

She scrolled down the list of recorded shows and quickly became overwhelmed. There were literally two months of unseen episodes of her favorite shows stored on the DVR. Danielle had no idea *what* to watch first. CSI Miami was by far, her all-time favorite. It's rare that she ever viewed an episode that she didn't like. You don't have to be a brain surgeon to know what her choice was.

An hour went by without her phone ringing and she loved it. Danielle was so into her show that she didn't realize her stomach was growling loud like a hungry bear.

"I'm so hungry!" she said as she tried to rub the hunger pains away. The thought of getting up from her comfortable spot on the sofa, only aggravated her but her stomach won the battle.

Danielle got up to go into the kitchen in search for *anything* to satisfy her hunger pains. As soon as she took a step in the direction of the 'feeding room,' her cell phone rung.

"Good lawd! Why does that always happen? I always seem to get a phone call, right when I'm about to do something!" Danielle sucked her teeth, irritated to the gills. "Whoever this is, your timing couldn't be any more off!" She picked up her phone, checked the caller ID and a huge smile spread across her face. In a seductive voice, Danielle says into the phone, "You dear, have such perfect timing." Nervous chatter streamed through the earpiece. Danielle decided to reclaim her comfortable position on the sofa, temporally forgetting about how hungry she was.

"So, what did I do to warrant such a delightful greeting?" the caller asked, stirring up the playful side of Danielle. Even though, she was in a humorous mood, Danielle learned early in the game of dating, to never allow feelings and emotions to become overly transparent. When she allowed her suitors to put forth a little effort in finding out how she felt, their initiative only added more interest and excitement into what they were trying to establish. This also, was a wonderful deterrent for monotony. Dullness was a slow death to any relationship.

"You feel like you have to *do* certain things to get a person's sincere acknowledgement?" Danielle indirectly probed Felicia's mind. She's trying to find out if Felicia, unconsciously revealed a side of insecurity, on her part. An inferiority complex will bring toxicity into the lives of everyone that person interacted with.

"Oh, *nooooo!*" Felicia belted out a strong laugh. She ensured herself that she was every bit as confident as Danielle expected her to be. Felicia had no doubt, she would pass every test, this highly intelligent woman threw her way. "Your question just took me off guard, that's all."

She's quick on her feet, I like that!

"So, how are you this lovely, evening?" Felicia inquired earnestly. Danielle was momentarily struck with a tinge of guilt about spending the night *and* morning, making passionate love to her best friend.

Whoa...but wait! It's not like we're in a relationship or anything like that.

161

Danielle's certainly in denial, by trying to convince herself that she's done nothing wrong. The reason Danielle felt guilty about flirting with Felicia in the first place, was due to the sexual encounter she had with Cynthia. They had forged a spiritual soul tie by engaging in sex, which should have never come into fruition. Sex brings people together in a way that was divinely designed for married couples, only (man and woman). Sex was not created to be committed outside of marriage. This is the reason there are many people who suffer from emotional and mental breakdowns from knowingly and unknowingly connecting to one another through illicit sex. The only way these connections are broken, is by the power of God through, Jesus Christ. Receiving gifts from people is another form that soul ties can come into existence. These gifts that are accepted, can keep you connected to an individual even after the relationship has long ended. Be careful what you confess to others. For example, statements to avoid; *"I can't live without you," "I'll die without you," "I'll never love anyone, like I love you,"* and so on and so forth. These statements can and *will* create bonds between you and the person you are confessing them to. This is the reason it becomes extremely difficult to move on with your life, after the relationship has come to a wane. Expressing to someone, that *you can't go on without them* or *you can't live without them,* is the *worst possible* thing you can ever say to another living being. You are essentially placing them in the position that *ONLY* God is suppose to have in your life.

"Well, actually I was about to get myself a bite to eat. I'm so hungry, I'm surprised I haven't fallen out from starvation." Danielle purposely left out the part about drinking all night and sleeping with her best friend. Alcohol steals nutrients from the body, causing great hunger.

"Oh! I'm sorry! Is there anything I can do for you? I mean, it's not a problem at all." Danielle was surprised by Felicia's show of concern.

Is she offering to bring me something to eat or is she just trying to make up an excuse to come over? Either way, is fine with me!
"If it's not a problem, then yes. I would like something to eat. I don't have the energy to do anything today, let alone cooking

162

something." Danielle held her breath as she awaited Felicia's answer.

"Okay, it's not a problem. I can certainly do that." Danielle exhaled with a smile.

"Thank you, *so much*. I really do appreciate this. You're a lifesaver."

"No problem, lady. I know you would do the same for me, you know what I mean?"

"Of course, I always extend a helping hand to a friend. Did you have a place in mind? I know of a terrific Indian restaurant on Venice Blvd., near Hauser Avenue. I always forget the name but I have their number. I can call them, if you like."

"That is quite all right, I got this," Felicia said. "I have the best driver in town. If that's not enough, we can always resort to GPS. My woman-" Felicia stopped herself.

Your woman! Danielle sensed dread coming from Felicia. That was a huge slip up! Danielle was trying to figure out what her next move was. Should she play it off and continue talking as though she didn't hear make another Felicia slip-up? *I know she wishes she kept that tidbit to herself! Oops! So, sorry but you did that boo-boo.* Danielle decided to remain silent, to allow Felicia to regain her confidence.

"*Ummmm*, I meant, my friends don't have to worry about anything when I'm around."

Ouch! That is so embarrassing! Why are people so easily embarrassed when their true feelings are exposed? I mean, I've done that myself. Maybe it's the act of assuming that person feels the same way and that's what brings the shame. Oh well, she'll live! Better her, then me. Danielle chuckled inwardly. She came to Felicia's rescue by changing the subject, "Oh! I'm sorry, did you want Indian food, too?"

"Don't worry about me, I'm never afraid to try *something* new. I've never eaten Indian food in my life but you never know, I just might like it," Felicia said with a hint of naughtiness. A sexy smile spread across Danielle's face. She was growing fond of Felicia's innuendos.

"I'm sure you will. You come off like the adventurous type." Pause. "*Are you,* adventurous?" Danielle asked. Felicia released a sexy laugh to match Danielle's sensuality. She's looking forward to knowing where this conversation will wind up.

"I'm going to tell you like this, I *give* as *good* as I get."

"*Okaaay,* good answer." Danielle felt her entire body get flustered. It was time to cut off the erotic bantering. "That was a very good answer but if we continue down this road, we're *both* gonna be on this phone, horny *and* starving." Felicia laughed out loud.

"Well, we don't want that to happen. I mean, with me being so far away, to do doing something about it." There were no hints in that response, at all. Danielle didn't know what she wanted more, food or Felicia naked, sitting on a platter. She was saved from having to decide when Felicia says, "Let me get off this phone so I can be on my way with your food, sweetie. Stay where you are, I'll be there shortly."

"Oh, don't worry, I'm not going anywhere." The phone went silent in Danielle's ear. She slowly removed the phone from her ear and stared at the high-tech device like she hoped it would give her answers to what was happening in her life. After hearing nothing, she sat the phone down, stood up and headed towards the kitchen, again. "I gotta put something in my stomach! Good lawd, I'm hungrier than a run-away slave who ain't ate a ting in fo' days!" Danielle reached for a box of Ritz Crackers that were sitting on top of the refrigerator. She didn't hesitate to tear into the package like a savage beast, shoving two crackers into her mouth at one time. "It's amazing how things taste better when you're hungry like a mug!" She haphazardly sat the box on the countertop and walked out the kitchen with a pack of crackers in hand.

Danielle resumed her position on the sofa and pressed play on the remote control to continue watching her show. *Ring! Ring!* She put the phone up to her ear without even bothering to look at the caller ID.

"For real! You just told the detectives you think he killed your friend, now you gon' let him in your house! Stupid! Who does that!" Danielle was so engrossed in arguing with the character on the television that she forgot someone was on the phone. "Hello!" she hissed, still agitated by the show.

"What's wrong, baby? Am I taking too long?" Hearing Felicia's voice diminished her irritation towards the character's lack of common sense.

"Oh no!" Danielle laughed. "You're all right. I was just caught up in CSI Miami." Felicia let out an exaggerated sigh of relief.

"It's all gravy, then?"

"Yup, gravy and mash potatoes."

"Good, I was just calling to make sure you didn't change your mind and decide to make yourself something to eat," Felicia said in a mocked disciplinary tone. Danielle was two seconds from stuffing another cracker into her mouth.

"Huh!" she mumbled, like she was caught with her hand in the cookie jar. They both laughed. "I'm *really hungry.*"

"I'm only teasing, silly." Danielle didn't care if Felicia was playing or not. She was going to continue chumping down on crackers until the food arrived. "Okay, we just pulled up in front of the restaurant. I'ma call you when I'm on my way." Danielle tried to say, okay, with a mouth full of crackers but she let out something that sounded like,

"*Ohay.*"

"Bye," Felicia said while bursting in laughter.

After devouring most of the buttery tasting crackers, Danielle says, "I hope she hurries up. A woman can't live off crackers alone."

COMFORT FROM DARKNESS

....unloving, unforgiving, slanderers, without self-control, brutal, despisers of good, traitors, headstrong, haughty, lovers of pleasure rather than lovers of God... 2 Timothy 3:3-4 NKJV

REGINA

An hour passed and Tommy still had not returned.

"I hope he's all right."

Regina paced the small bedroom floor wondering if she's really concerned for his safety or was she more concerned about something interfering with her getting high. Regina shrugged her shoulders not allowing herself to dwell on negative thoughts, for fear of realizing something dark about herself. And, there was absolutely nothing she could do about it, anyway, if he happened to run into trouble.

"I hope Tommy gets here soon. I want to get high!" Regina was shocked by her own admission. *Did I just say that!* The voice coming from her mouth sounded nothing like her. The voice she heard, sounded cold demonic. Regina's freaked out. Chills ran down her spine. She was disturbed by the lack of concern she displayed for ex-boyfriend. Regina wrung her hands together as she sat down on the filthy unmade bed.

"What is wrong with me!" Deep down, she knew where the lack of concern stemmed from, drugs was the culprit. "Lord help me, please!" Her pleads were immediately turned to thoughts of condemnation. That's when she heard an audible voice say,

"If you were getting high right now, you wouldn't even be thinking about asking for help."

She couldn't dispute the dark truth. Regina enjoyed getting high. She was just too ashamed to admit it. In fact, the realization of what she's doing, infuriated her. Regina frantically paced the floor, while crying out to God for His sovereign help.

"Lord, Almighty God! Please forgive me for what I'm doing to myself! I know this is *WRONG!* I know this is not Your will for my life but please don't forsake me! Please God. give me a chance to do right by You! I know about You. You've always stayed in my heart." She placed her hand over her heart. "Even though my parents never really talked about You, they still let me go to church with my friends and their families. My parents never thought it was important to have a personal relationship with You. You were only an afterthought to them. They were more interested in education and how they appeared to others than how they appeared to You, Father God. You *still* found a way to introduce Yourself to me, regardless of my parents' ignorance. Please God, never let my heart turn against You! Please!"

Regina didn't know much about prayer and what she did know, she learned from Lisa. She never heard anyone pray like her before. Lisa prayed like she has a personal relationship with God.

The prayers Regina grew up hearing, were simple prayers that came from people who didn't have a real relationship with God. She also learned, that many people only prayed because it *seemed* like the "right" thing to do. They never believed their prayers would come to past, anyway. This was why Regina never really took an interest in praying. It wasn't until she met Lisa and first heard her pray, that she learned, there *really* was something more to prayer than she *thought* there was. What Regina also learned from her dear friend, is when you pray with sincere conviction in your heart, God will always hear you. He delights in the prayers of the righteous; *(The sacrifice of the wicked is an abomination to the Lord, but the prayer of the upright is His delight. Proverbs 15:8)*

Regina was very sincere and her heart was filled with conviction. She put her faith into action as she pled for God's mercy. Regina didn't exactly know how to explain what just happened but she knew that God heard her cry. He will not forsake her, nor will He ever leave her. She will see shortly, how much God has honored her cries for help.

Regina felt a strong peace surround her. She could have easily picked up her belongings and walked away from that den of iniquities but the desire to satisfy her flesh was too powerful. She wanted nothing more than to smoke crack until she was oblivious to reality. Regina yearned to inhale the intoxicating smoke deep within her lungs, causing her body to experience ecstasy that many have killed for and died for.

Her spirit warred against her flesh, telling her to 'RUN! Get out now!' After contemplating what to do, Regina heard the front door slam shut. Her heart raced in her chest as she called out to Tommy but there's no answer. Panic gripped Regina, she's momentarily paralyzed. In a haste, she glanced at the window thinking she might have to use it to climb out to safety. Then, the thought of being shot or stabbed in the back as she tried to flee, made her abort that idea altogether.

Regina frantically searched the room for anything that could be used as a weapon.

I ain't going down without a fight!

She could hear footsteps getting closer. They were growing louder and so was the sound of her heart pounding against her chest like a jack-hammer. Her eyes zoomed in on Tommy's basketball trophies sitting on the corner of his chest of drawers. Regina darted to the dresser retrieved one, then she wedged herself in the corner behind the bedroom door.

The sound of her breathing escalated, filling her ear drums. The door knob slowly turned, Regina braced herself and raised the trophy high above her head, ready to crack the intruder's skull wide open. Just as she was about to attack, the red color of Tommy's jacket sleeve caught her attention. This recognition made her stop dead in her tracks. Tommy stepped into the room. He was startled when he saw Regina hiding behind the door. The look of terror on her face made him terrified. He thought she was hiding from an intruder in the house.

"What! Is someone in here!" he yelled out in fear as he held his chest.

"No Tommy!" Regina bounced up and down and jogged in place. Adrenaline was pumping through her veins with lightning speed. "I thought *you* were the intruder!" Regina screamed and tossed the trophy on top of the bed. She's angry and relieved. Regina clutched her chest while taking in deep breaths, trying to calm herself down. "I called out to you!" She punched Tommy on the arm. He laughed. "It's not funny, Tommy! You scared the shit out of me! I almost sharted on myself." She dropped down on the bed. "And yeah, while you're laughing, you almost got busted in the head until the white meat showed." She pouted. Tommy held her in his arms, rubbing her back tenderly.

"I know and I'm not making fun of you. I'm laughing at how we both almost peed our pants." Regina exploded with laughter.

"That would not have been funny at all."

"No, it would not have."

"Don't ever do that again! Next time I call you, you better answer!"

"I will, I'm sorry," Tommy said as he continued to comfort her.

Okay, enough of this mushy gushy stuff. I've been waiting entirely too long. My body needs this. Regina pulled away from him and asks anxiously, "Did you get anything!" Disappointment filled Tommy's eyes. It frustrated him to no end when he thought Regina was using him to get high.

"Yeah," he said through clenched teeth. Regina absolutely did not care that Tommy might be salty.

He knows he likes getting high just as much as I do! I don't know why he's trippin. He'll be all right, Regina tried to convince herself that Tommy would be all right but his demeanor said otherwise. Regina watched in awed silence, as his disposition change from light to dark. Tommy secretly battled with something vile within his soul and he's struggling to keep it at bay. Drugs had such a stronghold on Regina and it made it damn near impossible for her to see the truth. She ignored the signs that something foul, something wicked was residing inside Tommy and it would soon reveal itself. Regina brushed off the ominous, imposing feelings by saying to herself,

It's nothing, I'm probably just tripping. Instead of heeding the morbid warnings, she planned to reward Tommy with sex for his efforts, *after* she got high.

If Regina hadn't allowed herself to become so wrapped up in satisfying her flesh, she would have been fully aware of the subtle warnings that were becoming crystal clear, before her eyes. On several occasions, she caught Tommy looking at her in ways that under normal circumstances, would have unnerved her.

Regina's flippant attitude was a normal reaction for someone who put drugs over their better judgment. They wall easily look over the tell-tale signs of danger. Their judgment is so warped, that they have no problem giving a known serial killer the time of day, that is *until* the drugs wore off. Regina's problem, was the fact that she *wanted* to stay high, not having a sober moment. Her goal was to steer clear of sober thinking, for fear of having clear thoughts, which brought hurtful feelings. A drug induced state of mind had Regina blind to the unhealthy attachment to one another. Since the death of Tommy's mother every relationship he's had has been unstable and short lived. Regina's presence was a welcoming distraction. He's willing to do whatever it took to avoid being lonely again.

Tommy had a little surprise for Regina. He removed a small thin piece of foil from his pants pocket. She returned his mischievous smile with a look of bewilderment.

"What?" the question slipped out of her mouth. "That's not a rock!" she protested and began gathering her belongings to leave. "I waited all this time and this is all you brought back!" Tommy was too busy gathering his tools to get the party started. He's not paying Regina's protest any mind. One thing she absolutely detested, was being ignored. It just made her angrier. Regina wanted to knock the hell out of him. "Tommy!" she yelled at the top of her lungs. Tommy was startled that he almost dropped the contents in his hands onto the floor. He gave Regina the evilest glare, it scared the hell out of her.

"Look woman! You don't wanna make me drop this!" Regina had not personally met a serial killer. She could image that a killer's facial expression would look the way Tommy was looking at her, before he plunged a fourteen-inch hunting knife through her gut. Regina's insides trembled but she refused to let him know how terrified she was of him.

"Look at that, Tommy! Whatever that is, doesn't look like it's enough to get a dog high, let alone two adults," she said challengingly. He looked at her incredulously, then Tommy erupted into an odious laughter that would have made the devil's imps run for cover. Regina shrink back. *He sounds so damn evil!* Her knees trembled from an overwhelming feeling of terror. Regina folded her arms across her chest, hiding her insecurities. "I don't like being mocked," Regina said as she watched him intently, hoping that she recognized the Tommy she loved. The person sitting before her, was a complete stranger.

Tommy glared at Regina with dead eyes that were full of brittle cold. Seconds later, his icy stare quickly changed to warmth and love, right before her eyes. A sinister smile laid claim to his gorgeous face.

"Don't worry Gina, I'ma take really good care of you." His words oozed an icky sticky sweetness that made the hair on the back of Regina's neck stand on end. She was instantly overcome with a sickening foreboding in the pit of her stomach. She heard the faint subtle voice of Holy Spirit telling her to,

"Leave now!"

Tommy's back was facing Regina as he removed more items from his pants pockets. She was able to see a small glint of something silver in his hand. It was difficult for her to make out what it was but it looked similar to a spoon or some sort. Seconds later, Regina heard the distinct sound of the striking of a cigarette lighter.

Tommy placed whatever he had in his possession on top of the chest of drawers. Regina still couldn't see much of what he was doing. She tried to peep around Tommy's tall slender frame to see what he was doing without looking suspicious. If Regina's not mistaken, she could have sworn she saw him remove something from his breast pocket that resembled a hypodermic needle.

Is that a needle? Just then, the word *"RUN"* flashed before her eyes. Before her brain processed what was going on, it was too late. Tommy dropped to his knees in front of Regina, taking a firm hold of her wrist. *What in the world? Wait a minute!* "Tommy! What are you doing!" Regina tried to pull away from his strong grip but it was useless. He was entirely too strong. Tommy was thoroughly focused on the large vein pulsating between the crease on the inside of Regina's arm. "Tommy! Tommy. let go of me!" Her protest fell on deaf ears. There was no stopping Tommy was determined to do what he wanted.

Regina panicked! Fight or flight mode kicked in. Regina punched Tommy in the face with her free hand. It felt like she hit a brick wall. There was not too much Regina could do with her legs besides trying to squeeze him to death. But in Regina's predicament, it would probably work against her and turn him on instead of doing any real harm. Regina attempted to use her teeth and try to take a chunk of flesh out of his shoulder. As she proceeded to put her plan of survival into action, Tommy beat her to the punch! Using his long nimble fingers as a tourniquet around her upper arm, he took no time jamming the needle into her vein.

Regina instantly felt the rush of the drug enter her body. She went limp as a surge of indescribable pleasure rocketed through her medium frame. Regina involuntarily let out loud painful moan.

Satisfied with his malicious work, Tommy picked up her legs and laid them across the bed. He watched her intently, proud of his decision to get her high on heroin. He rubbed her head endearingly, like a child.

"That's right baby, take it all in. Let it take control of you." Regina was alert but unable to speak. Her body felt like it weighed a ton. She fought with every fiber of her being to thwart the effects of the vicious drug but it was to no avail.

"Stop fighting it, baby. Relax and let it have its way." Tommy gingerly placed her hand over his heart. "I did this for us, baby. You'll see…I can't let you go again," Tommy said somberly to a drug induced sleeping Regina. He began to beat and slap his head. Tommy often abused himself, to rid his mind of the ugly thoughts that tormented him every waking moment of the day. "Noo! I can't bear losing you again!" he sobbed.

Regina felt her body grow weaker. It will not be much longer before the drug took total control of her being. Before she slipped into unconsciousness, Regina asked God for forgiveness. Tommy whispered in her ear,

"It's okay, baby. This is the best high you'll ever feel in life."

With that said, Regina lost the fight and succumbed to the drug. It would be hours before she regained full consciousness. There's no doubt about it, Tommy would make it his duty to be by Regina's side when she awoke.

RIGHT IN YOUR CORNER

A man of many companions may come to ruin, but there is a friend who sticks closer than a brother. Proverbs 18:24 NKJV

LISA'S

spirit had been so wearily laden that she hadn't been able to go about her daily routine. God was keeping Lisa's mother content while the spiritual warfare brewed, for that, she was most grateful. Attending to her mother's needs while under heavy prayer would have been unfavorable, to say the least.

Lisa had several dreams about women in great distress. But when she woke up from the dream, Lisa was unable to put a name to the women's faces or even go into depth about the dreams. What she did remember, was feeling unbelievably disturbed by the dreams along with an urgency to contact her friends. Whenever Lisa called her friends, the only contact she made was leaving multiple voicemails. She tried to keep her mind content by saying,

"They're probably busy getting ready for work."

Lisa went into the kitchen to prepare dinner when she suddenly had a quick thought to call Danielle. She promptly made a beeline for her bedroom. "When I get this girl on the phone, boy! She knows better than to go so long without calling me." Danielle's phone rang three times before going to voicemail,

"This is Danielle Stevens, kindly leave a message and I'll call you at my earliest convenience. Thank you." Beep.
"Hey girl! This is Lisa, I've been trying to reach you for the longest. How are you? What's going on? I miss you. Oh! When am I going to see you guys? Call me! Hugs and kiss! Muah!" Lisa ended the call and scrolled down to Regina's number. Less than a minute later, she got her voicemail,

"Hey Regina, it's me. Where are you guys? I've been calling and I can't get a hold of neither of you. Call me and let me know that everything is all right with you. Love you! I wanna see you, call me!" Lisa dropped the phone to her lap and rolled her eyes at the phone like it's the culprit. She dialed the last number, when it went straight to voicemail, she sucked her teeth.

"Are you kidding me! This is unbelievable," Lisa said before leaving a message. "Hey Cynthia, this is Lisa. Are you guys all together? Seriously, I've been trying to reach all three of you and no one's answering their phone. What's up? I'm beginning to get a little concerned about you guys. All right then, love ya, call me!" Lisa sat still on the bed looking off in the distance.

"They'll call soon...hopefully. Father God, I ask that You please cover my friends, Your children, with the love and the blood of Jesus Christ. Father, I ask that You correct them in love and in patience. They lack wisdom when it comes to Your commands and statutes. Don't allow the enemy to be successful in whatever wicked plans he has for their lives, Father. You've had me praying for them Father God and being the best example for You that I know how to be. Do not permit the enemy to gloat over us and say God isn't strong enough to deliver His children from all danger. Father God, please keep their souls and keep the enemy at bay. You didn't bring us this far to leave us. I thank You Father God, that the words I speak are Spirit and Truth and they do not return to You void but accomplish what they are sent out to do, in the Mighty Majestic name of Jesus Christ. Thank You Father God for covering this prayer in the love and the blood of Jesus Christ so that the devil cannot interfere with it or stop it from doing what it is sent out to do. Thank You Father God, in Jesus name. Amen! And Amen!"

After Lisa prayed that divinely powerful prayer, she stood up and returned to the kitchen to resume prepping dinner. Lisa took every concern that she had to the Father and left them for Him to bear. When you pray, you have to know, beyond a shadow of a doubt, that He has answered your prayers, no matter what you think, no matter how things look, or no matter how you may feel.

It's a wrap, as far as Lisa was concerned. Now all she had to do was sit back, be patient and watch God reveal the truth to her, in a way she couldn't deny, because He is forever faithful and true to His word.

Tears welled up in her eyes and rolled down her cheeks. She was in distress over the sadness she felt deep in her soul. What Lisa suddenly realized was, she didn't feel the onset of the heart wrenching grief until *after,* she attempted to contact with her friends. As Lisa wiped fresh tears away, she says,

"God! Please, have mercy on my friends and Your saints."

TRUST IS THE ONLY OPTION

Who is among you that fears the LORD, that obeys the voice of his servant, that walks in darkness, and has no light? Let him trust in the name of the LORD, and stay on his God. Isaiah 50:10 NKJV

REGINA

slowly came to consciousness after the drug slowly began to wear off. Tommy was immediately stirred awake by Regina's sublet movements. With the grace of a stellar athlete, he jumped to his feet and ran to get the heroin stash. Tommy's plan was to keep Regina high as a kite, unconscious and disoriented to the point where she's physically unable to leave him on her own accord.

Drool rolled down the corners of Regina's mouth, her eyelids fluttered as she desperately tried to open them. She attempted to wipe the saliva from her mouth but it was a struggle due to the fact that her hands felt like cement blocks.

"Tommy?" she slurred. He was in deep concentration, fixated on preparing another dose of heroin to shoot into her veins.

"Yes baby," Tommy finally said, as he suctioned the chiba into the syringe. "Give me a sec, baby." Regina's head weighed heavy but she tried to lift it to look in the direction of his voice. Her eyes were squinted, everything was so blurry. She waited for them to

177

focus. When things began to slowly become clearer, Regina caught a glimpse of what Tommy was holding in his hand. He approached the bed, tapping the hypodermic needle with his finger.

She opened her mouth to protest but her throat was dry, her tongue felt like sandpaper and her voice was seriously hoarse. Regina could barely muster the strength to say,

"No Tommy!" He shushed her and kneeled down beside the bed, taking hold of her arm. Her strength was completely depleted, trying to fight him was futile. Resisting Tommy was equivalent to a two-year-old, trying to push a full-grown adult off of her. Tears streamed down Regina's face. "Tommy, no!" she said weakly, as she tried to shove his hand away.

"Baby, don't worry. I'll take good care of you." He tied a belt around her arm roughly, and jammed the needle into the *same* pulsating vein he used the first time. Regina tried to protest, once again, but she was stopped by the incredible soothing force of the drug streaming through her veins, at an accelerated pace. Words couldn't escape Regina. It was as if they were seized in the back of her throat. Her eyes rolled to the back of her skull. Regina's breathing slowed drastically as her eyelids flickered wildly. Seconds later, she was out.

Tommy's diabolical plan appeared to be working fine. He wanted full control of Regina's mind, body and soul. There was nothing he was not willing to do to carry out his heinous plans.

LAUGH NOW PAY LATER

DANIELLE

Her nap was short lived when the alert from her cell phone buzzed so rudely in her ear. She woke up feeling nauseous from the intense hunger pains arguing in her stomach.

"Ugh! I can't stand when I'm hungry like this." She went for her cell phone and discovered that she had a new voicemail. "A voicemail? I didn't know I had been sleeping *that* hard." Danielle scoped out the time, then she listened to the message. "It's 7:30? I hope this is Felicia telling me she's two seconds away with my food." As Danielle listened to the message, she heard a sweet familiar voice in her ear that almost brought her to tears.

Danielle missed her friend dearly. Lisa's voice was filled with such love and concern that it touched her heart. She really wanted to call Lisa but Danielle was afraid that her wrong doings would be exposed. There was something about Lisa that made a person want to come clean and confess every detail of their sins. Danielle was not in the mood for a confession session. The thought of conveying to Lisa about the goings-on in her life brought heavy conviction. She knew that her friend only wanted the best for her but disclosing her waywardness seemed like a difficult task.

Although Danielle wasn't raised to be a devout God fearer like Lisa, she still loves her friend's total devotion to God. What Danielle loves the most about Lisa, was the face that she's remained consistent, not only to God but to family and friends since the first time they met at a Women's Fellowship at their local church. Danielle was nowhere near ready to serve God on that level. Honestly, she really didn't think she needed God like that. Danielle believed that as long as she treated people fair and tried to be a good person, that's all that mattered.

Lisa's dedication to God befuddled Danielle. She didn't understand the big deal about making God your, 'end all-be all.' That's a little farfetched to Danielle. Then again, she remembered the difference in how the two were raised. Danielle grew up exposed to the finer things in life and all the possibilities one was privy to when they have stacks of money on racks. While Lisa grew up in poverty and endured trials and tribulations that went along with being financially disenfranchised.

Danielle often wondered if what she overheard her parents say, as a child, was true or not. In conversations with their friends, she overheard her mother and father say,

"...God is only for the poor and needy." Danielle was neither. She came from an affluent background and had traveled the world before she was ten. She studied abroad, rubbing elbows with the top echelons. Danielle is young, single, beautiful, bodacious, intelligent and her body was knock out gorgeous. Danielle has a lucrative career that she obtained through hard work and a *little* help from those who have desired her. She has a man in her life and *two* women who want her desperately. She owns her home and has recently purchased a $100,000 vehicle. Danielle's question for anyone who cared to listen was, where is God needed in her life? Yes, Danielle went to church as often as possible. She gave offerings to the church and she helped those who were less fortunate than she. Danielle believed those charitable actions alone, ought to guarantee her a spot behind God's pearly gates. If it didn't, well, at least she did her best.

Danielle contemplated sending Lisa a text message letting her know she was all right but she quickly abandoned the thought. Her once content disposition was quickly replaced with anger. Danielle felt convicted about having sex with Cynthia and being close, *very* close to sexing Felicia, too. She tossed the phone on the couch and pouted like a defiant child.

"Why do I have to feel like the bad guy! I have a right to

choose what *I* want to do with *my* own *damn* life! I am a grown, responsible adult. I pay my own bills. I don't have to rely on anyone, I'm not hurting anybody so what's the problem? I shouldn't have to walk around feeling guilty for not living up to someone else's expectations!"

This was how Danielle tried to validate the decision she made to live an alternative lifestyle. The anger she displayed was a typical defense mechanism that people routinely used when they knew or had an inkling of an idea, that what they were doing was wrong. It's also another way to deflect conviction away from them and hold onto stubbornness and pride that would keep them lost and bound in darkness.

Danielle's mind was riddled with thoughts of Lisa and her God. She welcomed anything that would keep her mind off both of them. Danielle accomplished that task by finding another episode of CSI Miami to watch. Satisfied with her decision, she went to the bar to make herself a stiff one, to help take the edge off. Liquor was a vice Danielle used to rid her mind of things she wanted to avoid.

When Danielle was just about finished pouring herself a glass of straight vodka on ice, the doorbell rang. She abruptly sat down her glass, went to the door and opened it without checking to see who it was. Danielle was beyond annoyed. To her surprise, she was greeted by an angel of light, standing before her with a bewitching smile. Felicia stood in front of her looking like a top model. She was wearing a pair of faded Levis, a sexy form fitting custom-made t-shirt, rocking black soft leather mules and a pair of dark shades concealing her beautiful green eyes. Felicia's her hairstyle was flawless! She looked like she just stepped out the salon.

"Are you gonna let me in or are we going to eat this fine cuisine on the porch?" Felicia said jokingly. Danielle expertly snapped out of her daze. Felicia's sheer beauty rendered her speechless.

"Oh! Come in, I'm Sorry about that. I'm so starved, that my brain temporarily froze up on me."

Felicia knew good and darn well that, her momentary lapse had nothing to do with food. Danielle was checking her out so tough that she couldn't take her eyes off her. Felicia's arm gently brushed across Danielle's breast as she passed her, going inside the house. She considered giving Felicia the benefit of the doubt, seeing that both her hands were occupied with bags. But Danielle knew the *"accidental"* touching of her breast was intentional. She closed the door and trailed behind Felicia into the kitchen.

When they entered the kitchen, Felicia took her sweet time looking Danielle up and down, enjoying every inch of what she saw.

"Where should I put this?" Danielle returned the favor by taking *her* time to answer. Don't think she didn't notice Felicia thoroughly checking her out.

Who am I to deny those gorgeous eyes a look at this delicious eye-candy? Dressed leisurely, Danielle still had what it took to make men *and* women speechless. "Here..." she said as she helped Felicia with the bags, "...we can sit them on the counter." In an effort to break the awkward silence, Felicia tried to make small talk while she removed various size food containers from the bags, meticulously sitting them on the counter.

"It looks like you are definitely enjoying yourself at home."

"Yes, I am." Danielle opened each container, looking inside them and sampling the scrumptious food. Her mouth was salivating. "Did you like what you saw?" Danielle turned to face Felicia, and her eyes told it all. Felicia wanted to devour her. Danielle smirked. "I mean, did the food look good to you?" she clarified, as she opened a container of Indian rice.

"Oh, everything looked well prepared. Indian food is quite interesting. I'm sure I will enjoy it. But the only way I'll know for sure, is to try it, you know what I mean?" Felicia's question commanded Danielle's full attention again. She was met with piercing eyes that bore holes through her soul, Danielle didn't flinch.

"You *will* soon find out, *if* you like it or not," she said with a wink as she handed Felicia a plate. Danielle gathered the different size containers of food and a beverage and went directly to the living room, plopping down on the sofa. It was ill mannered to eat in front of the TV but Danielle wasn't necessarily known for playing by the rules. If she wanted to sit on the couch in front of the TV and eat, she didn't care who liked it. Home was meant for relaxation and that's what Danielle planned to do.

Felicia finally strolled into the living room with a plate of food. Instead of sitting on the sofa next to the lady of the house, she elected to sit on the floor beside Danielle's feet. Although Felicia's actions confounded Danielle, she chose not to make a big deal out of it. Besides, she was too focused on eating to care either way.

If she's comfortable, who am I to complain? Felicia looked up at Danielle with a winning smile.

"So, what's on the telly?" Danielle's response was to offer Felicia the remote control but she shook her head. "No! I'm cool. I was just wondering what you are watching." Danielle really didn't want to give her a recap of the show because it would interfere with her gettin' her grub on but she wasn't trying to be a rude hostess.

"Oh, I'm watching, *ummm...*," she pushed the info button on the remote control, "...CSI Miami." Danielle forgot that quick, hunger will do that to you.

"Oh yeah, that's right. You said you were trying to catch up on your episodes."

"You know how it is with work. I rarely have a chance to watch too much of anything. I've missed the whole season."

"It's like that with me too. I'm a Walking Dead fan and I've just about missed the whole season." Their attention was directed to the TV once again and Felicia seized the opportunity to create light conversation when a commercial came on. "Girl, there's nothing like being at home, doing *what* you *want* to do and enjoying it."

"I know, right?"

"You don't have to deal with annoying schedules, deadlines and phone calls."

"For real!" Danielle laughed. Felicia sat her plate on the floor and shifted her body around to get a better view of Danielle. Felicia then, rested her elbow on the sofa, gently touching

Danielle's thigh. A sudden surge of electricity passed between them causing instant arousal.

Unable to hold back her instant activation, Danielle sat her food on the table, in front of her, giving Felicia her undivided attention. A person that could cause her body to jump with excitement by the slightest touch, deserved the spotlight.

"You know," Felicia paused and bit her bottom lip, "...you have the sexiest laugh." She said nothing else but continued to gaze hypnotically into Danielle's eyes.

Everything about you screams sexy! is what Danielle wanted to retort but she kept her cool. She couldn't deny the feelings of attraction that she had for Felicia. Danielle never felt this way for anyone, let alone a woman but she's not ready to admit it to herself and she's certainly not going to admit it to Felicia.

Instead of responding to the sensual compliment, Danielle resorted to stuffing her mouth with a fork full of food. Felicia laughed at her antics. She watched Danielle as she suddenly became engrossed in a commercial. She needed a distraction to avoid looking into Felicia's eyes. Danielle was nervous as hell! Her overt display of insecurity stroked Felicia's ego which encouraged her to proceed to the next level.

Danielle put the last bite of food into her mouth as stretched and rubbed her belly.

"Whew! I am so full, I'm about to burst!" She covered her mouth and let out a loud belch. "That was an indication of some good eating. Thank you *so much,* Felicia. I was going out of my mind from lack of food." Felicia chuckled.

"Why were you so hungry?" Danielle gave her the "you know why" look. Felicia understood all too well about what Danielle *didn't* want to say. Her mouth fell open wide. "*Ooookkaaay!* Say no more, I get it." Felicia laughed again. "Well, I'm just glad you're satisfied." Danielle smiled and another burp slipped out.

"Oops! Sorry." Felicia stood to her feet with a half plate of food in her hand. Danielle assumed Felicia was going for seconds. "You're hungry too, huh?" Danielle asked. Felicia stretched out her hand, asking for the empty food containers.

"No, I wasn't really that hungry. I mainly ate because I didn't want you to eat by yourself." Danielle wondered why Felicia's hand was extended until she pointed to the containers.

"Oh! I'm sorry, here you go!" Danielle said as she handed them to her. "I was trying to figure out what you were doing."

"Ha! I was wondering the same thing, myself." Felicia carefully balanced everything in her arms and walked in the direction of the kitchen.

"That really isn't necessary, Felicia. I was going to take it in the kitchen myself...eventually." Her protest fell on deaf ears.

"It's all good," Felicia yelled from the kitchen. "This is my way of thanking you for inviting me to your lovely home."

"Anytime," Danielle yelled back. *She has manners, she's appreciative, she's considerate and respectful! Now, she's a keeper!* Danielle could hear running water coming from the kitchen. "Are you washing the dishes too!"

"Yes, I am baby!" The water was shut off.

"Come on, now! You're too much."

"Don't be silly, I got this," Felicia yelled back. "You don't need to do anything but relax." Danielle was about to interject but her cell phone rang.

"Please, sit down and don't do anything else when you're done, please!" Danielle studied the caller ID. She didn't recognize the number flashing across the screen but she answered the phone anyway. "This is Danielle Stevens." She's greeted by laughter from a male's voice. With a look of confusion, Danielle says, "I'm sorry but may I ask who is calling?" He laughed again.

"It's me, baby!"

Huh! She panicked.

"It's been *that* long, that you don't even recognize my voice! *Awwww!* My heart just dropped to the floor baby!"

OMG! "Justin!"

"The one and only. How you doing, boo? Did you miss me?" Danielle wished she didn't answer the phone. Guilt filled every crevice of her being.

"Heeeeeyyyy!" Danielle feigned excitement. She jumped to her feet as Felicia entered the living room. Danielle held up a finger indicating that she had to take the call. She went into her bedroom, closing the door behind her. Danielle made a mad dash across the room to the window and looked out, praying that Justin wasn't calling her from outside of her front door. Many of times, he had surprised her by popping up, unexpectedly, at her doorstep while talking to her on his cell phone. *Good! He's not here.*

"Heeeeyyyy, yourself. Did I catch you at a bad time? I can call you back if you like. It's just that, I'm back in town and-"

Back in town? I didn't know you left!

"...I was hoping we could get together, later this evening. I've missed you, baby," Justin crooned sweetly in her ear. Now that Danielle thought about it, she really didn't missed Justin at all. She's been too preoccupied with work and her new found interest in women. You could say, she didn't have time to think about anything else.

"Hey! Okay, ummm..." *try not to sound so interested Danielle geesh! I'ma break this po' man's heart if he finds out he's no longer the center of my universe.* One of the main reasons, Danielle was no longer interested in Justin, was because she could finally admit to herself that brotha man was most definitely married, possibly with two and a half children. She psyched herself out long enough and she's way pass tired of playing the role of his whore.

"You must be busy or *something,*" Justin said sounding deflated. Danielle's questionable behavior made him a little suspicious. Where she was usually so eager to see Justin, now she's distant.

"Well, actually I was-" he cut her off.

"It's all right, I know you have a life of your own. I can't expect you to sit around and wait on me."

Yeah, you do. You pretty much want me to sit here and be your mistress while you probably have a wife and children at home. Danielle's not feeling him and his so-called disappointment didn't faze her in the least. "I was about to say-" she tried to explain again but Justin interrupted her once more.

"It's cool, no need to explain. I see the writing on the wall." Danielle was slightly confused by the way Justin's acting. She's totally turned off by his insecurities.

Ugh! What is wrong with him?

"Just call me when you get the time, I'll be around." The phone went silent in Danielle's ear and she sat down on the bed, stunned.

"What the...! Is he serious?" Danielle burst out laughing. "Did he really try to play me like that? Ha!" Justin was nowhere near hurt like he pretended to be. To sum it up in a nutshell, he didn't get the response he was looking for, so he conveniently used that as an excuse to do what he *really* wanted to do. "Umph! That's so sad when men have to resort to playing tired childish psychological games just to go play in the next woman's yard. He's such a loser." Danielle smiled and tossed the phone on the bed feeling like she shed a thousand pounds. Justin made it so easy for her, by saving *her* the trouble of finding an *excuse* to break up with him. "Now a sista can do what *she* really wants to do."

Danielle opened her bedroom door and walked into a living room that no longer resembled hers. Every blind in the room was drawn. Scented candles were lit and sitting in the middle of the coffee table. The sweet aroma from the candles were breathtaking, acting as an aphrodisiac to Danielle. She loved smelling beautiful fragrances. They do something to her senses that mere words couldn't describe. The combination of the soft music and the sweet aroma left her speechless.

Danielle was tempted to call out Felicia's name but she decided against it, not wanting to disturb the atmosphere with loud talking. She elected to take a seat on the sofa to take it all in. Danielle folded her hands behind her head and kicked her feet up on the table.

"Can't beat this with a stick." Danielle inhaled, taking the wonderful scent deep inside her nostrils.

Felicia suddenly appeared in the door of the living room holding two frosted wine glasses filled with white wine. She beamed with delight as she approached Danielle giving her a glass, then Felicia claimed her seat on the sofa, a few inches away from Danielle.

"Wow! This is absolutely breathtaking, Felicia," Danielle said as she tasted the chilled liquid. "*Mmm,* there's nothing like a glass of Chardonnay after a fine meal."

"I couldn't agree with you more, and thank you," Felicia said as she took a sip from her own glass. "You're right, there's absolutely nothing like it. I thought I'd surprise you with a bottle of wine from my private collection."

"You certainly thought right." They both leaned back and drunk their wine in silence, enjoying the intoxicating effect of the sophisticated beverage. As if finally waking from a coma, Danielle suddenly realized they were listening to one of her favorite tracks, "Spend The Night" by Rashaan Patterson. The rhythmic melodious sound track had Danielle down to do whatever.

"*Ooooh!* That's my song!" she said as she grinded her hips, ever so sensually, to the rhythm of the beat.

Felicia watched with deep yearning, being very pleased by what she saw. Her mind was overloaded with thoughts and images of what she thirsts for. Felicia could no longer resist the alluring lyrics that Danielle sang along with Rashaan,

"*...spend the night, it's all right and I'll be good to you...*"

Felicia finished her drink, in one swift gulp, sitting the empty wine glass on the table and proceeded to make her move. Danielle was no longer singing, she's completely mesmerized by Felicia's sheer beauty. Disempowering lust clamped down on Danielle with a force that left her wide open and at Felicia's mercy.

She moved in closer, keeping eyes locked on Danielle making, sure their desires were mutual. Felicia need not be concerned about how Danielle felt because her body begged for release.

Guards were relinquished, heartrate increased, their breathing became shallow and their eyes plead for sever gratification. When their lips finally met, it felt like magic! There was nothing that could stop the consuming fire taking over their flesh, silencing all rationality.

The moonlight spilled through the opening of the blinds casting a soft light on their countenances. They laid in bed basking in the afterglow of their love feast. Danielle laughed softly as Felicia shared the most embarrassing moments of her childhood.

"I'm *sooooo*, serious! They really fell down!" Felicia screamed in an animated voice. "I always dreaded going to the front of the class!" Danielle tried to stifle her laughter until Felicia finished her story. "I mean, as soon as I picked up the chalk, my panties dropped!" Danielle erupted in gut-wrenching laughter. She laughed so loud, that she thought the neighbors would bang on her front door asking them to keep it down.

"Please stop! Please!" Danielle pled.

"What made it even worse, was the whole class went insanely quiet! I couldn't do anything and I was too ashamed to cry. It was horrible!" Danielle held her stomach while kicking her legs uncontrollably, almost falling out bed. Felicia laughed along with her. "Some tried to look away and others looked at me like I was the most hideous thing on the face of the earth. The teacher told me to get myself together and take my seat. It was obvious he was trying to keep a straight face, too."

"Wow!" Danielle expressed, still laughing. "Oh wow!"

"Okay, you got your laugh on, now tell me something about your lovelier moments."

"Whoa, can I get a pass?" Felicia shook her head wildly, in protest.

"*Noooooo!* I spilled the beans it's your turn, now."

"*Okaaayy*, you can't blame a girl for trying." Danielle sucked in a deep breath and says, "Here it goes…it was recess and I was sitting at the lunch table eating some Lorna Doone cookies. Those are my *favorite* cookies. Anyways, I was down to my last two, when this lil bad knuckle-head boy, that I couldn't stand, came up behind me and popped me on the back of my head. He hit me hard too! I started coughing and choking. Cookies and milk came flying out my mouth and my nose started to run. Man! That ain't even the worst part! *All this* happened right in front of Bobby Taylor. I *loveded me* some Bobby Taylor! You know, I thought I was gonna die! I was coughing and spitting all over the place. Bobby was horrified and disgusted. He looked like he wanted to throw up! I was mortified!" Felicia was laughing hysterically, she almost peed on herself. "I mean the little asshole had the audacity to laugh and point at the mess that *he* caused!" Felicia yelled,

"Uh uh! I gotta go to the bathroom." She leaped out of bed, doubled over, holding her stomach while trying to keep from falling to the floor. She barely made it to the bathroom.

"Gurl, let it out!" Danielle said as Felicia closed the door. She could still hear Felicia laughing uncontrollably. Danielle got out of bed and wrapped a robe around her as she left the bedroom on her way to the kitchen. "I had no idea I was that funny."

Danielle opened the refrigerator and shuffled things around looking for something to eat. "I'm hungry again." Her eyes fell on a pack of Cracker Barrel Cheese. "Yes! Cracker Barrel Cheese and Ritz Crackers is da bomb." As Danielle reached for the cheese, she felt something press against her ass, causing her to jump forward. "Ooh!" She looked over her shoulder to see Felicia standing behind. "Would you like some cheese with that, ma'am?" Danielle said jokingly.

"I want more than that, baby," Felicia said, slowly licking her lips. Danielle turned her body around to face Felicia, closing the space between them.

"So, you're down for a third round?" Danielle felt the warmth of Felicia's breath lightly seducing her neck.

"I'm always ready." She smiled slyly.

"*Mmmm.*" Danielle closed the refrigerator door and opened the freezer, pointing to a bottle of vodka, "How 'bout a lil something to help us out? What's your poison?" Felicia wrapped her arms around Danielle's waist.

"For the record, I don't need *anything* to help me out when it comes to you." Felicia kissed Danielle's lips.

"I'll keep that in mind."

"Please do."

"So, vodka it is?" Felicia let out a sexy chuckle.

"Vodka *and* you."

"Excellent choice," Danielle said as she took the chilled bottle out the freezer and closed the door. She reached for the box of crackers on top of the refrigerator. "Baby, will you get two glasses, please?"

"Sure, I'll meet you in the room. Don't make me wait too long," Felicia threw over her shoulder.

"I'm right behind you." Danielle grabbed a roll of paper towels before she exits the kitchen. As Danielle crossed the living room floor the doorbell chimed, causing nervous butterflies to dominate her stomach. "What in the world?" Danielle looked at the wall clock sitting above her 60-inch flat screen television. "It's 11 o'clock at night! Who's at my door?"

Felicia walked into the living room looking just as confused as Danielle. Then, she remembered that she's naked and ran back in the bedroom. Danielle laid the contents of her hands on the sofa and made her way to the door.

"Who is it?" she yelled, not bothering to hide her annoyance. *Why did I do that? Nobody had to know I'm at home.* Danielle reluctantly looked through the peephole and her breathing stopped. "OMG!" Cynthia stood on the other side of the door, looking like she knew Danielle was going to let her in.

"It's me, I just came by to check on you," Cynthia said, staring at the peephole.

"Damn!" Danielle whispered. "Hey!" She scratched her head trying to figure out what to do.

"You gon let me in or what?" Cynthia asked irritably.

"*Ummmm...!*" *Well, it's too late now. I should let her in so she won't make a scene.* Danielle unlocked the door slowly opened it. Feeling self-conscious, she tightened her robe around her waist and says, "Hey now!" They embraced awkwardly. When they separate, Cynthia walked into the living room, scanning the large area.

"So, what are you up to?" she asked, while studying Danielle intently. "You just got out the shower or something?" Danielle's insides quivered. Something about Cynthia made her tragically nervous. She continued to examine Danielle suspiciously, while Danielle stood at the front door not knowing what to do with herself. She prayed that Felicia would stay in the bedroom.

Danielle felt so uncomfortable, she couldn't find anything to say to her friend. Cynthia's eyes drifted to the sofa and she noticed the evening snacks that Danielle sat down on her way to answer the door. Cynthia's head sprung up with deadly eyes trained on Danielle. She stared at Danielle accusingly and Danielle broke out in a cold sweat.

"Did I interrupt something?" Cynthia asked challengingly.

Good grief! Why did I answer the damn door! Before she could form the words to answer, Felicia walked into the living room wearing one of Danielle's *most* expensive robes. Dead giveaway.

Cynthia was startled, obviously by finding out that she and Danielle were not alone. She quickly regained composure and bore holes through Felicia. "Who...!" Cynthia swirled around, looking at Danielle with eyes ablaze. "What the!"

"Cindy I-"

"Cindy...I, *what Danielle!"* Danielle instantly became defensive.

Wait, one hot damn minute! I haven't done a dame thing wrong! We are not exclusive! I don't know what we are. "Cynthia-"

"Danielle!" Cynthia shot back with heat. Felicia cleared her throat.

"Danielle, is everything all, right?" Danielle wished Felicia hadn't said a word. She only added fuel to an already burning inferno.

Cynthia felt betrayed that this stranger was trying to defend someone she had known for years, like she was some kind of threat. "Is everything all right!" Cynthia repeated savagely. "Who is Ms. Einstein, standing over there!" Felicia looked at Cynthia like she wasn't feeling the dig. Danielle tried to push Felicia off the tracks of the runaway freight train by saying,

"Everything is cool, I'll be okay." Cynthia became even more infuriated.

"What do you mean, is everything cool! Who the hell are you supposed to be? I'll tell you what, it'll get better once you bounce outta here!" Cynthia pointed to the front door, emphasizing what she meant. Felicia opened her mouth to protest but Danielle raised her hand, pleading with Felicia to not say a word!

"I got this. Look Cindy, as you can see I have company and right now, is not the time for this," Danielle said as calmly as possible. "We can discuss this tomorrow, okay?" Cynthia eyes roamed from Felicia, then back to Danielle who was holding her breath, hoping Cynthia wouldn't explode. Cynthia was so angry that her body was visibly shaking. *My God! How am I going to calm her down and get her out of here!*

"I got a better idea, how bout we talk about *this,*" Cynthia pointed wildly at the two, "...right now?" she said, folding her arms across her heaving chest. "I got all night." Felicia had enough of Cynthia's temper tantrums.

"No, you see... *like* Danielle's idea much better." Danielle shot Felicia a look, begging her to be quiet. Felicia wasn't trying to hear it. Felicia was tired of Cynthia yelling and putting demands on Danielle like she was a child. Danielle is a grown woman, who was more than capable of making her *own* decisions. Cynthia was totally out of line and Felicia felt she had every right letting her know this. "So, why don't you leave, right *now,* like you were asked. Danielle will talk to you tomorrow, like she said." Felicia took on a defensive stance like she was more than ready to back up the bravado she so daringly displayed.

Cynthia cut hurt filled angry eyes at Danielle like she expected her to put her new friend in check but she didn't say a word. They both knew she was out of line. Cynthia pointed to Felicia and says,

"You had your chance, now I'ma beat the stupid off yo' ass!" In one fluid move, catching everyone off guard, Cynthia lunged at Felicia like a panther going after its prey.

Danielle, acting on pure adrenaline, moved forward grabbing Cynthia's jacket, pulling her back with all her might. Cynthia barely missed grasping Felicia's neck. Her body slammed against Danielle's body, almost causing them to tumble over the sofa straight to the floor. Danielle quickly regained her footing creating a barrier between Cynthia and Felicia, who's standing still, totally unfazed by Cynthia's actions. Felicia laughed daringly, taunting the beast.

"Look at you, embarrassing yourself. You're ridiculous!" Felicia sneered. "I grew up in the streets of Detroit, where we ate chicks like you for breakfast...literally."

Danielle raised her eyebrow in a questioning gesture. Cynthia, of course, used Felicia's revelation as an opportunity to make her look as ratchet as possible, by turning up her nose like Felicia stepped in cow shit.

"I don't give two rat ass where you dragged yourself from. You are here and you're about to get beat down in L.A."

Cynthia went for Felicia's throat, once more. This time, Felicia shoved Danielle out the way, snatched Cynthia by the arm, twisting it behind her back, sending surges of pain throughout her body. If Cynthia made one wrong move, Felicia could easily snap her arm in two. Cynthia's face was twisted up in agony. She fell to her knees, paralyzed by sheering pain while Felicia kept a firm grip on her arm, cutting off the circulation.

"Baby," Danielle said cautiously, "...please, let her go." Felicia heard absolutely nothing Danielle said. She was completely focused on keeping her target immobilized. Danielle tenderly rubbed Felicia's back. "Please baby, let her go." Felicia broke out of her trance and released her nemesis. Cynthia tried to get up from the floor too fast and stumbled. She spun around, flaring her arms wildly, almost hitting Danielle in the head. "That's enough, Cindy!" Danielle screamed. "I want you to leave...now!" Tears threatened to fall as she pushed Cynthia towards the door. "You gotta go, now, Cynthia!" Danielle couldn't stand seeing Cynthia behave like that.

"That's how you feel, Danni! All these years!" Cynthia wailed.

"Cindy, please!" Danielle's voice cracked. "Don't make me-" Danielle's words dissipate.

"Choose?" Cynthia finished what Danielle couldn't. Tears rolled down Danielle's face.

"I could never do...please don't make...me..." The pain was unbearable. Cynthia's bottom lip quivered as she tried to hold back sobs.

"Well, sweetheart...you just did."

Heartbreak, hurt and shame filled Cynthia's eyes. She walked to the door, Danielle wanted to faint. Cynthia turned the door knob and didn't bother to look back at her friend as she exited through the front door.

Danielle moaned from a deep stabbing pain in her gut as she fell against the wall for support. Felicia locked the door. The clicking sound from the deadbolt locking into place, felt like a shotgun blast to Danielle's heart. Felicia held her tight.

"Everything will be all right."

"I hope so." Felicia felt the warmth of Danielle's tears on her chest.

"Come on." She led Danielle to the bedroom where she laid her down, covering her with a comforter.

A FRIEND WHO STICKS CLOSER THAN A BROTHER

Above all, love each other deeply, because love covers over a multitude of sins. 1Peter 4:8 NKJV

LISA

was disturbed.

This isn't like them to not return my calls, she said to herself. "Something isn't right." At that split-second, Lisa heard Regina's name in her spirit. "Lord? What's going on with her?"

"Pray," was the only response. Lisa's spirit was full of sorrow.

"Father God, I ask that You please have mercy on Regina's soul, wherever she may be and whatever she is doing. Please be with her in the Mighty Majestic name of Jesus. I ask that You surround her with Your Angels, Father. Put a fiery hedge of protection around her to protect her from all harm that the enemy will try to send against her. I remind you devil, that you are powerless and defeated in the Mighty name of Jesus Christ. I rebuke you and bind your wicked spirits in the name of Jesus Christ. No weapon formed against Regina or any of God's people shall prosper in Jesus name! The desires of the wicked are not granted. *Praise You Father God! Hallelujah!* You are more than worthy God! Thank You Jesus! Praise Your name Jesus! Thank You for dying on the cross for me! Jesus, You said who the Son sets free is free indeed. I thank You that all Your children are set free from all bondages of the devil and his demons. Praise You Father God! Praise Your Mighty name!"

Lisa stood to her feet, pacing the floor as she spoke in her heavenly language to her God.

FROM OUT OF THE DARKNESS COMES THE LIGHT

DREAM

Regina ran as fast as her feet would carry her. She didn't know where she was but she knew she was in imminent danger. She felt hot breath on the back of her neck and heavy panting thrashing her eardrums. For fear of tripping and falling she refused to look behind her to see what was chasing her. Regina was running so fast that she couldn't stop soon enough to keep from falling over the edge of a huge drop, not less than three feet in front of her. There was no way she could avoid going over the edge. Regina dropped to the ground hoping her quick thinking would keep her from going over. Fail! It didn't work. The momentum propelled her over the edge and off into what appeared to be a dark abyss that led to a place she would never escape.

"Lord God, please help me!" Regina screeched from deep within her soul as her body was propelled further down. Out from nowhere, a large hand reached down and caught hold of her, rescuing her from eternal damnation.

Regina stared into the eyes of such a beautiful face that radiated love, in the form a brilliant illuminating light. His beauty was unlike any person or thing she had ever seen before.

"Jesus!" she whimpered from shock and wonderment.

"Peace, be still my child." Jesus stood Regina to her feet, looking at her with much love and compassion. "It is time that you get up, Regina. I have made a way of escape for you. Know that I

will always love you and I will never leave you, nor will I forsake you."

When the dream ended, Regina regained consciousness as the breath of life was blown back into her lungs. Her heart raced and her clothes were drenched in cold sweat. It took time for her eyes to adjust to the darkness. Now she remembered exactly where she was.

"Tommy!" Regina whispered to herself in shock. He was lying beside her sound asleep. "Thank you, Jesus!"

She carefully lifted herself and scooted to the edge of the bed, making sure not to wake her captor. God only knew what his plans were for her. The opening of the blinds allowed light to stream through the dense room. Regina was barely able to make out the shapes on the floor. She feared she might trip over something or make a sound that would wake Tommy's crazy ass. Regina had an inkling to run out the house without anything in tow. She could only imagine the attention she'd draw to herself if she ran out, barefoot, looking like a deranged woman, Lord knows she certainly smelled like one.

"Come on Regina!" she said in an attempt to amp herself up. She suddenly remembered where her purse and jacket were. They were sitting on the chair near the window. Regina crept up to the chair to retrieve her belongings and her foot grazed over an object. She leaned down and picked it up. "My shoe! Yes!" Regina could just about make out the other shoe sitting against the chair's leg. She grabbed everything and jetted out the house never, looking back.

Regina had been holding her breath not realizing it until she stuck her key into the ignition.

"Oh, my God!" She mashed down hard on the accelerator causing the tires to burn rubber and the car sped off like a bullet. Regina made a sharp right turn at the end of the block and cried like she never cried in life. "Thank You! Thank You Father God, for saving me! Thank You! Thank You!" She cried a river of tears all the way to Lisa's house.

Ten minutes later, Regina was parked in front of her friend's house in a trance like state. She was so deep in a daze that she couldn't tell you if it was day or night. In between sobbing and thanking God, she hadn't noticed that someone was peeping through the blinds watching her. Moments later, a figure appeared outside her car window. Regina's eyes peered up. It took a few seconds to process that someone was standing outside of her car door. When Regina recognized the familiar face, with eyes watching her filled with an abundance of compassion, she began crying all over again.

"Regina!" Lisa called out to her through the closed window. "Hey! What's wrong?" Regina wanted to open the car door but shame weighed heavy on her, not to mention that her body odor made her want to seal the car doors shut forever. "Sweetie, please open the door!" Lisa pled. Regina didn't move, she sat in silence as the terrifying events she just experienced overtook her mind, leaving her in a state of confusion. "Talk to me, Gina. I'm here for you." Humiliation almost won the battle inside her head, Regina couldn't move if she wanted to. She felt a force take hold of her hand, assisting her in unlocking the door.

Lisa opened the car door and the crisp night air hit the side of Regina's face, engulfing her body reminding her that she's still alive. When Lisa wrapped her arms around Regina, pulling her into a loving embrace, she knew everything would be all right.

"Oh honey! It's all right, I'm here." Regina sobbed heavily in her arms. "Come on." Lisa removed the keys from the ignition and gently helped Regina out of the car. "Let's go inside. I made homemade vegetable soup and wheat bread. Does that sound good to you?" Regina nodded her head, yes. She was too weak to speak. Lisa held onto to her waist as they walked to the house. Lisa couldn't help but to notice how much weight Regina shed. She was nearly skin and bones. *Thank You Lord, for Your help!*

Lisa sat at the kitchen table in total disarray. She was mortified by what Regina just confessed. They almost emptied an entire box of Puffs Tissues. Regina couldn't help but to unveil her heart to Lisa after receiving so much love. Lisa wished she could take Regina's pain away and bear her burdens. She had no idea what her friend was going through!

"Oh sweetheart, I'm so sorry! Why didn't you tell us?" Regina shrugged her shoulders and avoided Lisa's caring eyes.

"I, I didn't think it was a problem. I mean, I did do hard drugs in college but that was so long ago. I haven't had any dope until now." She wiped tears from her eyes. Lisa was discombobulated. Her mind was wheeling a million miles a minute.

I didn't see it! I mean, I knew something was wrong but nothing like this! A quick thought came to her mind. *Ooooh! That's why You had me praying for her. Lord God, You are awesome!* "I just wish you talked to someone!"

"I, I-"

"What happened? I mean, what...!" Lisa was severely affected by what Regina revealed.

Regina shook her head in total disbelief, as she tried to process what made her go so far to the left. She couldn't believe that she allowed something so small and insignificant to cause her to do such grave and harmful things to her mind, soul and body.

"Do you know that I died, Lisa!"

"What!" Lisa felt like she's just been slapped in the face with a wet towel. "Regina, you died! How!" Lisa looked her up and down, examining her closely.

"I had no control! It was like something took over me. I just wanted to get high and stay high! I couldn't fight it. As soon as I'd come down, I couldn't get high fast enough. I was a fiend. I would have done *anything* to stay high. The last time Tommy-" Lisa cut her off.

"Tommy! Who is Tommy?" Regina realized that she explained everything that happened but failed to mention the person she was getting high with.

"Tommy is my ex-boyfriend." She avoided Lisa's eyes. "We dated in high school and it continued on through college. After getting involved with drugs, we were expelled from college and we had to return home. We were forbidden by our parents, not to have contact with one another. I haven't seen him in years." Lisa squeezed Regina's hand reassuring her friend that she was not there

201

to condemn her. "The whole ordeal became eerie and dark. I mean, I initially went to his house just to get high but when I saw him, I realized how much I missed him but then strange things began to happen. He started changing before my eyes." Lisa saw fear looming in Regina's eyes as Lisa watched her try to explain what she saw. "His eyes Lisa, his eyes were pitch black. I saw evil in them. I should have left but it felt like I was trapped inside that house."

"What happened! Did he do anything or did you just start feeling different about him?"

"No...yeah, well...I...yeah he, ummm...he tied me up." Lisa gasped. Regina shook her head in disbelief as the reality of what she was saying registered in her mind. "I kept feeling to leave, Lisa! The warnings felt like life or death but I chose to stay. I can't believe I didn't leave!" She fought back tears.

"It's okay, it's all right."

"Tommy left to get more drugs. As soon as he left, I heard a voice telling me to *"leave!"* Of course, I brushed it off and waited for him to come back. He was gone for hours. I thought something might have happened to him. The thing that bothered me the most, *Lisa,* was thinking something might have happen to him and I would not be able to get high. I didn't feel one ounce of guilt, either!"

"The drugs, it was the drugs, baby," Lisa said trying to help ease Regina's feelings of shame.

"When he got back home, I noticed that he wouldn't look at me and he kept his back turned towards me. I couldn't tell what he was doing. Next thing I know, he was restraining me. I tried to fight him but he was too strong."

"Did he hurt you Gina!" Lisa asked again, making sure she wasn't holding anything back out of fear or shame.

"No! No." Regina blew a forceful stream of air out of relief. "Honestly, I don't know what would have been worse, being raped or continuously being shot up with heroin?"

"Ohhhh, my Lord, Regina!" Lisa's heart ached. She had tremendous compassion for her friend. Tears threatened to fall from her eyes.

"He kept shooting me up with heroin and when I'd wake up, he'd just give me more. Every time he shot that stuff inside my veins, I felt my heart grow weaker. I was so high and so weak that I couldn't pray or open my mouth to say a word. I thought I was dreaming but the more I share what happened to me, I know it wasn't a dream. I was being chased by what, I don't know. But I do know, I was filled with *terror* that I've never felt before. I knew that whatever was chasing me, if it caught me, I was never waking up again. I was running so fast that I couldn't stop soon enough to avoid the drop-in front of me. I fell and slid, hoping it would slow me down to keep me from going over the edge but it didn't. I slid over, I couldn't see anything but darkness and despair. It felt worse than any despair you or I have ever felt on this earth. I think I went to hell, Lisa." The look of horror on Regina's face, told Lisa that she really believed what she was saying. Lisa gripped Regina's hand tighter. "I cried out to God and I begged Him to help me. He caught me before I fell further down. His face, Lisa...!" Lisa saw so much love beaming through Regina's eyes. "He is so beautiful! You can't possibly imagine His beauty and how much He loves us. He's surrounded by an immense illuminating light, just being in His presence alone, made me feel whole. I knew at that point, that I didn't need drugs or anything else to make me feel better. All I needed and all I wanted, was Him." Regina shed tears of joy. Lisa felt the anointing of God coming through Regina. "He told me to leave and always know He will be with me. Lisa! He kept me from dying in my sins! He saved me, even in my darkest hour. He was there for me,for me!"

"I know, Gina. He loves you more than you'll ever know. He really does."

"I know and I want to do all I can to show Him how much I appreciate His love and forgiveness."

"Receiving God and obeying His word and allowing Him to use you however He chooses, is what He wants from you. God has been waiting on you for a long time. He never gave up on you."

"I know, I really see that now. I love Him *sooooo* much, for what He's done for me. *I love Him!*" Regina emphasized. "I could have died today and I have no doubt that hell was my final destination. He is faithful."

"God has so much for you to do. He wants to use you to reach out to others who are in need."

"I know, I know."

They remained seated at the table, talking about God and His mercy until the morning hours. Lisa let Regina sleep in her bed and she slept on the sofa. Regina stayed at Lisa's house studying and reading God's word. Her spirit thirsted for God and she desired to serve Him to the fullest. Regina never knew that giving her entire heart to God would be so fulfilling. Seeking a higher education never made her feel so complete.

HURT DISGUISED AS ANGER

A hot tempered man must pay the penalty, for if you rescue him, you must do it again. Proverbs 19:19 NKJV

CYNTHIA

blew through every red light, driving in a blind fury, turnt up on New Amsterdam Gin. She was so drunk and enraged that she couldn't see straight.

"Who do you think you are!" Cynthia howled, as she whipped through another red light at Jefferson and La Brea. It would be a blessing if the police got to her before she injured someone or herself. "You will never hurt me like that again! *Neevver!*"

That statement was covered in anguish. It wasn't only directed towards Danielle, the bearer of the bulk of Cynthia's anger, those words were towards Cynthia's parents for abandoning her and they were aimed at every dirty dog of a man who violated her. She abhorred being exposed to such overt perversion as a little girl. No little girl should ever be exposed to the atrocities that she endured. Cynthia's foster parents didn't get off that easy either. They definitely were included in Cynthia's 'bouts of unbridle rage. Her foster parents swore to protect her and give her love. Sadly, they only saw her as a dollar sign, an extra income to finance their material desires.

"Ahhhh! I hate all of 'em!" Cynthia shrieked, banging on the steering wheel until she broke down and cried. It's a wonder she even made it home.

The once full liter of gin was now empty. Cynthia opened her car door and the bottle crashed to the ground, breaking into pieces. She got out the car and stumbled up the walkway, to her front door. Cynthia's car keys and purse took a tumble to the ground.

"Damn!" she cursed as she bent down to pick them up, swaying back and forth allowing her eyes to adjust. Everything was blurry as hell! Cynthia's head was spinning so fast that she was nauseous. "Come on!" she slurred and clumsily unlocked the door. "That's right!"

Cynthia forcefully slung the door open, it slammed against the wall causing tiny bits of plaster to spray the air. She shut the door and floundered across the floor when her right foot got caught on the edge of the dog-eared generic rug. Cynthia immediately lost her footing and was sent her hurling to the floor, landing flat on her stomach. The wind was knocked out of her, black spots appeared before her eyes. Cynthia felt the liquor rumble inside her belly like a sea of restless waves. She covered her mouth sensing an eruption getting ready to spew from her mouth. Cynthia managed to push herself up from the floor and ran to the bathroom where she dropped to her knees in front of the porcelain throne. Instead of vomiting she began crying again.

"Why! Pleeeaase!"

Cynthia had been dodging her pain most of her life. People who were hurting tend to abuse drugs, alcohol and sex to escape. This was common and an easy way to temporarily cover pain but it *NEVER* resolved the turmoil within. The only thing these vices were good for, was creating *more* problems, adding to other unresolved issues. Unresolved issues are the devil's playground. He wants you bound hopeless and depressed and depression is anger turned within. When we hold anger inside, the results are outward destruction. The enemy would love for us to destroy ourselves rather than being set free by the power of Jesus Christ.

Being set free and delivered is what the devil fears because you become a danger to the kingdom of darkness.

Cynthia slowly lifted herself up from the bathroom floor and wobbled down the hall to her bedroom where she collapsed on the bed.

"Please, God, take the pain away. I can't take it anymore," Cynthia's voice became faint as she drifted off into a deep slumber.

DREAM

There was nothing in the world that could make her happier than being pushed on the swing by her father. She looked in the distance and she saw her mother beaming with joy as she watched her husband play with their baby girl.

"Push me higher, daddy! Higher!" Cynthia shrilled in delight.

"Okay, baby! How high do you want daddy to push you, sweetheart?"

"Hiiihhggg! Mommy, look mommy!" Cynthia shrilled as her little frame was pushed higher into the sky. It seemed like she could touch the edge of the sky with the tips of her toes if she stretched far enough.

When Cynthia fell back to earth she called out to her mother once again.

"Mommy, do you see me!" But this time, when she called out to her mother, there's no answer nor did she feel the loving hands of her father catching her and gently pushing her from behind.

Fear gripped Cynthia's heart. She turned and looked in the direction of where her mother was standing. The look of happiness and joy that once covered her face, was now replaced with sorrow and pain. Cynthia was confused. She didn't understand why her mother looked so sad.

A loud snap ricocheted in her ear followed by the bottom of the swing breaking away, propelling her into the air. Cynthia fell to the ground, sliding through the sand that felt like tiny razor sharp pins, piercing the flesh on her legs and the palms of her hands. She came to an abrupt stop on the concrete.

Cynthia's eyes strained to look at her father and mother. She eagerly waited for them to take her in their arms, cradle her and kiss her telling her that everything would be okay. That never happened. Instead, her parents remained standing in the same spot, no more than twenty feet away from Cynthia, looking tattered and dirty. The bright colored clothes they wore to the park, were now replaced with filthy rags. Cynthia's father's, once strong healthy frame, now resembled that of a skeleton. Her mother's voluptuous curves have disappeared and what was left was barely enough to fill out the tattered clothing hanging from her body.

Their appearance was not what devastated Cynthia. It's the distant, uncaring look her father gave her as he injected a needle into his arm. Her mother grabbed him, pulling him away like Cynthia meant nothing to them. She cried and begged for them to come back to her. Her throat was raw and horse from yelling and screaming like her life depended on being acknowledged as their child.

Cynthia's cries fell on deaf ears. Rosette and Eddie continued walking away, ignoring their child's distressful cries. Out of nowhere, a man clothed in the brightest of whites appeared to Cynthia, stretching out His hand to help her to her feet.

She looked at Him with eyes full of pain and hate. Cynthia refused His help and stood to her feet on her own. She folded her arms tightly across her small chest and turned her back to Him. He looked at her compassionately with warm eyes. He understood she was hurting and it was impossible for her to accept His love at that time. He looked down at her tiny fragile body with so much love and says,

"I will always be here for you, Cynthia."

The sound of Cynthia's own crying was what woke her up. When she was fully awake, she realized that she was only having a dream. She then heard a loving voice say,

"Cynthia, I am still here." She drew her body into a fetal position and says,

"I know, Lord. I know. Thank You." She cried herself back to sleep.

DANIELLE'S

stomach felt like it was twisted in knots. She thought she was going to throw up and have a bowel movement at the same time. Danielle looked at her cell phone wanting to call Cynthia but she fought the urge. As if Felicia, sensed Danielle's agony, she woke up and held her tightly in her arms.

"Don't do this to yourself." Tears rolled down Danielle's cheeks.

"I know, it's just-"

"...she's your friend," Felicia finished Danielle's sentence. "I know sweetie but Cynthia is grown. You asked her to leave, she wouldn't and look what happened." Danielle cringed as flashbacks of last night's events assaulted her mind.

"I did ask her to leave, and I'm not blaming you but I just wish you let me handle it," she said between sobs. Felicia tenderly lift Danielle's chin staring, into her eyes.

"Heeeyy, I did what I felt I needed to do. I don't care how long she has known you. Cynthia had no right storming into your house making demands like that."

"I know, I just feel it could have been handled differently."

"Danielle look, don't do this to yourself. You and I both know that alcohol and emotions don't mix." Cynthia had been drinking before she stepped foot into Danielle's house. "When Cynthia sobers up, she'll realize her mistake." Danielle anxiously reached for her phone but Felicia pulled her hand away. "Give her some time. If she's still upset, you'll only make matters worse."

Danielle knew what Felicia said was sound judgment but she couldn't help to feel that her friendship, of almost fifteen years, was over.

I hope she's all right. We've had plenty of arguments but they've never been as horrible as this. I mean, she was humiliated in front of me when Felicia damn near had her begging on her knees for mercy. Danielle sighed and rested her weary head on her lover's breast. Felicia kissed her softly.

"It'll be all right." Danielle nodded her head, tightly closing her eyes, trying to keep last night's bad scene from playing over in her head like a ratchet B movie.

"Remind me to never challenge your Detroit street skills. That's a side of you I never want to witness again," Danielle told her.

"Believe you me, that's a side I never *want* you to see again."

IT ALWAYS FEELS BETTER IN THE MORNING

CYNTHIA

woke up with a horrible hangover and a heavy heart but she couldn't remember why she was so troubled. The phone rang, causing her head to pound even harder.

"*Geesh!* you have impeccable timing," Cynthia said angrily to the person who dared to call her so early in the morning. She looked at the alarm clock and growled, "7:30!" Cynthia yanked the phone up, without checking at the caller ID, which was something she rarely did. *"Hello!"* Cynthia barked into the phone.

There was a brief moment of silence on the other end of the line. A calming voice broke through the thick silence.

"We'll, good morning to you too sunshine." Lisa knew the way to soothing a savage beast was with kindness. Plus, she wasn't trying to get cussed out early in the morning.

"Lisa!" Cynthia asked sounding surprised and a little embarrassed.

"Hey you, it's nice to *finally* hear your voice. I've been trying to call you for a while. How's everything?" Lisa asked, even though it was clear that her friend wasn't in a good mood. Just as Lisa asked her friend how she was doing, Holy Spirit flashed a scene in her spirit, of what took place between Danielle, Cynthia and another individual, Lisa had never seen before.

"I'm good. I just didn't sleep too well last night." That's the only explanation Cynthia was willing to give. She's definitely not about to tell Lisa the *real* reason behind her displaced anger. I mean, how would she sound, telling Lisa that she got into a brutal confrontation with Danielle and almost got into a fight with Danielle's *female lover* because she was jealous and *is sexually* attracted to her best friend, who they *both* have known for years? Lisa would have been at Cynthia's door in 0.2 seconds, ready to perform an exorcist. Cynthia's lips were sealed.

"Okay, well if you ever want to talk, you know I'm only a phone call away."

"I know." Cynthia's soul screamed for release! A release from every burden she carried for far too long but she didn't. Cynthia was full of too much shame and regret. The devil had her wedged between a rock and a hard place. "Thank you for checking up on me. I'm sorry for not returning your calls but you know how things can get. You think you have all the time in the world but then it slips right pass you."

"I know all too well, but if we don't find time to reach out to the ones we love, we'll never have the time."

"I hear you."

"Hey, have you talked to Danielle?" Hearing Danielle's name felt like a thousand daggers piercing Cynthia's heart.

"I saw her the other day but she was kinda busy. We really didn't have a chance to talk."

"Oh, okay." Lisa could tell by the sound of Cynthia's voice that there was something else she was not saying. "Well, I'm not going to keep you much longer. I called early not expecting you to answer the phone. I sincerely apologize if I disturbed your sleep. I just wanted to hear from my friend." Lisa's voice was so sweet and sincere that Cynthia wanted to cry.

"Thank you, Lisa. Thank you so much for being a friend. I really appreciate you."

"No prob."

"Thanks again for calling me," Cynthia told Lisa.

"Take care."

They both hung up. Lisa knew it would be a long time before she heard from Cynthia again.

IT FELT SO REAL

DREAM

Regina was sitting on a sofa in a living room that had no walls. The foundation was shabby and falling apart. Regina was engaged in fun-filled laughter as she joked with a male companion.

A faint noise coming from the rear of the house drew her attention. Just as Regina's about to spark up the pipe, sudden fear struck her heart, beads of sweat formed on her brow. She sat the pipe down, stood up and slowly made her way down the hall to the rear of the house.

The hall was pitch black, non-translucent. It was so dark that she couldn't see her hand directly in front of her face. This darkness, felt alive, animate like it bred evil. It was the mother of all abominations. Noises became amplified. Her heart pounded like a sledge hammer against her chest.

Regina stood frozen in front of a closed door. Devilish laughter, god-awful screams and unceasing chatter surged through the door. She was horrorstruck fearing, what was on the other side. Even though she was petrified, intense curiosity kept her bound, not allowing her to retreat. As Regina finally gathered the courage to run, a gentle voice says,

"Open the door. I am with you."

Regina gripped the doorknob, slowly turning it open. The stench of death violated her nostrils and the visual was far worse than the smell. She nearly passed out from the horrid smell.

Her knees buckled. An immensely strong hand held her steady. The scene before her eye was total chaos! Regina stared with her mouth agape at an average size room. The activity and the mass amount of people that she saw, there was no possible way that space was large enough to hold them.

An enormously large gaping hole sat in the middle of the floor with intense heat emanating from it. It's deathly hot! If the heat didn't cause you to fall unconscious, the horrible gut wrenching smell would. There were tables scattered about the room in no particular order. People of various sizes, shapes, colors and ethnicities sat around the tables. Some were lying haphazardly around the edge of the sweltering heat emanating hole.

One thing that dawned on Regina, was the fact that everyone was stark naked! Some were walking about talking to others, laughing and going about their merry way as if their appearance was normal and not a scene straight out of a horror flick. Others were engaged in orgies and the rest were practicing perverted sex acts. Every person's body was decomposed with gaping holes in their midsections. Some had heads partially detached from their necks, hanging by thin strips of flesh. They're grotesquely disfigured but no one seemed to care.

Horrible looking eight-foot-tall creatures with unnatural strength erupt into hideous laughter throughout the room. These gruesome beings picked people up by whatever mangled body parts they had, whether it was broken legs, half detached torsos, skeleton exposed fingers, severed scalps, and tossed them high into the air as they kicked and screamed terrifyingly and plunged into the fire breathing hole. The foul creatures roared with wicked laughter at each victim's futile attempt in trying to evade the torture that awaited them. The more terror and pain that they inflicted upon their victims, the more the massive atrocious beast enjoyed it. Regina heard a gentle voice say,

"Go closer to see what's in the hole." Fear gripped her. She was unable to move.

"Please no! I don't want to. They will throw me in there too!" The endearing voice says,

"They can't see you, Regina. I am protecting you." Even after being reassured, Regina was still afraid but she was compelled to see what was inside the hole. She pried her feet from the floor and carefully stepped inside the room.

Regina was so terrified that if she made a noise the demon creatures would hear her and snatch her up, kicking and screaming. The fear slowly began to subside when Regina noticed she wasn't visible to them. She watched in horror as the wicked beast continued tormenting the damn, hysterically laughing at their agony.

The closer she got to the middle of the floor the more putrid the smell became. Regina was amazed that she hadn't fainted due to the awful stench. The foul odor seemed to have tentacles that strangled her lungs, causing her to cough and choke. When Regina was within a few feet of the hole she stepped, closer and peered over the edge. What she saw was beyond frightening.

There were people stacked on top of each other. Regina realized that the screams she heard were from people that were tossed into the hole. Dead flesh covered their bodies like a morbid blanket. Massive amounts of bodies were lying on what appeared to be some sort of conveyer belt that moved painstakingly slow. There were hundreds, possibly thousands of wicked entities aligned along both sides of the wide stream of bodies. The damned were trying, with all their might, to forage their way off the moving apparatus but they were viciously intercepted by the evil entities and thrown back onto the massive sea of bodies. Regina didn't know where they were going but she felt it was a place far worse than the room she stood in.

Regina was submerged in deep sorrow. The anguish that engulfed her was unbearable, she quickly ran away. As she ran towards the door, what she saw from the corner of her eye caused her to stop dead in her tracks. Regina felt the blood drain to her feet. Two of her friends were seated at one of the tables, engaged in laughter, having a grand ole time, oblivious to the chaos and smells of decay.

Regina stumbled, nearly falling on her face. She couldn't believe her eyes!

"Cynthia! Danielle! You have to get out of here, now! Danielle!" Her pleading went unheard. The hideous creatures were within inches of her friends table. Regina watched in horror as the entities stared, with unadulterated hatred and unearthly fury, at Danielle and Cynthia. No mere man could handle such vile hatred and fury that poured out from the creatures. Regina covered her mouth sobbing uncontrollably. She knew it would only be a matter of time that her friends would be captured and furiously cast into the dreadful pit.

Regina was about to collapse from the weight of the tremendous grief and sorrow she felt for Danielle and Cynthia. Before she could be completely overcome by immobilizing sorrow, she heard a gentle voice say,

"Fret not my child, I AM with them."

Regina jolted up from sleep, the fear that held her captive dissipated at once. She sat in bed with her hands over her face trying to sort out what she just witnessed.

"Oh, my GOD! It felt so real!" Regina looked at the clock, it's 3:30AM. She reached for the phone, dialing frantically and put the phone to her ear. Regina waited anxiously as the phone rang several times before it was answered.

"Hello?" Lisa answered with a groggy voice.

"I'm so sorry for waking you but I didn't know who else to call. I just had a dream that shook me to my core!" Lisa instantly became fully alert when she heard the desperation in her friend's voice.

"What's wrong, honey!"

"I, I believe I just had another dream about hell. This time, Cynthia and Danielle were in it!" Lisa listened intently as Regina gave details about the terrifying dream. She remained silent and heard the Holy Spirit confirm that the dream was real. "I saw them Lisa! They were sitting at a table laughing and talking to other people unaware of the deplorable indescribable things that were happening around them." Lisa could tell Regina was obviously shaken by the dream God has given her.

"Your dream was very graphic, that was a God warning dream. He's telling you to pray for them. Keep them covered in the blood of the Lamb of God and in the love of Jesus. Regina, thank God that He trusts you enough to confide in you about the lives of others. He knows you have a heart full of love and compassion for His people." The image of hopelessness and death lingered in Regina's mind. She was saddened. Lisa spoke soothing words that brought comfort to her soul. Regina knew she was given the dream by God to pray for her friend's salvation. "Are you all right?" Lisa asked. Regina gave a sigh of relief.

"Yes, most definitely! I feel liberated after sharing my dream with you. Thank you."

"You can call me anytime, sweetie."

"It didn't feel like a dream, Lisa! It felt like it was really happening. I can still smell the stench in my nose and I can still see the disfigured bodies! There are no words to describe it!"

"Now, you're ready to see and know the truth. It's the truth Gina. There *is* life *after* death. The choice is ours, where we will spend eternity, whether it will be eternal life or eternal damnation. God wants you to pray without ceasing for Cindy and Danni. They'll be all right."

"I know, when I get off the phone I'm going to pray. I'm going to pray for all of us."

"Amen. I'ma let you go so I can pray too."

"Okay, good night and thanks again."

"Good night."

Parts of the dream continued to play over in Regina's mind. She shuddered outwardly thinking about the lost souls that have *no* idea what awaited them after death. When she thought about how ignorantly and rebelliously she lived her life, she immediately began praising God for helping her to escape an eternity of total damnation.

"God have mercy on us. Thank You, for Your grace and mercy that You've bestowed on me. I know that's exactly how I was, unaware of the terror that awaited me but You had faith that I would make it through. You knew all along that I would answer Your call. I Thank You, I love You with all my heart Lord, Jesus.

Thank You Jesus!" Regina continued pouring out her heart to God until she fell into a sweet sleep.

THE MORNING AFTER

DANIELLE

woke up for the second time that morning hoping it was just a nightmare and not a reality. When she opened her eyes and saw Felicia lying next to her, she knew what she dreaded really went down.

"Man-O-Manischewitz!" Danielle moaned in a state of shock. Felicia turned over onto her back.

"Hey baby, did you sleep well?" Danielle didn't answer. Felicia examined her closely. "Not that good, huh?"

"I'm okay," Danielle mumbled as she climbed out of bed and went into the bathroom. Felicia had a thought to join Danielle in the shower but she quickly banished that plan.

"I'll let her have her time alone." Felicia glanced at the clock. "I know what I'll do. I'll have a nice breakfast waiting for her when she gets out the shower." She sprung to her feet, got one of Danielle's robes out of the closet and headed to the kitchen to prepare breakfast.

Danielle was greeted by the delicious aroma of food cooking as she stepped out the bathroom. A smile adorned her face when she pictured her lover preparing breakfast.

"Awwww! That's so thoughtful of her." Danielle was so anxious to eat that she didn't bother putting on a stitch of clothing.

She stopped at the kitchen's entrance and leaned against the door's frame watching Felicia with admiration. An alluring smile infused with appreciation, strong like and lust spread across her face as she studied Felicia. She slightly turned her head in Danielle's direction, her mouth curled into a tantalizing smile.

220

"Oh, so now you're a psychic?" Danielle asked as she walked up behind Felicia, encircling her arms around her waist and kissing the curve of her neck.

"Oh! Did I leave that out?" Felicia said jokingly. She turned around and gave Danielle a hug. They're standing so close that their noses touched. *"Mmmm,"* Felicia moaned, kissing Danielle's lips. "You have the body of a goddess." She took a whiff of Danielle's breath. "You use Crest too?" Danielle bursts out in laughter. "I'm serious! I smell it on your breath."

"What were you expecting my breath to smell like?" Felicia was embarrassed.

Yeah, what did I expect her breath to smell like? Duh! "I expect it to smell sweet, like you," she said, giving Danielle a peck on the cheek. "And if you must know how I knew you were standing behind me, I could smell the scent of your body wash." Felicia buried her face in between Danielle's breast, inhaling like she was trying to pull the skin off her chest. "You smell divine." The smell of bacon beginning to burn snapped them back to reality.

"Oh baby, the bacon!" Danielle shrieked. "It's about to burn!" she said laughing. Felicia hurriedly turned around to remove the pan from the fire.

"Caught it just in time. A few more seconds and it would have burnt to a crisp."

"And we wouldn't want that!" Danielle says as she took a bite of the sizzling bacon. *"Mmmmm!* Not bad for *almost* burnt pork." Felicia shooed Danielle away and motioned for her sit at the table.

"Sit down so I can serve you." She ran ahead of Danielle to pull out a chair for her. "All I want you to do is relax and prepare yourself to sample a taste of paradise on a platter."

"Paradise on a platter? I'm glad I brought my appetite." Danielle watched Felicia in delight as she poured pancake batter in the pan.

"How many pancakes do you want?"

"As many as you want to give me," Danielle said with a smirk. Felicia turned around with her hand on her hip and spatula in the other.

"Pancakes aren't the only thing I want to give you, baby." She grinned mockingly.

"Really?" Danielle taunted.

"Yes...really."

"Well," Danielle leaned seductively on the table, "...you can give me the rest, *after* breakfast," she said with a raised eyebrow. Felicia smiled and turned back to the stove.

"I'ma definitely hold you to that."

"You do that, right now, all I can think about is food. You're the blame for my ferocious appetite." Felicia let out a chuckle.

"How is that?"

"You made me work up an appetite last night. A sista woke up *hungrier* than a run-away slave!"

"Oh!" Felicia laughed hysterically, almost dropping the frying pan on the floor.

"Yeah...*oh!*" Danielle said joining in the laughter. "You *know* what I'm talking about."

"I certainly do." Felicia piled Danielle's plate with eggs, sunny side up, bacon, two Jimmy Dean Maple Sausages, blueberry pancakes and melted cheesy topped hash-browns with a side of sour cream. When she sat the plate in front of Danielle, her eyes opened wide as saucers.

"Oh, my, baby! This looks scrumptious!" Danielle squeezed Felicia's face and kissed her passionately on the lips. She pulled back, cupping Felicia's face tenderly in her hands. "Thank you." Felicia planted feather like kisses all over Danielle's hand.

"You're welcome, baby." Danielle picked up her fork and commenced to eating like there's no tomorrow.

"I am *soooooo* hungry! I might eat everything on this plate and then some."

"Go right ahead, enjoy yourself. There is plenty of food." Felicia took a piece of sausage from Danielle's plate and put it in her mouth. *"Mmmm,* I love Jimmy Deans," Felicia said as she untied her robe preparing to walk out the kitchen. Danielle was puzzled.

"You're not having breakfast with me!" Disappointment filled her eyes.

"Enjoy yourself, baby," Felicia said as her robe slightly opened revealing the front of her gorgeously toned body. Danielle blushed. "I'm going to take a quick shower." Felicia pecked her on the nose.

"I'll be right back, don't go anywhere. I'll feel so much better being around you after I take a shower." Danielle didn't protest. She knew all too well how one would want to take a shower after a night *and* morning filled with *extracurricular activities.*

"Okay, hurry up then."

"I will," Felicia yelled back as she raced out the kitchen.

The food was even better than Danielle imagined. As she savored every delicious morsel in her mouth, her mind wondered about what the day would bring.

"Maybe, we can take a stroll on Santa Monica Pier, *hmmmm,* that sounds nice." Danielle chomped on a piece of bacon, and just that fast, her mood changed from upbeat to somber. Regardless of how great the food taste, it wasn't enough to keep her mind from going back to last night. Danielle shoved her half-eaten plate away and contemplated calling Cynthia but, it was too soon. *I should give her more time.* "It's too soon," Danielle said out loud to herself.

"Too soon, for what?" Felicia asked as she walked into the kitchen towel drying her hair.

"I was just thinking out loud about whether or not I should have a second helping of your incredibly tasting food but I decided against it." Of course, Danielle was lying but she didn't want to damper Felicia's morning by moping over her friend. She's in pain and she could only imagine how betrayed Cynthia must feel. Calling her on the phone wasn't going to be enough to mend a broken-heart. Tears threatened to escape from her eyes. Danielle fought tooth and nail not to let them roll down her face. When Felicia's back was facing Danielle, she quickly wiped her eyes and carried her plate to the counter. Felicia had a piece of bacon dangling from her lips while she studied Danielle closely.

"You're leaving me?"

"Huh?" Danielle was taken aback.

"You asked me to hurry and take a shower but now you're leaving me to eat all alone." Felicia pouted her lower lip. Guilt shot through Danielle. She sniffled and tried to avoid looking directly at Felicia.

"I'm so sorry, baby. I, all of a sudden, started feeling drowsy, honey." Felicia rubbed Danielle's shoulder endearingly.

"Niggeritis?" she said jokingly. Danielle snickered.

"Hell, to da naw! And everyone gets 'niggeritis,' *after* eating. It happens because our digestive system depletes all our energy to digest food. But seriously, I don't think I'll be good company right now. I'm sorry, baby." Danielle stepped to Felicia, taking her in her arms and leaning her forehead against Felicia's. "Is that okay?" Felicia nodded her head, yes.

"Go lie down, I'll be in there shortly to give you a massage." Felicia winked. Danielle slowly exit the kitchen. When she was out of Felicia's eyesight, she made a short detour to the bar to get a bottle of Jack Daniels.

"This will definitely do the job." Danielle tucked the bottle underneath her arm and headed to the bedroom. Self-medication was Danielle's choice for dealing with emotional pain. Her plan was to keep drinking until the pain in her heart subsided. If that didn't work, sleep would be the next best thing. You can't feel hurt when you're asleep.

Felicia found Danielle fast asleep, still holding onto a bottle of Jack. She removed the bottle from her hand and covered Danielle with a blanket. She turned on her side, snoring.

"I hope this helps you," Felicia said as she tenderly rubbed her lover's head. She drew the blinds close and quietly walked out the bedroom, closing the door behind her.

IT FEELS SO MUCH BETTER TO NUMB THE PAIN

CYNTHIA

sat on the edge of the bed cradling her head in her hands as if the world had come to an end.

"God!" she said, wiping angry tears away. "Forget it man!" Cynthia picked up her cell phone and dialed a number. "Hello," she said in a sultry voice.

"Hello? How are you?" Cynthia smiled to herself.

"I'm doing fine. How are you?"

"I'm good. It's been a while since I've heard from you. I thought you forgot about me."

"No, I haven't forgot about you, sweetheart," Cynthia whispered.

"Are you sure about that?"

"I'm very sure," Cynthia said pouring on her sexual charm.

"Humph! Okay, what did I do to be graced with a call from the illusive Cynthia?"

"Illusive?" Cynthia laughed. "Is that what you think of me?"

"Well, that among other things." She giggled.

"Hmmm, I hope the *other* things are good."

"That depends on what your interpretation of *good* is."

"Interesting, well how 'bout we meet up today? Maybe you can shed some light on those *other* things you mentioned." Cynthia's heartrate accelerated, thinking about the other *things* they could get into.

"Oh, so you're trying to come and see me?"

"Yes, that is…if you're not too busy."

225

"No, my schedule is light and easy today. What time would you like to meet?"

From that day forth, Cynthia and Lori were inseparable. They did *everything* together and Cynthia loved it. Between sex, popping ecstasy pills and downing tons of alcohol, there was no room for Cynthia to think about Danielle.

Lori introduced Cynthia to ecstasy one night during their lust filled sexcapade. Lori told her that if she wanted to have crazy intense orgasms she should have sex on "E." Cynthia hasn't had sex without them.

All was well, so it appeared. Cynthia and Lori hit up every popular night club and after hours' spot in L.A., choosing people to take home for an all-night alcohol and drug induced orgy. Cynthia's world was fine, just as long as she kept her mind altered with alcohol, ecstasy pills and sex on top of sex. But soon everything would come crashing down in a New York minute.

They left a trendy club on the posh side of Downtown L.A. with a trail of ten people following them. When they got to Cynthia's house, it took no time to get the private party cracking!

Some of their guests separated into different groups throughout the house. A man and woman were seated on the sofa in the living room. The man had a book lying across his lap with a thin white powdery substance on top of it. He whipped out a debit card to cut the powder, separating it into two lines. He handed the woman a neatly rolled up bill. She leaned forward placing, the bill at the tip of her nostril and sniffed one of the lines up her nose. She wiped the residue away and leaned back on the sofa. The man snorted the second line and says,

"Cocaine always makes sex better." He began to grope and kiss the woman while she remained still as a mannequin.

Cynthia and the rest of the partygoers were in her bedroom. Loud music blared from the high tech stereo system as they took turns drinking from a large bottle of brandy, undressing each other and participating in activities that they wouldn't dare speak about in public.

Cynthia's room was a sexual smorgasbord. She couldn't be happier than a pig in slop. She excused herself from the group and went into her closet to fetch a bag of tricks. The bag contained

226

various styles shape and various size dildos and strap-ons. When Cynthia emerged from the closet wearing a well-endowed black strap-on, everyone's eyes were fixated on what hung between her legs. The group stared at Cynthia with carnal excitement in their eyes.

"*Ooooh,* come here baby!" an older man crooned. "Daddy's been waiting for this all day. How did you know what I wanted!" Cynthia strutted to the man. When she's within reaching distance of the older man, he eagerly reached for the strap-on, stroking it like it was the real thing. His action intensified Cynthia's appetite for satisfaction. She grabbed his shoulders, pushing him to his knees and bending over,

"*Yeeesss!*" he yelled with anticipation. Befoee Cynthia got busy, Lori whispered into her ear and walked away heading to the bathroom. Lori's mind was so focused on relieving herself and getting back to the party that she didn't notice she had an audience. Lori pushed the bathroom door close and it was suddenly stopped. She jumped startled and pulled the door open, thinking she smashed someone's hand in between the door. When Lori looked up, she saw the sexiest smile, on the sexiest face.

"Oh, I'm sorry! Did I close the door on you? I was about to use the bathroom really quick," she said smiling. "I won't be long."

"I know," sexy chocolate said. Lori was puzzled.

Okay, well what do you want?

"I just want to watch," he said with empty eyes that quickly turn to a piercing glare, making Lori's insides tremble.

Something's not right here. "Okay," she said with a raised voice, hoping someone would hear her over the loud music and moans. "Let me to take care of my business first, when I'm done, I'll do whatever you want me to do, all right?" Lori said, calmly trying to deter him from what, she didn't know but she could feel that something was indeed wrong.

"Sure," he said with a slight bow of his head. He then, looked Lori square in the eyes and says, "I'll tell you what..." in one powerful push, the intruder forced the bathroom door open, causing Lori to stumble almost fall into the bathtub. He slammed the door shut and locked it, "...I'm coming in and you're *still* gonna do whatever I want!" he bellowed with such force that could match a steam pipe explosion

Lori's heart felt like it was going to erupt inside her chest. She wanted to scream but she knew no one would hear. Lori decided to play it smart.

"Okay," she said, lifting her hands indicating that she's not a threat. "This is a pleasure party, baby. Whatever you desire, we can try to make it happen. Please, just let me use the bathroom, first." He violently grabbed Lori's waist, yanking her body close to his. He reeked of liquor. She wanted to turn away but she's afraid that would only infuriate him more. "It doesn't have to be like this. We don't have to fight to get off. Let's just do this nice and sweet, okay baby?" Lori said pressing her hands against his muscular bare chest.

Of course, under a different set of circumstances, Lori would have considered him to be an extremely handsome man. His caramel complexion glistened under the bright light. What hair that was visible on his body was perfectly manicured. His light brown eyes simmered in anger. He certainly was eye-candy but his good looks were the last thing on her mind. Lori's thinking about how many women he had done this to.

"I know what I want to do," he said with a voice cold as ice. He took her by the neck and threw her naked body to the floor. Pain ricocheted down her spine making her believe her back was possibly cracked. She let out a piercing cry. Urine gushed from between her legs, forming a puddle underneath her.

"Wait a minute!" Lori pled, as she tried pushing him off her. He pinned her hands behind her head. "No! Wait! Please! You don't have to do this!" Lori begged. *Oh, my God! I'm about to be raped on my girlfriend's bathroom floor! God help me, please!*

Lori was about to scream but his large hand came crashing down on the side of her face with so much force that she temporarily blacked out. She could taste the blood as it formed a small pool on the inside of her mouth. He wrapped his fingers around her neck and squeezed tightly. It felt like her eyeballs were about to pop out of her head.

"Shut up whore!" he hissed. "Try to scream again and I'll break your neck." Lori whimpered. She dared not say another word.

I'll let him do what he wants, so I can walk out of here alive. Her body went limp, preparing for the worse then she heard a loud knock at the door.

"Who's in there?" It's Cynthia. She wondered why Lori was taking so long in the bathroom.

"Shut up!" he spat in her ear. "Keep your damn mouth close or I'll kill her too." She froze in utter terror.

"Hello!" Cynthia yelled while banging on the door. "Hey! Turn that down." The music instantly shut off. "Lori!" Cynthia yelled again, you could hear the fear in her voice. "Come here and help me with this." The sound of movement and muffled voices could be heard on the other side of the door. Lori's sobbing so intensely that her body convulsed.

"Get da hell up!" the perpetrator barked. He snatched her up to her feet. Lori felt a cold stream of urine run down her legs and she cringed. "You better act like everything is cool when they open this door or I'll kill you and everybody in this damn house! You hear me!" Lori nodded her head frantically.

"Please don't hurt her, please!"

"Well then, do what I tell you if you don't want to die!"

"All right, already! I will!" He pushed her body against the cold ceramic sink and kissed her forcefully. Lori fought hard not to gag. Tears rolled down her face.

"Stop crying!" he said harshly.

"I'm sorry," she whimpered.

Seconds later, there was a loud bang against the door and it bursts open, crashing against the wall. Cynthia stood in the doorway looking perplexed and angry as hell. The partygoers gathered behind her looking even more confused.

Mr. Personality played his roll well, by pretending to be so engrossed in making out with Lori, that he didn't even notice the loud commotion around him.

Lori looked at Cynthia with eyes pleading for help. Something about this scene didn't sit well with Cynthia. She stepped into the bathroom and pulled the man off her woman. Feigning confusion, he says,

"Whoa! Whoa! What's up!" His eyes shift between Lori, Cynthia and the rest of the partygoers. "What's up!" he demanded.

"You mean to tell me, you didn't hear us banging on the door?" Cynthia asked in bewilderment, all the while keeping her attention fastened on Lori. Her eyes travelled down Lori's body, down to the yellowish puddle of liquid on the floor. Cynthia slowly followed the liquid up Lori's legs. *What is that!*

"It's okay, baby," Lori said unconvincingly. "We didn't hear you." Her body revealed the terror that she felt. She was shaking like a leaf. Cynthia couldn't hear a word Lori said. She's confused by the sight of the wet floor and Lori's wet legs.

Is that piss!

"You know how I get when I'm ready baby," Lori added, still attempting to convince her partner that everything was all right.

Cynthia glared at the perv like she could kill him. Without thinking, Cynthia snatched the top off the toilet bowl tank and brought it down on top of the assailant's head. Cynthia watched in rage and sheer delight when she saw him drop to the floor like a ton of bricks.

The earth stood completely still. No one knew what to do. Once Cynthia saw blood gushing from the hole on the top of his head she wanted to faint. But that would ruin her image as "the bad chick" that people thought she was.

"Come over here!" Cynthia barked at Lori. She quickly snapped out of her semi-comatose state, jumped over her assailant's body and ran into the arms of her *she-ro*. "What the hell was going on in there!" Cynthia needed answers. Lori couldn't hold it together any longer. She broke down like a fragile porcelain doll in Cynthia's arms.

"He-he...," Lori said between sobs, "...he tried to rape me!" A loud gasp filled the room.

"Oh, my God!" the partygoers said in unison. "I can't believe this!" was heard throughout the room. A male partier says, "We gotta call the police before this bastard wakes up." The room was suddenly filled with the scuffing sounds of people moving frantically to put underwear and clothes. One man was so distraught that he put on a woman's pair of thongs and was about to put on his pants when the owner of the thongs protested in disgust.

"Hold up! Let me think," Cynthia shouted, to no one in particular. A naked man standing next to her says,

"We gotta do something before this fool wakes up. I got a feeling, he's not gonna be happy about getting clobbered upside the head with the top of a toilet bowl tank!" All was still.

"Call the police."

Cynthia's house was filled with police officers guarding various areas of her home. Two detectives interviewed a few of the partygoers who had a conscious to remain at the scene of the crime.

When the police officers apprehended the perv from the bathroom floor, he went berserk like a wild mustang resisting captivity. His violent actions towards the officers obviously worked against his presumed innocence.

Lori was a total wreck. She rocked back and forth in her chair while being interrogated by a middle aged black detective. She's trying to grasp the reality of almost being raped.

"Did you know the assailant ma'am?" Lori wanted to yell,

"Hell no!" But she was too weak and in utter despair. All she could offer was a barely audible, "No officer." Cynthia couldn't stand what was happening to Lori.

"Can you hurry this up! She's in no state to be interrogated right now!" The detective was unfazed by Cynthia's torrents. His 'no nonsense' facial expression said it all. The detective continued interviewing Lori as if Cynthia wasn't there.

"Well, Ms. we have all the information we need, as of now. If we have any more questions, we will be in contact with you." He reached inside his breast pocket for a business card, handing it to Lori. She took the card, still oblivious to what was going on.

"Thank you, Detective," Cynthia said. He nodded his head and walked out the room.

Moments later, the entire crowd dispersed and Cynthia was left trying to process everything and comfort Lori at the same time. She held Lori in her arms and rocked her ever so gently.

"Baby...I'm so sorry," Cynthia said, almost in tears. Lori sniffled and buried her face inside the crease of Cynthia's neck.

"I don't know why he-" Cynthia hushed her.

"Shhhhhh, don't, just relax. I got you baby. He can't hurt you anymore." Lori cried from her soul. Cynthia felt helpless and furious. *Why wasn't I there to stop this from happening! Damn it!* They held onto one another for hours.

After Lori fell asleep, Cynthia laid her on the bed, escaped to the living room and opened a bottle of brandy to nurse herself into a numbing state. She curled up on the sofa with her drink allowing her mind to drift off to nothingness.

Cynthia immediately went into a deep sleep and dreamt that she was lying in a hammock under the warm sunrays. A beautiful bird came to rest on the side of her face. Cynthia laid motionless as the bottom of the bird's wing lightly brushed across her cheek. She woke up to Lori standing above her, rubbing the side of her face with such endearment. Cynthia's bottom lip quivered, tears threatened to fall from Lori's eyes. Cynthia shot up to attention.

"What's wrong baby!" She reached out to Lori but she pulled away. Cynthia was confused. "Baby, tell me what's going on!"

"I, I can't," she managed to say, "...I-" Lori's voice trailed off. Cynthia attempted to sit Lori on the sofa next to her but she resisted.

"I don't know what's going on Lori, please...talk to me." Cynthia wasn't use to being vulnerable, openly displaying her emotions. She cared deeply for Lori and she couldn't bear seeing her in so much turmoil.

"I just want to tell you that...I can't do this anymore, Cindy," Lori said in a shaky voice. Her heart felt like it was going to break into a million pieces. Lori loved the time that they've spent together but she knew Cynthia was running from something. It would only get worse for them if she stayed. The horrible situation was a warning that something had to change. Lori knew the only way to help Cynthia, was to let her go.

Tears brimmed Cynthia's eyes. She's didn't know if she wanted to run and hide from Lori or get on her knees begging her not to leave.

"Please baby! I'm so sorry for what happened but-" Lori interrupted.

"Don't," it's Lori's turn to comfort Cynthia. She held Cynthia in her arms. Cynthia sniffled trying to hold back tears, "...I can't be your cover anymore. You have to deal with what's causing you so much pain." Cynthia pulled away from Lori, stood up and walked to the furthest side of the room. With her back facing Lori she says,

"Don't do this to me. I need you."

"You don't need me, Cindy." Silence. Cynthia's back remained to Lori. "Will you look at me, please."

I can't. She walked up to Cynthia, wrapping her arms around her waist pulling her near her heart and whispers,

"I have to go. I-" Lori's voice trailed off and she reluctantly removed her arms from Cynthia's waist.

The next thing Cynthia heard was the sound of the front door closing. A part of her felt like it left too. She dropped to her knees and cried like an abandoned baby. Cynthia's at the end of her road. There was nowhere to turn, nowhere to go and there was nothing she could do about it.

In the meantime, on the other side of the tracks, Danielle and Felicia carried on like they had no cares in the world. When they weren't home entertaining one another, they were having lunch in the park or at the beach watching the waves beat against the shore or driving up the coast reminiscing about their college years. Things appeared to look real nice for the happy couple, until Danielle began battling strong convictions.

It seemed as though their relationship went from "marital" bliss to a living hell overnight. No amount of alcohol took away her inner turmoil. Thoughts of the way she kicked Cynthia out of her house kept playing over in her mind like a bad ratchet B movie. When Danielle couldn't stand it any longer, she attacked the next closets person to her. Felicia would bear the brunt of her frustrations.

Danielle's irritations manifested through small things, like copping attitudes with Felicia when she left the top off the toothpaste, when she tripped over a pair of Felicia's shoes sitting in the middle of the bedroom floor, when Felicia forgot to leave the garage door opener or failing to return Danielle's phone calls promptly. The lists of her sudden annoyances were endless. It's clear to Felicia that whenever she's in Danielle's presence, her lover suddenly became overtly obnoxious. Felicia resorted to staying out of her way but her decision didn't stop the world from crashing down around her.

Everything came to a volcanic eruption one evening, while Felicia washed dishes, after preparing a lobster dinner with stemmed broccoli, sautéed shrimp and a caser salad. Felicia had slippery hands and accidently dropped Danielle's favorite coffee mug into the sink causing it to shatter in pieces.

Danielle was reclining on the sofa listening to soft jazz and drinking chardonnay straight from the bottle. To say the least, she was inebriated, close to drunk. Danielle's feet were propped up on the coffee table. She's nodding her head to the fiery breakdown of one of her favorite jazz track's when she heard a loud *CRASH* come from the kitchen!! She jolted to her feet like a volt of electricity shot through her.

"What the!!!" Danielle yelled like she was on fire. *"Felicia!!"*

"It's okay!" Felicia screamed back from the kitchen. "I'm okay!" She foolishly thought Danielle was concerned about her. "My hands were soapy and I dropped your mug in the sink."

My mug!! Did she say she dropped my mug?! Danielle howled to herself. She totally hyped the minimal situation up, blowing things way out of proportion. *"My favorite mug!"* She was out of order. You would have thought Felicia admitted to slapping Danielle's mother and stealing five dollars from her purse.

Danielle stormed into the kitchen, already in combative mode when she got within the doorway. Hands on her hips, she growled,

"Why are you so damn clumsy!" Felicia spun around and eyed Danielle like she hit Felicia in the face with a filthy diaper. *What!! She's not coming in here to see if I'm okay! She's really tripping off a silly mug! Wait a minute...let me calm down. Breathe in...breathe out. One, two, three...ten.* Felicia's facial expression softened, "It's okay, baby. I'll get you a new one tomorrow." She turned back to the sink and rolled her eyes up to the ceiling.

"Uh-uh! What was that! Oh, so *you're* bothered right, now? You broke my mug and *you're* supposed to be bothered!" With her back still facing Danielle, Felicia says,

"Danni! *Dannniii*...I said I'll replace it tomorrow!" She swung around to face Danielle, looking her square in the eyes showing signs of frustration. She hoped that would make Danielle back off and leave it alone. Felicia didn't mumble a word as she turned her attention back to the dishes.

"I don't want a *new* one! You should not have broken this one!" Danielle marched up to the sink, lifts up a piece of the broken mug and dropped it down in sheer disgust. A piece of glass flew in the air and somehow hit Felicia just above her left brow. The disdain on Danielle's face didn't change in the least when she saw a tiny trickle of blood oozing from the small cut on Felicia's face.

Felicia covered the wound with her hand and went to the other side of the kitchen snatching a paper towel off the roll. When she wiped the blood from her brow, she brought the paper towel to eye level, staring at it like she couldn't comprehend what she saw. Felicia looked at Danielle like she was a complete stranger.

"Have you lost your mind?" Felicia said with a calmness that could make Freddy Kroger shudder. "What in the world is wrong with you!?" she screamed, taking Danielle off guard but she's a pro. She quickly regained composure, looked directly into Felicia's eyes and says,

"That's what happens when you break someone's favorite mug." Felicia was incensed.

"What is your problem, Danielle!" she yelled. "You betta check the *real* reason why you're angry, because I don't have *anything* to do with it!" She turned to leave out the kitchen.

"Uh-uh!" Danielle said, staying close behind Felicia's heels. "Don't walk away from me!" Felicia responded by throwing her hands up in the air. She's too through with this nonsense. She pepped up her steps, keeping as much distance between her and Danielle as possible. Felicia attempted to close the bedroom door but Danielle threw it back open, making it crash against the wall with a loud bang. "Don't nobody close doors in my house, but me!" Danielle knew she was wrong but she had gone too far to turn back.

"What do you want from me!" Felicia demanded. "I'm not about to stay here and let you beat me with your guilt about what happened between you and Cynthia!" Danielle's eyes betrayed how she really felt. She was truly shocked. The fact that Felicia knew Danielle was treating her as her whipping girl suddenly made Danielle feel deathly ashamed.

They stood toe to toe, glaring at one another, both pleading for understanding. Felicia broke the silence,

"Please tell me, Danni." She reached out to touch her arm but Danielle pulled away. "What do you want?" Felicia hoped Danielle would try to understand that she was ripping her heart apart but she would have been better off talking to a brick wall.

Danielle was still as a statute peering at Felicia with emotionless eyes. If she ever cared about her, there were no traces of it now. Felicia was determined. Danielle's cold disposition wouldn't deter her.

"Tell me, please. Why do you have so much animosity towards me? I'm not your enemy, baby! I promise you, I'm not. All I've done was try to love you and this is what I get back? Huh!"

Danielle was unmoved. Felicia dropped down on the bed like dead weight. The situation took its toll as Felicia wondered where the woman was that she fell in love with. Danielle fought not to run to Felicia and fall to her knees begging for forgiveness.

I'm so sorry. Tears blinded Danielle's sight. When she parted her lips to speak Felicia's heart skipped a beat. She hoped that Danielle would say something to soothe the tremendous pain in her heart. Instead, what Felicia got was, "Pack your things and get out of my house." She was crushed. Before Danielle turned to walk away, she adds, "And out of my life." That final statement left Felicia in total despair.

WHEN IT'S THE END THINGS LOOK WORST

Cynthia and Danielle were on identical paths of destruction. Danielle spent her days at work appearing to have everything under control but she spent her nights being wined and dined by whomever tickled her fancy. And if they were lucky, they got a chance to spend the entire night with her, not just a couple of hours.

Sex and alcohol were Danielle's drugs of choice. Hard liquor, wine or champagne, it didn't matter. As long as whatever Danielle decided to use altered her state of mind, she was fine. Most nights, all it took was a simple glass of chardonnay and off to bed she went with one of her suitors.

Danielle operated like she was without a conscious. Right and wrong were no longer a part of her reasoning. Physical gratification was what she *thought* she needed. If one of her suitors couldn't perform to her liking, that's quite all right, she'd quickly dismiss them right on out the door and it was on to the next one. *Next!!*

Cynthia always wanted Danielle to cross over to the dark side. Now that she had, Cynthia was nowhere to be found. If Cynthia witnessed what Danielle had become she surly wouldn't enjoy it in the least.

Cynthia competed with herself about how long she could continue having a stream of sex partners before her body and mind gave out on her. She used sex to block everything out that she didn't want to deal with. Cynthia wanted to be lost in a world far from reality. She wanted to love nothing and feel nothing. All one needed to gain access into Cynthia's world, was a bottle of Jack and possibly some "E" pills. What took presidents over those two things, was having exceptional skills in bed.

Cynthia enjoyed turning out the youngins who were twenty years plus. She could smell their innocence like a dog smelled fear. The more experience they lacked, the more Cynthia thrived off of turning them out, introducing her companions to sexual games that they would be ashamed to brag about the next day.

Cynthia's conscious died right along with her heart. She had no problem converting the innocent to full fledge sex addicts, with no boundaries. Her heart turned colder than it already was. And her selfish logic was,

"Hell, it was done to me and I turned out fine!" Cynthia was blinded to the truth. At the rate, she was going it didn't seem like she cared to know the truth at all.

Danielle was lying in bed exhausted after a second round of sex with her new lover, for the night. She reached for a bottle of Hennessey that sat on the nightstand. She twisted off the cap and guzzled it down like water. Danielle became a professional at taking it to the head, without showing signs of discomfort as the fiery liquid rolled over her tongue, singeing the back of her throat. She slammed the bottle down on the nightstand and leaped on top of her barely awake suitor. Startled, he opened his eyes and smiled.

"Oh baby." He yawned. "Can I get a little more shuteye? My energy is gone." He chuckled and delicately pinched her chin. "Girl! You wore a brotha out!" Danielle looked at him with disgust, confusion covered his face.

"This is not a room and board. I brought you here for one thing and you *half* did that right!" He flinched. Danielle's words ripped his ego to shreds.

"All I'm saying is-" Danielle interrupted.

"And *all I'm saying is,* do your job then, get the hell out of my house! It's as simple as that." she said, sounding as heartless as she felt. He grabbed her arm and tossed her on the bed like a rag doll.

"You stupid...! If I didn't have a conscious I'd break your-" he stopped his self before he said something he might regret. He's heard too many stories about brotha's getting caught up in strange situations because they allowed their anger to take control of them.

239

This woman might be recording this trying to get a brotha locked the hell up! I'm out this bitch! He bounced out of bed, took his clothes and went into the bathroom to get dressed. Danielle clumsily shot up like lightening, and staggered, stumbled to the bathroom door, banging on it like he stole something.

"Open this damn door! Who do you think you are! You ain't nothing! I brought your sorry ass here and you think you can treat me like this!"

BAM! BAM! She hit the door so hard it sounded like it cracked. The door was yanked open in a fury. All she saw was a huge blur charging at her like a quarterback. She's violently thrown down to the floor, he pinned her neck under his foot. Danielle couldn't move and she could barely breathe. He pressed his foot down harder with a wicked smile plastered in his face. She thought she was going to die. Danielle clawed at the hem of his pants leg and he pressed down even harder. She saw black spots before her eyes.

"I told you to leave me the hell alone!" he spat.

Please help me! Danielle didn't know if she was crying out to God, the one she denied, or calling upon her inner strength. *He's going to kill me!* The assailant had a deranged look in his eyes. Danielle knew her life meant nothing to him at that moment. He laughed at her vulnerability.

"How does it feel? I could break your neck." His own admission snapped him out of the violent trance. He instantly removed his foot off her neck, retrieved his keys from the dresser and scrammed out of the room and out the front door.

Danielle remained lying on the floor too numb to cry. When she realized how close she came to death, she drew her knees to her chest and screamed.

Cynthia's unadulterated lifestyle did more than caught up to her, she was dragged to the bottom of the pit. For the first time in her adult life Cynthia spent her days and nights alone. She roamed around the house in a daze. Her mind was in a dark and lonely place. If she wasn't battling paranoia she was tormented with thoughts of dying.

All day she ran from room to room looking out windows and making sure the blinds were drawn. Liquor didn't make it any easier. Alcohol only made her more paranoid. She hadn't bathe in almost a week and her hair hadn't been combed in nearly two weeks.

After wearing herself out from running around the house, she finally fell out on the sofa to watch TV. An episode of Good Times was on. Cynthia cradled the remote control in her arms staring at the show intensely. This was one of her favorite shows as a child. The episode she was watching is where Penny was being abused by her mother. Cynthia didn't see Penny in this graphic scene, she saw herself. When Penny's mother burned her with the iron, Cynthia screamed out in pain.

"*Ahhhhh* momma! *Wwwhhhyy...wwhhyy* did you leave me!" She hurled the remote control against the wall smashing it to pieces. Cynthia bolted from the sofa, charged into the kitchen and returned with a knife. She dropped to her knees putting the tip of the knife to her wrist. "I don't want to live like this anymore! I'm tired!" Cynthia sobbed. "I can't take it anymore, God! Please, help me!"

Ending her life was not what Cynthia actually wanted to do but she felt compelled to do so. She had convinced herself that all hope was gone and there's no way of escape. Cynthia believed she would feel so much better if she wasn't breathing any longer, that isn't true. If Cynthia thought for one second she could take her own life and end up in spiritual utopia, she was wrong. In her mind, she felt that she participated in too many corruptible things.

What kind of life can I possibly live?

As Cynthia prepared to slit her wrist someone banged on the front door, frantically turning the door knob. The distraction barely did a thing to interfere with Cynthia's plans in taking her own life. She ignored the interruption, continuing with her deadly mission.

There's another bang at the door and this time, it was followed by a voice.

"Cindy, open up! I know you're in there. Please, open the door, Cindy!" She stared at the door.

"Danni!" Cynthia whispered. "Is that you!" She dropped the knife to the floor, covered her mouth and cried. Danielle banged on the door again.

"Please Cindy, please open the door! I need you, I need my friend!"

Cynthia heard a loud thud, like something or someone hit the door. The thud, was the sound of Danielle's body falling against the door. She was crying so immensely that her legs became weak. Cynthia opened the door, causing Danielle to fall into her arms. They held onto one another for dear life.

"I'm so sorry, Danni," Cynthia said through tears of anguish.

"I'm sorry too, Cindy."

"God was absolutely right, He said He would never leave me nor forsake me." Cynthia pushed the door close, shutting the world out.

FIN